The End of Hardship

Based on a true account, Curt Conrad's team has three weeks to locate and defuse a nuclear bomb in North Korea dropped by General MacArthur which is what caused him to be recalled by President Truman. Their failure may cause world condemnation and US allies to withdraw from the Korean War, resulting in a humiliating defeat by the communists.

Little did he know that this mission would not only change his life, but he would meet the woman of his dreams.

Danyl A. Doyle

Ideal Books—Durango, CO
ISBN: Pending
Library of Congress Control Number: pending
Title: *The End of Hardship*
Author: Danyl A. Doyle
Digital distribution | 2024
Paperback | 2024

This is a work of fiction. The characters, names, incidents, places, and dialogue are products of the author's imagination, and are not to be construed as real.

Disclaimer

In 1982, a Korean War veteran told me a breathtaking account that has haunted me for over forty-two years. At the time, he was the director of my department, responsible and liked by all. He was sharp, and compassionate and taught me a lot. We became good friends.

One night, his eyes were dark and sunken into his brow. He looked burdened. He said, "There's something I went through during the war that I've never told anyone, and I'd like to get it off my chest."

He gathered my eyes into his deep brown ones. "You have to agree not to tell anyone else or write and publish it as long as I'm alive."

I promised.

He began – hesitating and speaking slowly.

I listened with horror and fascination as he told of going on a top-secret mission and being captured and tortured by the North Koreans. I became convinced it was true when he showed me his missing fingers and his badly scarred eyebrow. He began sobbing. His shoulders shook, and he couldn't go on. It took many difficult and long meetings over weeks for him to tell the whole story. When he finished, he again made me promise not to share it with anyone until he was long gone.

As he acknowledged, there is no way to independently verify the truth of his experience since the Navy appears to have destroyed all evidence of the top-secret mission, including sanitizing his medical records. He remembered what happened in bits and pieces over the years after the Navy "deprogrammed" him, using methods that pretty much erased his memory of being on the mission.

When he finished, I was shocked at the implications. If true, it explained the real reason why Truman recalled MacArthur. It has international implications even today.

I tried to get him to write and publish his story, and offered to ghostwrite it, changing all names. He refused, "They'll come after me. I could be killed like two of the other guys on the mission." He caught my eyes. "And you could also be killed."

All names and most locations have been changed to protect anyone who may be affected by this publication. The romances are a product of my imagination, however, I have faithfully recorded his account of being in Korea, the Navy deprogramming, and his efforts to discover what he went through.

Curt gave permission to write this story when he passed.

The time has come.

Book I
The Mission

Chapter 1
Saving General MacArthur

April 9, 1951, Ten months into the Korean War

Stars twinkled in the night sky and the Sea of Japan was calm. The carrier deck rose and dropped slowly. A dark storm appeared over the horizon. The restless sea beckoned with low fingers of waves as if to warn of a waiting doom.

They heavily overloaded Curt with equipment, weapons, and canned food. He crawled into the Douglas AJ Savage Bomber's belly where, instead of bombs, four other men on the top-secret mission waited for their night drop into North Korea. He caught Taylor's dark eyes as he buckled in. Taylor Hawkins was the oldest on the team at twenty-eight. He was from Billings, Montana. Without Taylor and the metal detector Curt packed, the mission was pointless. A bomb specialist, Taylor reluctantly volunteered when they promised to clear his crappy record resulting from too much boozing after his wife divorced him.

Nineteen-year-old Carl Brooks was his buddy from the spy ship. Jack Honeycutt was eighteen like Curt and from Sacramento, while twenty-five-year-old Adam Spoker, or Spooker, grew up in San Diego. Nodding to the other men, Curt fist-bumped Carl and got buckled to the bomb rack.

He felt giddy with excitement: he had only jumped using a static line and this was a free fall from a plane not designed for parachutists. The last time he bailed out was in the middle of "A" training in September. He loved parachuting but his CO called him in. "You blew the top off the language proficiency test. You're going to an intensive Korean language school. You'll be in naval intelligence."

It sounded exciting. He imagined infiltrating North Korea in black clothes, a knit cap, and black leather gloves with a silencer on his pistol.

They pulled him and Carl from the frogmen program and after the language school, assigned them to a 105-foot, lightly armed spy ship monitoring North Korean radio transmissions and tracking military movements. It was a converted fishing trawler and could have passed for one except for all the antennas and a mounted fifty-caliber machine gun. There were forty-three on the crew. Most were old fat dudes or geeky-looking guys with pimples who didn't mind staring at screens, smoking, and eating all they wanted. They liked the safe environment.

"Fuk a duck," was all he could say.

Carl agreed wholeheartedly. "Yeah, when they said we were going into naval intelligence, I thought we'd be spies on secret missions. This is boring as hell."

Instead of being in the heat of the war, they puttered up and down the coast of North Korea in the Sea of Japan, listening to the action. Maybe that's why they became best friends. Carl was a big, funny guy with a hard stomach and wide shoulders. Two years older than Curt, he was from Oklahoma and spoke with a southern drawl.

The Captain asked, "Both you boys from the south? You look like brothers."

"Nope," Curt grinned. "I'm from western Colorado and he's from Podunk, Oklahoma." He laughed when Carl slugged his arm.

"I'm from Norman. There's no Podunk, Oklahoma."

Everyone on the spy ship smoked except for the two of them. They worked out on the deck to stay in shape and bet their free Lucky Strikes in poker games, taking the other men's military script. Carl was also an athlete, having relinquished a football ride to Oklahoma State. Had Curt accepted the football scholarship to CU Boulder, they might have played against each other. They competed to see how many push-ups, sit-ups, and pull-ups they could do in fifteen minutes, three times a day.

Carl told him, "Hell, man, when the commies overran South Korea, I couldn't live with myself playing it safe in college, knowing our boys were getting shot up over here."

Exactly Curt's sentiments. His father served in World War II and his grandfather in World War I. It was a family tradition.

When the spy ship captain announced the Navy was looking for volunteers with jump training for a top-secret mission, their hands shot up.

They were loaded onto a helicopter. Onboard the carrier, the briefing officer said, "This could be a suicide mission. You may be captured and tortured. This secret mission is the most critical of the entire Korean conflict. If you are unsuccessful, our U.N. allies may abandon us and millions of innocent civilians could die. If they torture you, you *must not* reveal the purpose of your mission. Tell the cover story to any allies, but only give your false name, rank, and serial number to the communists."

He scanned the men as he said with certainty, "We will not acknowledge your mission and there will be no record of it anywhere. You have three weeks max, then we'll assume you are dead and report you lost at sea. We will do everything possible to get you out safely and you'll get combat pay and bars no matter the outcome."

The subtext was: you're gonna die.

He and Carl took it as "This will be fun. We'll be heroes." Both men admired General MacArthur and were thrilled to be on this mission that would save his reputation.

The fleet admiral said, "If you make it back, I'll personally see to it that your Navy careers are secure, and I will make you officers."

Curt barely made the cut because he hadn't free-jumped like Carl. At the last minute, a man dropped out after learning his wife was pregnant. He and Carl high-fived. "Way to go brother!" They promised if either of them got wounded or killed, the survivor would do everything possible to haul his body out.

Their aim was the south fork of the Taedong River. The mission: Save the United States from international condemnation. They were to locate and defuse a nuclear bomb that General MacArthur ordered dropped, intending to poison the entire riparian system to P'yŏngyang. It was the unreported, real reason that President Truman had recalled him.

After an intolerable delay, the twin props of the AJ Savage bombers picked up speed, then the rear jet engine roared, drowning out nervous chattering. The smell of jet exhaust hit, and he brushed his nose and mouth. Curt had never catapulted from a carrier or been in a jet, but ever since he was a kid listening to his father and grandfather's war stories, he imagined doing something heroic like this. His hands shook with excitement, not fear.

They moved into the catapult lane. Screaming engines, then sudden G-forces slammed men into one another, although they were clipped to the bomb rack. Curt felt like he was on a wild roller coaster ride as his cheeks pinned back, exposing his gums. He glanced at Carl. In the dim blue light, he had the same shit-eating grin, loving every minute.

The hybrid propjet bomber left the carrier behind as it clawed into the sky, and the men smacked into the bomb bay bars in rough air currents, fighting to hang on. The plane banked toward North Korea as hundreds of other AJ Savage bombers swung into formation.

The AJ Savage is a bomber without windows. The briefing officer said, "This mission requires stealth. Your plane needs to fit in so the North Koreans won't think you're invading paratroopers. If you're lucky, you'll make it to the ground without being detected."

The plane wasn't built for paratroopers and when the bomb bay opened, standing on slick stainless steel bars, they'd dive out as if into a swimming pool, pulling their ripcord as soon as they cleared the jet exhaust. No one had ever done this before.

The men didn't talk because it was too loud. Curt wrapped into private thoughts, reviewing the steps of the mission, and anticipating what to do when things went wrong as was sure to happen. *It will be one of those challenges Mom told me about. God will protect me.*

He and Carl checked each other's parachute harness straps when the pilot announced, "We're dry," meaning they were over land. They had long minutes to anticipate the bomb bay doors opening.

Carl yelled over the noise, "Our drop zone is only sixty or so miles from the 38th Parallel. Hell, this will be a cakewalk."

He yelled back, "Sixty miles as a crow flies." He had studied the topo maps. There were steep, treacherous hills and rough, twisting valleys swarming with North Korean army units on the few roads. He imagined himself fighting off the communists and saving the team.

Waiting was the hardest part, and it was a relief when the red light came on. The pilot announced, "Five minutes to the drop zone."

Curt felt the urge to push ahead of the others to jump first but restrained himself. His legs twitched and his fingers shook, ready for action.

"One minute."

The bomb doors split open. Taylor yelled, "Let's go!" He nose-dived, quickly followed by Carl, Jack, and Spooker. Excited, Curt slipped on the bomb rack, and instead of swan diving, he tumbled forward as his toe caught. He flipped upside down and damned near hit his head on the open bomb door. Wind and prop wash spun him. The heavy equipment on his back faced the ground.

"Shit!" Curt fought to get turned over or the parachute would tangle and may not open at all. He was like a turtle on its back accelerating

200 feet a second at 122 miles per hour. He didn't have much time since they were much lower than normal to give minimal exposure to potential ground fire.

Curt remembered diving into the lake at home. Snapping his head, he flung his left arm to the side and rolled over, but it caused him to tumble again. He panicked since it was seven months since he last jumped. This was a free jump, not a static line, and he didn't have the experience. *Calm down and focus on the techniques.* Fighting the rookie instinct to curl into a ball, he spread his arms and legs wide, making himself into a wing. It allowed him to roll so he faced the ground. He immediately pulled the ripcord, deploying the chute. He glanced up over his shoulder. It fluttered in a streamer. He was dropping a hundred feet every three seconds. Oddly, he calmed. *If I die, I die. I knew this was a suicidal mission when I volunteered.* He reached for the emergency chute chord but stopped when the main chute unfurled and opened. *Thank God!*

Like a giant snapped the lines on a puppet, the harness jerked his groin, the straps cutting in. He was carrying a hundred-seventy pounds on his back because of the heavy metal detector, and the chute wrenched his body, knocking out his breath. He inhaled sharply, trying to suck in air as he swung and spun wildly in the night sky with stars twirling above. His risers twisted, then unwinding, he spun in the opposite direction, making him dizzy. The ropes pinned his head down with his chin on his rifle stock, preventing him from looking up to check the canopy.

The spinning stopped abruptly and as endorphins hit his brain, it was peaceful in the starlit night sky. Spots in his eyes. Nausea. Silence with only wind and the fading sound of the bomber looping back to the carrier. The mission planners were right when they said there wouldn't be a moon tonight and no rain with scattered clouds. Hopefully, the commies would think his chute was a passing cloud. Adrenaline in his veins, his muscles jerked with fear and excitement. This is exactly what he dreamed of when he joined the Navy: action, adventure, and a chance to be a hero like his father and grandfather.

He scanned the ground. The forested hills were black and he needed to find the river basin where the nuclear bomb was dropped. He wished there was moonlight reflecting off the water. He could barely tell the difference between the heavily wooded hills and the valleys. He packed the metal detector and if he didn't make it, if he didn't meet up with the other four men on his team, the mission was wasted. He saw the other men's chutes far above to his left, almost in a row. His unexpected free fall put him below the others, and the tumbling shot him way off course. Far to the north, he saw searchlights and tracer flak from North Korean antiaircraft guns and flashes from American bombs. It was only 120 miles from Seoul to Pyongyang, the industrial heart of Korea. Fortunately, there were no fires or lights from North Korean camps down below.

Where is the river? Ragged hills and narrow valleys everywhere. *Was that a glint of water reflecting starlight?* If so, he was way off course. He glanced up at the other parachutes. He was far to the east of them.

Cursing, he tried to guide the chute back to the west. Jerking on the lines, half the parachute folded in, and it damned near collapsed. *Fuk me. I'll kill myself if I keep doing that.* The ground was coming up fast because of all the weight he carried and he was a big man; over six feet five inches, and 245 pounds, all muscle and bone. They designed the parachute for an average man carrying a seventy-pound pack, and he had difficulty controlling it. He was way outside of the target landing zone. Again, he jerked the lines hard, trying to steer to the west. The damned thing nearly collapsed on itself once more, and he shook the lines to fluff them out. He looked down the same instant the top of a pine tree smacked him in the face. The top broke off. The parachute looped over, tangling in the tree. He flipped and fell headfirst twenty feet through branches. The lines wrapped around his ankles and jerked him to a hard stop, upside down. His .30 caliber carbine slid from the case. He watched it fall a hundred feet to the ground. Sweat popped on his forehead. He fought the lines for several minutes, but the pack was too heavy to do a sit-up. He didn't dare release it and possibly destroy the metal detector. Even if he tried, the parachute harness would trap it, making things even more unmanageable.

He blacked out, hanging upside down.

Curt came to after several minutes and tried to pull himself upright, but his backpack was too heavy. He couldn't decide: *If I cut off the pack, the metal detector might be destroyed, then we're screwed since the nuke might have buried itself in the ground.* He tried to pull himself upright but it was impossible. Both ankles were wrapped in the parachute chords. He wiggled out his knife but couldn't reach the lines. Swinging up and down, he exhausted himself and passed out just as he got the knife back into its sheath.

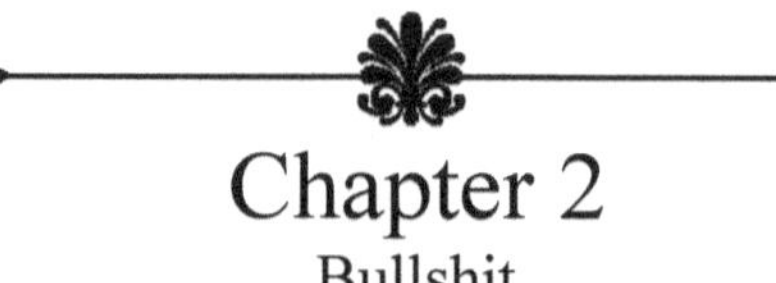

Chapter 2
Bullshit

As dawn broke, Curt came to and surveyed the area. He was in a thick pine forest near the top of a steep rocky hill. He heard small birds. A woodpecker tapped. The forest seemed to breathe in and out. No amount of military training could have prepared him for this. He was totally alone. He might have one or two days to get himself upright, then he'd die from being upside down. Headache city. Nausea.

If he cut himself off, he'd fall a hundred feet into rocks unless he could grab pine branches on the way down. Doubtful with the heavy pack nearly doubling his weight. His body would tumble down the rock-strewn hill, and he could die or paralyze himself. Couldn't see the river anywhere. *Shit!*

The other team members might be miles away. He tried to pull himself up, straining with all his might, trying to reach a line with his knife. He fell back exhausted and breathed to keep from blacking out. "Stay cool, stay calm. Think through the problem." It was his father's voice. Then he imagined Grandpa saying, "Sacrifice the backpack. It's better than dying up here."

The sun lurched down the mountainside. Guilt hit him. *They'll blame me for mission failure if the metal detector gets broken.* He grabbed a pine branch and pulled his shoulders and chest onto it. The sun was above the horizon so he could see better. The sky cleared and was very blue.

He studied the problem. His eyes traced the lines wound around his ankles in a counter-clockwise direction. Cutting one wouldn't make any difference. He examined the tension in the cords above his feet. One looked tighter than the others. Reaching for the next higher branch, he supported himself and, stretching as much as possible, nicked the line. He kept at it. Resting, nicking the line, catching his breath. He unfastened his helmet and let it fall, then tossed everything he could reach to lighten the load. He held his breath as grenades and the ammo belt bounced off rocks.

Back to nicking the line. The damn parachute cords were like tensile steel. A dozen efforts and one was down to merely a string. Suddenly, it released and jerked him from the branch, causing him to fall. The knife whipped from his hand, slashing his right thumb. Five feet and the other lines yanked him to a stop, stunning him. *Shit!*

Now he didn't have a branch he could pull his shoulders onto so he could get some blood back to his brain. Hanging headfirst, he saw the knife glinting ninety-five feet below at the base of the tree. He figured his team was still far away. *Did they see where I went down?* It was getting hot in the noonday sun as blood gushed from the wound on his thumb. He put pressure on it as he tried to think, forcing the terror down from his throat.

Now how the hell am I going to cut myself down? He fought panic.

When he calmed down, Curt mentally reviewed everything in the heavy backpack. He had a trench shovel with an edge, but it was impossible to get at it on his back. The parachute harness prevented him from twisting the pack around to his chest. *I'm going to die up here. Either I have to shoot off the lines or find a way to get out of this backpack. Even if I unbuckle it, the parachute harness will trap it. With my knife gone, I can't even cut myself out.*

He blacked out.

What felt like hours later, he came to when a woodpecker started hammering on a nearby tree. The sun was lower and his head pulsed with pain. It wasn't hot, but he was, and sweat seeped from his chest and neck into his eyes. He fought panic and felt like puking from the fear.

He wrestled the .45 from the holster. It might bring the North Korean military, but he was a dead man if he stayed hanging upside down much longer. Sweat and black spots in his eyes, he tried to aim. He had to shoot all the lines. At least four or five shots. The clip held six. He'd save the last one to kill himself. No wait, right there, the lines crossed each other and if he got a bullet in the perfect place, he might only have one line holding his ankles. *With any luck.* He was unsteady as he tried to do a sit-up with the pack dragging him down, and the pistol wouldn't hold still. As the sights went over the crossover place for the third time, he squeezed the trigger. A perfect hole.

In the tree.

He felt himself sliding into unconsciousness and stuffed the gun into the holster, getting it snapped before passing out.

Noises far off in the brush and trees woke him. Fear gripped him. *Fuck, the commies heard my shot. They'll kill me right here and leave my body hanging.* He got his forty-five out again and tried to look around but could only see to each side. The noise was coming from behind him. He was relieved to see a small group of wild boars rooting and moving in his direction. Relief flooded his chest.

He sited the pistol on the ropes and fired twice in quick succession, hitting a line but it didn't break. Got the gun back in the holster before he blacked out again.

He wasn't sure how long he was out but the sun was setting when he heard, "Well looky what the rookie did to himself." California Jack's voice.

Curt glanced down. "About time you guys showed up."

Jack had a mouth on him. "Now I know why you almost weren't allowed on this mission."

Carl snapped, "Shut up. It could have happened to any of us. We have to get him down." His pack was off, and he started climbing the tree.

"Bring your knife," Curt said in a weak voice.

"I've got it." He was athletic and came up the pine tree. When he got to Curt, he lifted his shoulders to get his head higher. He studied the parachute lines. "Hell man, you've got a real mess." He called down. "Spooker, I'm going to need your help. Drop your gear and climb up."

The pine top wobbled and swayed with the weight of two big men. Curt said, "Wait, try to get me to that branch." He pointed up. "If I can hold on to it, you could climb around the other side and cut the ropes. Once my ankles are free, I can get down."

Carl yelled, "Hold up, Adam. This tree is swaying and if three of us get up here, it might topple over." He did a military press with Curt's body, lifting him high enough to grab a branch. Without warning, the branch he stood on gave out. Carl dropped, but lower branches caught him between his legs. "Ouch, shit! That hurts." Groaning, he hugged the tree trunk.

Curt had a tenuous grip on a branch. He closed his eyes and, muscles bulging, pulled his shoulders up to rest on it. Taking long breaths, he looked down. "You okay?"

"Yeah, I got it." He breathed through it and then worked his way around the trunk opposite Curt and sawed at the parachute lines. "I better cut a length and tie it around the tree so you can hang on when I chop through the other lines." He got a five-foot piece and tied it off. He handed the end to Curt. "Get ready for a jolt."

"Do it." Curt nodded.

He chopped through the lines and with each one, Curt dropped a little. When he sawed through the last one, he fell like a cannonball. The weight of the backpack was too much in his exhausted state. He lost the hand line and crashed through twenty feet of pine branches before grabbing onto one. He nearly passed out again, his hands torn and bleeding.

Carl made his way down and clung to the opposite side of the trunk. "Think you can make it the rest of the way down, or do you need help?"

"I just need a breather. Didn't get much rest last night." An incredible sense of relief flooded over him, and he took deep breaths.

Finally on the ground, Curt sucked down a quart of water, then put sulfa and a bandage on his thumb. He closed his eyes. He felt dizzy and felt like throwing up from the retreating adrenaline. His ankles hurt. He pulled his boots off. The rope burns and bruises would be with him for a while. He rubbed them gently. They were tender and already turning purple. He felt like an idiot.

After catching his breath, he said, "Geez, sorry for the screw-up. I got my toe hooked on the way out and it tumbled me."

Jack said, sarcastically, "I seen you upside down, spinning like a wild man." He grinned like the wiseass Californian he was and blinked his blue eyes, mocking. This was his first mission as a frogman but the way he acted, you'd have thought it was his hundredth.

"You did a good job of righting yourself." Adam Spoker had heavy black eyebrows, a brown complexion, and a slender, lanky body. He carried the serious look of a spy, so they called him Spooker. "I saw a guy with hundreds of jumps die when something like that happened." Spooker served on missions all over the world as a frogman. He was quiet and took, rather than gave orders.

Curt glanced around. "Where's Taylor?"

The men glanced uneasily at each other.

Brow furrowed, Carl said, "He was the first out, and I wasn't much behind him. We spent half a day looking but couldn't find him. That's when I said we better search for you. I saw you hit the top of a tree and knew about where you were." He shook his head. "We heard your gunshots. Luckily, there doesn't seem to be any North Koreans around."

"How close are we to the river?" Curt asked.

Jack said with a sarcastic tone, "Hell, we're miles out of position 'cause of you."

Curt clinched his jaws and stood. "We need to find Taylor. He's the key to this mission."

Everyone knew it.

The tension thickened.

Sweat dripping from his face, Carl looked up at the parachute. "We need to get that down and buried. They could have spotter planes and would know we're in here. It would blow our cover story, then we'll get tortured if we're captured."

"We won't get captured," Curt said with confidence, "But you're right. We need to get it."

They had agreed to kill themselves with the suicide pills if the communists got the drop on them.

It was dark by the time they got the darned thing down and buried. A sliver of a moon formed in the star-studded sky. Carl said firmly, "Let's get going. Someone may have heard those shots. We need to walk until we can't see anything, then camouflage ourselves with brush."

Hell, they already couldn't see much. Carl made quick movements with his wide shoulders as he walked. A slightly hooked nose like a hawk and black stubble covered his square chin. Heavy eyebrows protected his deep-set brown eyes flecked with green.

They carefully swept their tracks with branches. It was slow going. They crashed into things. Carl whispered, "We're making too much noise. We better camp for the night."

After they settled under tarps, Curt thought about his choices. He could have been playing football at the University of Colorado next fall. It would have been fun, but nothing as exciting as this. He whispered to Carl, "Do you wish you were still at the University of Oklahoma, playing football?

A moment passed before he answered. "Not yet. I've never been so fucking scared. I love it."

In the morning, a few clouds fought to keep possession of the sky with clots of purple scattered in the centers while the edges glowed pink and scarlet. Carl reminded them, "We've got one week of food, then we forage. I hope we don't waste a lot of time trying to locate Taylor. Watch for nuts, berries, and anything to eat as we walk. No talking. Whisper and use hand signals. The last man brush out our tracks, and we'll rotate every hour. It will be slow going."

Curt said the topo maps showed the river was in a valley to the northwest. It was the general direction they figured Taylor landed. As they walked, he reviewed what the briefing officer told them. MacArthur received the authority to use nuclear bombs on April 1. He wanted to lay a string of them across the Yalu River to prevent any further ground invasions from China. He also planned to have nukes dropped on the main rivers to poison the entire riparian system clear to Pyongyang. He ordered one dropped but word got back to President Truman before he could deploy the others.

The briefing officer said, "Our U.N. allies could pull out of the war if they learn we used nukes on civilians. It's likely the Soviets will drop nuclear bombs on South Korea if word gets out. It could ignite World War III. It's a damned good thing it didn't denote. We have *one* chance to defuse it, then if the North Koreans find the bomb, we can deny it was live, and they can't reverse engineer it to produce their own. It's up to you men to save South Korea from communism and prevent the world from believing the U.S. is barbaric."

It was the real reason Truman recalled MacArthur. What the press published was total bullshit.

Chapter 3
Searching For Taylor

They hid in a clump of brush and quietly talked as they ate rations. The conversation was hushed. "We have to find Taylor. He's the only one that knows how to remove the trigger."

Jack said derisively, "They threw together this mission in a rush without proper planning. We should have two guys who could defuse the bomb."

Spooker frowned. "We work with what we have. That's part of being a frogman."

"It's a shame they didn't just turn MacArthur loose and let him nuke all of North Korea, maybe even the Chinese capitols." Jack flicked a stone. "Then, we wouldn't be here."

Curt shook his head. "I admire MacArthur, but I don't agree with killing civilians. These people don't want war, they just want to live their lives like us. This is a poor country raped by the Japanese. Korea is a pawn between the Soviets, Great Britain, and the U.S. It was traded-off so the Soviets would fight the Nazis. If they left it as one country, this wouldn't be happening."

Spooker nodded. "Yep. What they should do is make the leaders of countries get in a ring and duke it out. It would be an international sell-out. The winner gets the money. Leave the people out of it."

The men nodded.

Carl stood. "Let's get going. We have a job to do." Moments later, a pheasant flushed at his feet, letting off a two-note call – scaring the hell out of everyone.

Curt remembered hunting pheasants in his father's orchards. He thought of his ex-girlfriend. She proudly wore his class ring on a chain, yet constantly flirted with other guys – especially Bud.

He ignored it most days, but one noon as he walked out to the high school's front lawn where Darlene sat giggling with other girls, her former boyfriend, Bud, clocked him in the back of the head.

Curt stumbled, caught himself with his left hand, and came up with an uppercut that laid the jerk out on the grass like a sack of potatoes.

Students rapidly gathered in a circle, yelling, "Fight, fight!"

There wasn't a fight. Bud was down for the count.

Darlene was red-faced with excitement as her friends twittered, "They're fighting over you."

Mr. Stafford, the principal, ran down the steps yelling, "Knock it off, boys. I know you hate each other's guts."

"I don't hate anybody," Curt said as he helped Bud stand. "He hit me from behind so I punched him back."

Bud wiped the blood dripping from his nose. "He stole my girlfriend and had it coming."

The other kids excitedly described what happened, and Mr. Stafford made them sit in the office while he called their parents. He suspended them for one day, but because there was a football game tomorrow and the rules said you must be in school on the day of the game. Mr. Stafford said, "Don't come to school on Monday. And if you get in another fight, plan on more time off."

Curt smiled to himself. Bud was working at a gas station while he was on a top-secret mission to save the United States from a crime that shouldn't have happened. He'd return home as a hero.

At dusk, they located Taylor. He held his .45 to his head about to pull the trigger and looked up, surprised.

Terrified, Curt ran to him and gently took the gun. "Man, this isn't necessary. We're here, and we need you." He was still in his parachute harness and pack, lying in the scorching sun for two days. Dehydrated, he was on the edge of death. The team gathered around, watching his face.

Taylor slowly shook his head. "I broke my ankle when I landed and got knocked out cold. I can't walk and it hurts to move my foot. I decided to kill myself because I'll be a burden."

Curt's heart thumped in his chest. "Man, you're the only one that knows how to remove the nuclear trigger. Without you, the mission is a wash." He sat down beside him. "I'll carry you until you can walk." He had to help Taylor. He must give him the will to live. He was a good guy, a recovering alcoholic, and was depressed over losing his kids in the divorce.

He put his hand on his shoulder. "They said it was a suicide mission."

Taylor's eyes were on the ground. "I'm sure my ex-wife will be happy I'm gone. The kids would get a nice monthly check with me out of the picture."

"Listen, friend, there's a lot more reasons to live than die." He glanced up at an eagle flying overhead. "Look at that. Isn't it beautiful? We're in a beautiful part of the planet. There's wildlife all around us and we're on the greatest adventure of our life. We'll get you out of this." He looked at the other men, and they nodded.

Taylor's eyes shifted from the soaring bird back to Curt. "Thanks, man." His voice was weak.

Curt dropped his pack, then unlaced the boot on Taylor's left foot. "Take a breath." He pulled at it as Taylor gritted his teeth. It wouldn't come off due to swelling. "Bet you could use a drink." He gave him water and a morphine pill. "Let's let that take effect, then I'll get it off." He released the parachute harness and Taylor's pack. Gently lifting him like a child, he leaned Taylor against a tree trunk in the shade. "You're probably hungry and thirsty."

He shook his head.

After Taylor rehydrated, Curt opened rations and helped him eat.

Everyone dropped their packs and found undergrowth to settle into for the night, then came back to Taylor. Carl kept talking to him, telling him he was the most valuable member of the team.

Once the morphine kicked in, Curt worked the combat boot off Taylor's foot. The ankle was purple and badly swollen. A bone poked through the skin. He gently shifted Taylor's leg, and it retracted. "Shit, you did a number." He wouldn't be walking, even with crutches. He needed a wheelchair.

The men frowned.

"Can you move your foot?" Curt asked.

He tried and, despite the morphine, pain shot up. He could move his toes but not his foot. "It's toasted."

"Yep, it's a compound break." Curt shook his head. "Probably both the tibia and fibula."

Jack stomped his boots, sending up a cloud of dust. "Fuck, see, I told you, they shoulda sent at least two men who knew how to defuse a nuke. This mission is going south."

Carl got in his face. "Listen punk. You better get your head screwed on right. We're here, and we're in this together. We need every man to do his job. You're supposed to help dig up the bomb if it's buried and guard Taylor while he's working to defuse it, but you're expendable."

Jack's face colored, and he turned around, stomping off. He was short and wiry and it was clear who would clean whose clock.

Spooker walked to him. "Listen, Jack, even if we had two bomb experts, we'd still need to deal with anyone injured. I've been on a lot of missions and things go wrong. Be flexible and innovative. Come back and act like a team player."

The men talked about how to carry Taylor's gear and him without abandoning anything essential. They went through their packs, burying as much as possible with pit shovels. "I can navigate by the sun and stars," Curt said, "Although they're light, we can get rid of the compasses."

"Keep your pistols and Taylor's tools. We gotta have them." Spooker dug a shallow pit.

They decided Curt and Carl would rotate carrying Taylor as they were the biggest and strongest. They'd trade the metal detector among everyone and when they found a stream, sink their carbines. Curt said, "We need to find the river basin. Intelligence thinks the bomb might have landed on a soft sand spit or island. It should have detonated unless it's defective."

Jack's upper lip curled. "Wouldn't it be ironic if they forgot to install the trigger and this mission was a waste? I heard they don't stick them in until the last minute."

They all stared at him.

Curt knew where they were. He pointed at the map. "If I'm right, we have four steep ridges to climb, then we should see a wide valley. Creeks feed to the main river, and we'll follow the first one we find. We'll likely come across some small villages on the way. The maps aren't well marked, and they're old. There could be North Korean military installations on strategic high points for radio communications. It'd be easy to stumble into a patrol or an enemy camp." Thinking of his mother's faith, he said, "Relax. If everybody does their job we'll get home safely."

They slept restlessly. As sunlight cracked the horizon open, Curt tightly rewrapped and splinted Taylor's ankle, then hoisted him up. "Hell, you're not heavy. What, maybe a hundred-thirty pounds?" He told the other guys. "Put his and my pack on his back, and I can handle it if someone carries the metal detector."

They walked slowly, scanning for North Korean patrols and watching for edible plants. They didn't talk. Birds flitted and called from the trees and brush. Occasionally, a hare sprinted off and sat under a bush as if invisible. It would have been easy to have it for dinner, but they didn't dare shoot or start a fire.

At the top of the next hill, Curt whispered, out of breath, "I'm pretty sure once we get through this valley and up the next ridge, we'll see a creek." He pointed. "That valley looks greener over there." He grew up hunting and fishing in the Rocky Mountains and was never lost.

Carl offered to take Taylor, but Curt waved him off. "I'm good for a couple more hours since we took a break for lunch."

Taylor slept most of the day, knocked out from the morphine. Curt pulled off his commando cap to wipe the trickling sweat from his face and neck. But he couldn't keep the irritating black flies and gnats, attracted by the salt and odor, from plaguing his skin.

The sun mellowed, more orange than yellow. They rested under a red-barked pine tree, eating while using hand signals and short whispers. It was incredibly exciting. They were on a mission to save the world from communism. A part of him wanted to jump up in celebration as if he scored a touchdown. They would be heroes, and his career in the Navy would be something else! He'd have stories to tell his grandchildren like Grandpa.

There was a partial moon, and they traveled in the darkness, barely making out an animal trail. Guys kept stumbling and making too much noise. Carl whispered, "There will be more human activity the closer we get to the river. Stay alert." He took Taylor on his back. "Shit, Conrad, you're stronger than hell. You carried him and two packs the whole day. This is over two hundred pounds."

"Yeah, my whole body is sore."

They redistributed the contents of the packs among the men and buried all but two pit shovels and the grenades. Spooker stood with his ears twitching. He though he heard something. "If we get in a firefight, we're better off with ammo than grenades."

Jack complained, "Why the hell did they overload us to begin with?"

"Quit yer bitchin,' kid," Carl spat. "I don't hear Curt complaining, and you're the same age. He's been packing a hell of a lot more weight than you."

"He's a lot bigger and stronger."

"You want a turn carrying Taylor?"

He shut up. Usually, they put the wise-ass on point where he'd be the first one shot, but Spooker didn't trust him. "Curt, you're a mountain man, mind taking the lead?"

He nodded and carefully led the team, following rocky animal trails that might not show their footprints. The only sound was the rustling of equipment and quiet footsteps. It felt safe. A deer spooked and scared the shit out of the team.

Curt flashed on hunting near his home. Deer often foraged the apples in late fall. He was going for the state rushing record as the tailback while Bud was a pulling guard. Bud deliberately missed a block on a sweep, and the defensive end speared Curt in the thigh. Limping back to the huddle, he said nothing. He had high pain tolerance, and it took a maiden in distress to make him mad.

The quarterback said, "Bud, you missed that block on purpose. Do it again, and I'll tell Coach Ecklund to pull you. We can get by without you, but we gotta have Curt."

A farming community, the high school allowed boys to attend classes only three days a week if they kept their grades up while they worked the harvest. Wasn't a problem for Curt. He was in the running for valedictorian, and Dad needed him on the apple farm. He ran a flatbed wagon by himself, jumping off, and stacking apple boxes three or four rows high the Mexican workers filled. His one-eyed dog, Partner, was always with him. The collie lost an eye several years back when he and Curt ran off a mountain lion attacking their chickens. It once was a handsome dog, but now one side was disfigured. Made Curt love him even more. Like his father, he rooted for the underdog.

Darlene was the most desirable girl in the county. Guys drooled over her, and she knew it. She hung on his arm as if he were Prince Charming. Curt gradually got so he ignored Darlene's wandering eyes, her touching other guys on the shoulder, and her laughter at their jokes that weren't funny. Girls fawned over him after Grandpa helped him repair the 1935 cream-colored Lincoln convertible. He and Darlene cruised Delta's main street in it, turning heads as her long blonde hair flew wildly around the car. He always brought Partner despite Darlene's protests since they were best buds.

"It's so ugly, I'm embarrassed," she complained.

It loved hanging its head out the window, gulping air.

He liked Darlene because she made him laugh, and she laughed at his jokes, even the ones that weren't funny.

He mentally slapped himself. He needed to pay attention to where he was at.

Near midnight, he stopped at the top of a hill they climbed. He pointed. "See that red light on the next ridge? I'd bet that's a radio transmission station and there's probably a camp somewhere close by. We better stop here and camo up with branches, then scout the area before proceeding."

Carl was exhausted and accidentally sat Taylor down on his bad side.

He moaned loudly.

Jack slapped his palm over Taylor's mouth. "Shut the fuck up!"

Curt firmly took Jack's wrist, removing it as he signaled with a finger to his lips.

They camped after force-feeding Taylor, who was out of it from the pain meds. They rotated the watch every hour. After dawn broke, Curt woke to the sound of footsteps, laughter, and talking. He sat up with a start. The sky was pure blue without a cloud.

He crept to look over the ridge. A North Korean patrol walked along the hillside, joking with each other, completely unaware the American team was a hundred yards above them. He woke the others, gesturing to get their weapons loaded and stay quiet.

Jack was on guard. He dozed in the sun with his back to a big boulder, right out in the open. Curt touched his toes and cupped his palm over the big mouth's face.

Jack woke with a start and started to speak, but Curt kept him quiet. His heart pounded, and he wanted to strangle the idiot but silently motioned Jack to crawl around the other side of the boulder as he pointed down where the patrol rambled loudly. Someone started singing. The patrol sensed no danger.

After the North Koreans disappeared around a bend of the hillside, the team held a whispered conference. They sent Spooker and Curt to scout the area to locate the communist camp and figure out the best way to avoid contact. Curt was sure a creek lay over the next hill as it looked like there may be a wider valley but there also would be subsequent hills and valleys where the river ran. They agreed the other three would stay put even if it took all day and night unless they heard gunfire, which meant they made contact. In that case, the three men would make a wide loop of this valley, and they would try to reconnect to the northwest.

"We're fucked." Jack threw his hands in the air. "We're gonna die."

Everyone glared at him.

Curt was happy to go scout. He hated sitting around and wondered if Carl would end up smacking California Jack. He told Carl, "Maybe feed him some morphine. That'd keep him quiet. He's pretty worthless as it is."

Carl made a fist. "I'll just cold-cock him."

They were a good team. Spooker had mission experience, and Curt was a natural leader who spent years stalking animals in the pinon-cedars around Cedaredge and up the draws of Grand Mesa, a rocky country not dissimilar to this. Within an hour, they understood each other intuitively. Soon, they located the North Korean camp and plotted a course to avoid it. A creek likely fed to the main river. They followed it. Intelligence said their objective was in a broad valley.

They got back at dusk. No one spoke since the North Korean patrol had returned the same way. Everyone was tense. The scouts needed a break, and they took a nap. Everyone ate; they fed Taylor and gave him more morphine. They combined med kits and kept the suicide pill in a shirt pocket for easy access. No one wanted to be taken prisoner. The stories of North Korean POW camps were enough to make warriors shake in the night.

As the moon rose, they started with Spooker leading. The enlarging moon gave more light than the night before. It was quiet except for a few night creatures hunting for a meal. The crickets stopped sawing their legs when they approached. Curt carried Taylor and two lighter packs. Carl took the tail since no one trusted Jack to be alert and not do something stupid.

Making their way across the ridge above the North Korean camp, they walked quietly, taking a step at a time, pausing, and then stepping again. Spooker pointed out the direction of the camp when they were parallel to it. The breeze brought noises and the smell of cooking meat. It made them hungry.

Carl put his fingers to Jack's lips and shook his head. They moved on, winding farther around the camp. In the early morning, they bedded down in a thick brush stand. Exhausted, they crashed, but decided two men needed to stay on watch to ensure one was awake after Jack's fuckup.

Curt and Carl trusted each other and took the first watch. They were both sore from packing Taylor. They agreed to wiggle the sleeping man's boot if he snored. It started raining. Lightly at first, then it turned into a drenching thunderstorm. The rain was cold. They had ditched the rain tarps and every other parka to lighten the load so the two men shivered together under one rain parka. Figuring no patrols would be out until after the storm passed, Carl whispered, "Well, this is what we wanted, right? Adventure."

"Yeah. Can't say I regret it." Curt pointed a finger at his head. "Yet." He winked.

"As long as we don't get captured I'll be happy. I'd rather die fighting. I'd do a suicide run with my gun blasting."

"I'm with you on that."

Carl said with a slack expression, "Listen if I'm wounded, don't rescue me. Save yourself."

"Like hell. I owe you for pulling me out of that tree."

"Screw this kinda talk. Let's think about how we're going to locate the bomb."

They outlined a strategy to crisscross one side of the river basin in mile-wide squares. They'd do that for five miles, then cross the river and repeat the pattern. They would only use the metal detector where a bomb might have buried itself, otherwise, it would burn out the battery. "Sand spits or islands." Curt wore a tight-lipped expression.

"This might take us much more than a week. We'll run out of food and have to forage."

Curt made a silly face. "We'll live on love."

Carl punched his arm.

The storm passed, leaving everything soggy. Jack started to complain, but Carl stood over him. "Soldier up," he whispered fiercely in his ear with a clenched fist.

No one slept well since it was daylight and it got hotter as the sun moved overhead. The sky was mostly clear with scattered, fluffy white clouds. Periodically, someone got up to relieve himself. Whoever was on watch signaled it was safe. They didn't hear any patrols. Curt slept next to Taylor to comfort him when he moaned with pain. He'd need to be on a low dose of morphine to defuse the bomb.

The next night with a brighter moon smiling down on them, they followed the creek to a larger stream, camped during the day, then followed it again until the valley opened up. Success depended on the silence between your steps.

A small covey of black grouse flushed. Everyone froze. Carl winked and lifted his rifle and aimed at them, grinning.

Curt gave him a thumbs up, thinking it would be cool to go bird hunting with him when they got back to the States on leave.

He was the top scorer in basketball and last spring, broke the state record for the high hurdles. He was awarded a full-ride scholarship in football to CU Boulder, yet was almost as proud he won the County talent show. He fingerpicked guitar and sang in his best Bing Crosby voice, "Some Enchanted Evening." Even his normally reserved parents gushed. His mom said, "Curt, you're a natural and handsome. You should go to Nashville."

Dad huffed, "He'll be a sailor if anything. He will serve his country and make us proud." They often argued because the Cold War heated up, and McCarthy was finding subversives everywhere in the government and Hollywood. Dad served on a destroyer during World War II and received the Navy Cross for heroism along with several purple hearts. Grandpa was a decorated machine gunner in World War I. Military service was expected.

Dad said he should enlist immediately, but Mom wanted him to finish his bachelor's and then enlist. "He would go in as an officer. He's a natural leader." They constantly argued about their son's future since he was an only child. Curt wanted to make them proud, and this was his chance. He felt high on the adventure – it was more important than anything he had ever done.

They were getting closer, and Taylor was doing somewhat better but there was no way he could walk. When sure no Koreans were anywhere close, Curt interviewed him about how to remove the nuclear trigger.

"It's in the nose. This one is likely defective because it should have detonated in the air or on impact. They want us to retrieve it so if the North Koreans find it, they won't be able to reverse engineer it, and also, the government can claim it was not an armed device. It gives plausible deniability." He described removing the plate on the nose, unhooking the wires, taking more screws out, and so on until, at last, you removed the whole assembly. The men listened closely. It was a technical process with many steps. They looked at one another, wondering if anyone besides Taylor could carry it out. This bomb was the second generation of the Fat Boy dropped on the two Japanese cities. It had more explosive power and would spread radiation throughout the riparian system and, depending on the wind, much of North Korea. They had to keep Taylor healthy. Curt dripped sweat as he listened to Taylor describe the delicate process.

During daylight, they picked anything edible and dug for roots. Near dusk, Jack found a patch of elderberries and started stuffing his mouth.

Spooker whispered, "Man, you're supposed to cook those. They have small amounts of cyanide, and you'll get sick."

"These are great and there's enough for all of us." His mouth looked like a child eating a grape popsicle.

"You better stop now, Jack." Spooker shook his head. "You can die from elderberries if you eat them raw."

It was dark enough to move. "Come on, let's go." Carl walked away.

Jack fell behind because he kept shoveling elderberries in his mouth. Within twenty minutes, he began walking slower and slower, holding his stomach and dropping further behind. He sweated furiously. The next thing they knew, he threw up, then got the shits, barely getting his pants down in time.

Curt held his shoulders up so he wouldn't get it all over his pants. He crapped on the toes of Curt's boots.

Curt whispered, "Dang it Jack, I don't mind helping you, but spray it straight down."

They dragged him under some bushes after wiping his butt because he was so sick. They propped Taylor against a tree, and he said he'd stand watch. He laughed. "Stand, know what I mean?"

They would have cracked jokes about Jack but stayed quiet. Still, it was funny. They decided three of them would scout ahead. Taylor pressed his lips together. "Don't worry about me, I'll keep Jack Shit in line." He cocked his weapon. "Curt, you might want to find some big leaves and wipe that crap off your toes. They'll smell you coming."

Curt, Spooker, and Carl returned several hours later. Jack hadn't recovered. They camped that night as billowing clouds skipped across the sky.

Carl got in his face, whispering fiercely, "Jack, you're expendable. One more screw-up, one more complaint, and we're leaving you."

"Man, I'm sorry. I'll listen, I won't bitch, and I'll do my best from here on out."

They rotated the watch in pairs. The moon reflected the sun's rays brighter each night. During his turn with Carl, Curt sat staring at the pine forest, listening to small animals foraging.

After the spring prom dance, he took Darlene for a drive up the Grand Mesa, and they stopped at a look out where they could see the valley from Cedaredge to Delta and Montrose. After steaming up the windows, he asked her to marry him.

"Yes, but only if you're going to CU instead of the Navy like your dad wants. I can't see myself as a Navy wife."

He wasn't lying when he said, "I'm thinking about my options. Kinda depends on you."

As soon as they graduated, Curt spent his free time after farm work at Hart's Basin, the fruit grower's lake. A heavy rope was tied to a big cottonwood tree near the spillway. He and other athletes timed each other to see how fast they could climb up the branch holding the rope, swing out into the lake, and swim as fast and far as they could to the shallow end, a mile away, and then race back. His dog swam until he tired and then waited on the shore.

Curt always won because Partner swam out to meet him, encouraging him to give it his all. When they finished the swim, they exercised and ragged each other, saying, "I'll make the grade in the Navy, you won't." Everyone knew Curt could get into the frogmen if he wanted. He didn't. He wanted to play football at the University of Colorado.

Word got around about their activities, and Bud Hamilton showed up with Darlene in his new Ford pickup. He opened the passenger door for her, taking her hand as if she was a princess. She stepped out as Curt reached the top of the rope swing.

Partner growled at Bud, showing his teeth.

Curt looked down at them together as Partner tried to get between Bud and Darlene. She told him that she was going shopping today in Grand Junction with her parents. Anger coursed up his chest into his neck. He slid down the rope. His muscles bulged as he walked straight at Bud. Partner's neck hair stood up. Without saying anything, he stood, looking from her scared face to Bud's defiant expression. His feelings were mixed. He wanted her, and mostly, he wanted to punch Bud's face. Yet he felt betrayed and upset with her. He clenched and unclenched his fists.

"Cat got your tongue, Cunt-rad?" Bud said, sarcastically.

Partner growled, baring his teeth again.

Curt stared him down, then frowned at Darlene. "Take off my class ring. I don't trust you anymore."

"No, please Curt, it's not what you think. After shopping, my folks dropped me off at the Chocolate Shop in Cedaredge, and Bud was there. He asked if I wanted to go watch you guys swing off the rope swing. It's nothing, please, I'm not with him." She moved to Curt's side and tried to take his hand.

Grins on their faces, the guys watched, expecting a knockdown fight. "Bud will take Curt down."

"No way, Curt is taller and stronger. He'll punch Bud out before he has a chance."

They started taking bets. "A quarter on Curt, two-to-one odds."

Curt regarded her baby-blue eyes and shook his head. "I've been thinking. My mom says I need to stop being so naïve. You're going to Mesa College in Grand Junction and will be home every weekend, and Bud isn't going to college. I'm going to Boulder or the Navy and either way, I won't be around much." He held out his palm. "I think we should break up, then you can ride around with anybody you want. I don't want to control you."

Bud's face broke into a wide smile. "I told you, Darlene. Cunt-rad doesn't care about you. He's not committed to you."

"Stop that, his last name is Conrad." She smiled at Curt.

Partner growled.

Curt took a deep breath, then walked over to his car and felt under the driver's seat. Bringing out a ring box, he opened it and showed everyone a sparkling diamond he spent a fortune on. "Although you said yes, guess I was premature to buy this engagement ring. I don't think you're ready to commit."

Darlene reached for it, but he snapped the box closed. "No."

"I can be loyal, please, give it to me!" She bounced up and down, clapping her hands like a cheerleader.

Bud smirked. "You don't want to marry Cunt-rad. He'll go off to the Navy and get himself killed. His daddy is saying he will do the patriotic thing despite having a full-ride scholarship. Me, I'll be working at Eckert Motors, and I'll take good care of you."

Curt raised his chin. "Darlene, give me my class ring. I'm setting you free." He felt a sense of relief.

The guys sniggered.

Reluctantly, she did, then she turned to Bud. "Let's go. I never want to see this asshole again."

They peeled out, throwing gravel and hitting Partner as he chased the pickup. He came back to Curt, happily panting.

Curt kneeled and hugged the collie. "Good boy." He looked at the dog's good eye. It was glazed over with a cataract. "You can smell evil, can't you?"

The collie whined and licked his hands.

The fellows were disappointed. "Why didn't you punch him out? Geez. And why did you break up with Darlene? She's the most beautiful girl around, and she's got a personality that won't quit."

Curt shrugged. "I've never trusted her. She flirts with everyone, even you guys." He looked into each of his friends' eyes, then said, "I have a feeling she would fool around on me even if we were married. I'm better off without her." He had Partner. What more does a guy need than a dog?

That night in North Korea, the clouds strung out like links of sausage, hanging low over the hills. It felt pungent and rich, as if pregnant with the scent of flowers. Seven days after bailing out, they found the main river basin and each night, began crisscrossing the banks in mile-wide squares. They heard or saw several North Korean patrols but like the first one, the communists laughed, sang, and talked. They saw a lot of wildlife: geese, martins, rosy finches and cuckoos. The ducks paddled away, oblivious to the war.

Each time they saw a large sand spit or island, Curt unpacked the metal detector and scanned. Brown frogs sang love songs. A kingfisher snagged a small fish and took off. Three large geese looped over but didn't land. They ducked episodic North Korean patrols easily as the men were casual, their weapons slung over their backs as if out for a walk with a girlfriend. The team could hear them coming for miles.

Again sitting on watch, Curt remembered that on June 25, 1950, the North Korean communists invaded the south, quickly overrunning the country and pushing the U.S. and ROK forces into a small corner in the southeast of the peninsula around Busan. His dad was damned near hysterical. "You gotta join now. You gotta go fight those commie pigs." He was a staunch Republican who supported Senator McCarthy in his search for communists. He agreed with McCarthy that President Truman was a son-of-a-bitch.

"No! He has a full-ride scholarship to CU!" His mother yelled. She was a Democrat and couldn't stand McCarthy. They fought until midnight.

Curt felt conflicted as he watched them argue. He knew his mom was right, but he should own up and be a man. He was a risk taker and rode his bike over rough trails, taking jumps that sailed him high into the air. He was in his element on this adventure to find the nuclear bomb.

He recalled that Dad walked over to the wall where his Purple Hearts and Navy Cross hung with a photo of him shaking President Roosevelt's hand. He turned to Curt. "It's up to you, son. Hide at college for four years while brave men fight for our country, or help save the world from communism."

The next day, at his father's prodding, Curt made the trip to the Navy recruiter in Grand Junction. He took the tests, and the recruiter excitedly said, "You have the scores for officer's school. I'll sign you up for the frogmen and you'll have adventures most guys can't imagine."

He needed a parent's signature since he was seventeen.

On July 5th after he rubbed the collie's tummy and ears, his dad took him to Grand Junction and signed the papers. That afternoon, he rode a bus to Denver for the physical. He sang to himself, "Bell bottom trousers coats of Navy blue, Momma loves a sailor boy, and he loves her too." Nothing would happen to him. He'd come home a hero and find a good woman like Mom.

They ran out of rations. Spooker had wilderness survival training and was a pro at finding edible plants. They smelled fish in one section of the river, and Curt caught several using an improvised pole and line. The men cheered him, silently clapping their fingers. They could not make a campfire and pretended they had chopsticks, eating them raw like sushi. Silence became a habit. Even Jack fell into line— despite his frustration and red face, he didn't speak.

Two nights later, Curt scanned a large sand spit and the metal detector pinged a large object. He waved the men over. Carl sat Taylor down gently, and they started digging. The night was quiet, not even an owl hooted. The only sound was the soft lapping of the river. Their shoveling noises seemed to echo down the valley.

Soon, they struck metal. Guys waved their pit shovels in silent celebration, then got back at it. The damn thing was buried nose down, and they had to get it fully exposed and tipped to the side. The plan was to rebury it as soon as Taylor removed the trigger, so they dug a deep, long trench and eventually got the five-hundred-pound bomb toppled over in the wet sandy mud.

Curt carried Taylor to the nose and using a shielded flashlight, he began taking screws out. As he pulled the exterior plate, they heard a North Korean patrol coming. They weren't singing and laughing but were noisy as they tromped along.

Quickly, they shoveled sand over the bomb, and Carl hauled Taylor onto his back. They scrambled into some brush down the bank opposite from the soldiers and lay quietly. This was the first night patrol they had encountered. It scared them because the soldiers were quiet and serious. They carefully readied weapons without shoving in shells for fear the passing North Koreans would hear the clicking. Long minutes.

The patrol passed. An owl hooted. Curt remembered some Native Americans thought it was an omen that someone would die.

The men exhaled. They silently agreed to stay hidden. The bomb would wait. They moved further downstream in case the patrol spotted them. They hid in a thick bunch of overgrowth. They readied their weapons to shoot it out with the communists. If they got them all, maybe they could still defuse the bomb. They hoped the soldiers would stay on the side of the river they came up. If their luck held.

The sky grew darker in preparation for the first light of dawn. Curt felt a sinister presence in the darkness and tried to stay awake although he wasn't on watch.

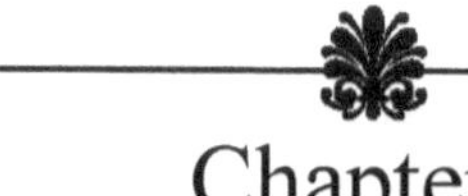

Chapter 4
Captured

As it broke dawn, Curt came awake to the sound of rifle bolts locking into place. They were surrounded.

No one spoke. A North Korean pressed an AK47 barrel against his forehead. He didn't dare pull his weapon. Jack and Spooker were on guard but had no chance. Soldiers held rifle barrels pressed to their backs. Their hands went up. The other men woke as an AK 47 barrel touched their heads.

A patrol leader yelled in Korean. It was clear what he meant.

Curt gave an involuntary shudder as he warned the others, "He said don't move, or we're dead."

They struck him in the face with a rifle butt for speaking.

His nose bled.

The communists gathered their weapons, then stood them up, excitedly taking their .45 semi-auto pistols, and then chatted happily to each other in Korean. "Look at this. Wow, what a weapon!" They argued about who got them. Five pistols among the twenty men on the patrol. The squad leader fired one and screamed in Korean, "We'll take everything to camp. The lieutenant will decide." He unfastened the holster from Curt and slid the .45 into it after buckling it to his waist.

Carl reminded everyone, "Give only your name, rank, and serial number. If you say anything, it gives them the incentive to probe. Act compliant and don't look them in the face, or they'll think you're disrespectful." They slugged him in the gut with a rifle butt for speaking. He stood stiffly, taking shallow breaths.

They kept trying to force Taylor to stand.

Hands lashed behind their backs with parachute chords, Curt and Carl looked at each other. He wondered if they should explain Taylor's broken ankle in Korean. Would speaking Korean help or make him a target? Taylor screamed in pain each time they made him put weight on his foot.

Curt knew it took eight to ten weeks for a broken bone to heal. It was only a week. If they forced him to walk on it, it'd break again, and he may lose the foot. Taylor yelped again as they slapped him, trying to force him to stand.

He pointed at Taylor's foot, "Mang-ga jyeoss-eo." It's broken.

The patrol leader strode to Curt. "Hangug-eohaseyo?" Do you speak Korean?

He realized speaking Korean made him look like a highly trained spy. He shook his head, No.

He punched him in the gut.

It didn't phase Curt. He just stared at the guy.

"Teopeu gai, eung?" Tough guy, huh? He hit him in the chin with his rifle butt.

Curt fell sideways to the earth. Wiping blood from his mouth, he shook his head and slowly got to his knees.

The Korean kicked him in the face as if punting a football.

He went down.

Looking around, the patrol leader said in Korean, "You're commando spies on a secret mission. We found your buried gear." He picked up the metal detector and squinted. His face went dark. "Sit up! Why do you have this?" He held it to Curt's face. "Tell me why you have a metal detector!"

He stated his name, rank, and serial number.

The squad leader kicked him in the face.

Blood ran from Curt's nose and mouth as he lay on the ground.

The team members stared at the earth. They were told if captured, "Don't look a North Korean in the eye. Bow and be submissive. They view us as animals and think beating us is no different from kicking a dog."

When Curt could stand, they loaded Taylor onto his back and lashed his hands around his chest so he couldn't let go. They looped parachute lines around each of the American's necks and marched them to a small camp. The unease he felt earlier slapped his face, mocking. He felt like a soft-shelled crab about to be eaten.

The North Koreans laughed like ducks. The camp leader rewarded the platoon with cups of soju, a strong liquor.

They bound the American's ankles and sat them in a circle in the center of camp. Facing outward, ropes were looped tightly around their necks and tied to a tree. Yellow forsythia bushes grew near their tents. A sparrow hopped from branch to branch, oblivious to the humans.

Soldiers happily took their boots and belts and put them on. They were far too large but better than their cheap Chinese boots. The heat fell on them like a wool blanket, and they sweated. A sergeant interrogated Curt in Korean. He smelled of alcohol and sweat. "You're a spy because you speak Korean, and you're muscled up. Special forces, huh? We found buried parachutes and other gear. What's your mission? Why do you have a metal detector with you?"

Curt said, "My name is Phil Brown, private first class, serial number 0658 913 G131."

The leader didn't understand English. He barked, "You speak Korean so I know you're on a secret mission. Why do you have a metal detector with you?"

Curt kept his eyes on the ground without speaking.

He hit Curt in the chest with his rifle butt.

Curt jerked back but didn't go down.

The North Korean looked shocked. He said to his men. "This man is like steel. These guys are highly trained commandos." He turned back to Curt. "Speak Korean. I know you can. You're a spy. What is your mission? Why were you on the river bank with a metal detector?" He held the pill he found in Curt's front shirt pocket. "Is this a suicide pill? You're spies!"

"My name is Phil Brown. Private first class, serial number 0658 913 G131." That's what his dog tags said. The Navy gave them fake identities.

They beat and kicked him unconscious.

The next morning, a military truck arrived. It was a crisp spring day without a cloud in the sky and began to warm. They blindfolded them. They were hauled bouncing and jostling in the back of the truck, their hands lashed to the wood rails out in the bright sun. They rode all day without food or water to a small, crude prison camp. When the blindfolds were removed, the jail appeared it was constructed in a hurry as a temporary holding pen, built of bamboo with a metal roof. Twelve-foot high barbed wire surrounded a roughly circular yard. In front of the jail sat a rectangular pad of concrete that may have once supported a building. There was an elevated office and a set of huts for the guards. A small patch of cherry and prune trees outside the fence formed small pink and white buds.

Curt thought they were somewhere northwest of Sinpyong, a small village on the south fork of the Taedong River.

Immediately, the short, pudgy camp commander began interrogations, starting with Curt. His translator spoke English.

"What were you doing in North Korea? What was your mission?" One of their .45s sat in a holster around his waist.

"My name is Phil Brown, private first class, serial number 0658 913 G131."

"You're spies that parachuted into our country on a secret mission. I know you're officers because you all carried 45s, probably CIA, huh? And you speak Korean. Why do you have a metal detector? You're all muscled up, tough sons-a-bitches, not regular troopers." He snarled, "What are these pills? Each of you carried one in your front shirt pocket. Are these suicide pills? You are spies!"

Curt wanted to say, "Why don't you take the pill and find out?" He said only his name, rank, and serial number.

They pounded him unconscious, then stripped him naked and shoved him into a horizontal bamboo rod cage.

When he came to, he saw Carl in a similar cage, his face bleeding and bruised. The horror of what they faced hit him. *Would the men say only their name, rank, and serial number or would one slip?* He wondered if they would survive. *This is God's ultimate test of me.* He tried to blow biting flies from his face. His feet and hands were tied and the bamboo bars pressed against his shoulders. *How did they force my body into this?* He couldn't see beyond Carl but imagined the other men were naked and in similar horizon cages. The scorching sun beat down. He was thirsty and hungry.

Carl's eyes flickered open.

Curt mouthed, "We're fucked."

He peeked around outside the fence as best he could. A thick evergreen forest with a few bushes surrounded the camp. Small birds hopped among branches and sang, establishing territory for their nests. Breeding season. A patch of cherry trees bloomed and bees anxiously awaited nectar. He thought of home. He wasn't a hero now. He was a fool to volunteer. His body hurt from the beatings. He inhaled the spring air and wished he was on the farm tractor with his dog running close behind.

A guard realized he was conscious and ran to inform the commander. He came out with his translator, strutting with self-importance as if his belly didn't hang over his belt. He smiled, showing bad teeth. "I know you speak Korean. Are you ready to talk?"

When Curt didn't answer, he pointed at the sharpened bamboo stake the guard held. "You need encouragement. We have your parachutes and the other things you buried. You had compasses, grenades, and suicide pills. You must have hiked a long way. Why do you have a metal detector with you? What were you searching for?"

"My name is Phil Brown, private first class, serial number 0658 913 G131." He glanced at the bamboo stake, trying to prepare himself.

"You're a commando team on some top-secret mission. Your .45s mean you're officers or special agents." He smiled as he pointed at Curt's face. "And you speak Korean, so you're highly trained for a special mission. Are you CIA, Rangers or Frogmen?"

Curt stayed silent.

The commander nodded, and the guard stabbed the stake through the bamboo bars into Curt's right thigh.

"Ouch!" He fought tears as hot emotions hit his chest. He'd like to...

"You either talk or enjoy my methods. I've been carefully planning what I will do to my first guests before they're transferred north. I will get your confessions, and they'll see how good I am. Now talk!" He yelled and someone brought an American parachute. He unfolded it and laid it over the bamboo cage. "How would you like a little shade? The patrol found this parachute and three others buried. We're only missing one. This is yours, right?"

He took a quick breath and fought through the emotions, saying his phony name, rank, and serial number.

The guard stabbed his left thigh with the stake.

Squeezing his eyes closed, he fought through the pain and rage, refusing to give them the satisfaction of an outcry.

The briefing officer said they shouldn't give captors any information. "They will take anything you say and twist it, trying to lead you to reveal more. They want to get you confused. They will get contradictory statements from different team members. They will write down what you say and force you to sign it. Soon you'll be trapped by your own words, and it won't stop the torture. The best strategy is to say only your name, rank, and serial number."

He gritted his teeth and tears ran as they tormented him until he was too exhausted to keep his eyes open. Jack and Taylor screamed as they were tortured. Carl yelled his name, rank, and serial number to remind them not to say anything.

Curt hollered, "Don't give them the satisfaction of screaming!" It earned him another round of stake punctures. By the time they finished, he bled from every major muscle group. He lay in the heat and flies, sweating, hurting all over. Rage mixed with fear. His thighs hurt the worst. He felt blood dripping from his skin. He closed his eyes. A guard poked him with a stake. He fought the scream of pain and stared at the hot blue sky, thinking of home.

That evening, the guards pulled Curt from the bamboo rod cage, tied his hands in the back, then dragged him by the ankles face-down across the uneven concrete of the compound. The guards dragged him straight into a deep divot. *Wham!* His right eyebrow bled. Two steps, and they lifted his legs high, scraping his eyebrow against the other side of the pothole. At the crude jail structure, they untied his hands, punched him, and threw him onto the dirt floor.

He lay barely conscious, listening as they hauled in the rest of his team. As his strength returned, he got on his knees and looked through the bamboo bars at the bruised and bleeding seamen in separate cells. He asked, "You guys okay?"

Immediately, two guards opened the cage door. One said, "Don't kick this one in the stomach. He's all muscle." They kicked him in the groin and pounded his face, saying in Korean, "No talking."

Curt wanted to fight back and cuss them out but the briefing officer said, "Be passive and act compliant. Don't give them an attitude, or they will cut your nuts off. Say only the name, rank, and serial number on your dog tags."

Later that night, a young guard brought him thin rice soup and a cup of water. The boy had kind eyes as if he didn't want to be there.

He tried not to gulp it so he wouldn't throw up. He saw Carl looking at him through the bars of the cage. They didn't dare speak.

Carl gave him a thumbs up and mouthed, "Hang in there."

Chapter 5
Losing A Finger

In the morning, the North Koreans fed them thin rice soup. The orange glow in the east turned a hot yellow. They got back their underwear along with straw slippers. Curt felt better. At least he wasn't completely naked. Probably their hairy bodies grossed out the Asians.

As the day warmed, the commander pulled him into the office. "Why are you in North Korea? Why do you have a metal detector with you? I know you parachuted in. Confess you are commandos and tell me what your mission was, and I'll go easy on you."

Curt stated his name, rank, and serial number.

Each time, they slapped, kicked, and punched him. Commander Park gave up and ordered the guards to beat the holy shit out of him.

He awoke inside a horizontal bamboo cage and heard Jack cussing in the office as he was interrogated. "Fuck you, bastards! Ow!"

They did the same to all the men, then left them moaning and sweating in the horizontal cages. Around noon, guards pulled Curt. They tied his arms behind the back of a wooden chair and tightly wrapped his ankles with barbed wire to the chair legs. He faced his men in the horizontal cages.

The commander interrogated each man, having a guard stab him with a sharpened bamboo stake in the chest and shoulders. When Curt tried to look away, guards held his head to watch the man being tortured. The translator called out. "Brown, you're the leader. It's up to you to tell the men to cooperate, or watch them bleed."

Jack screamed the loudest, and Curt said, "Jack, don't give them the satisfaction. Grit your teeth."

The commander asked the translator what he said, then strode to Curt. "You think you're tough because you're big and muscled up. You don't care about these men. You'll let them get tortured to death." Teeth bared, he pulled out a knife. He touched it to Curt's index finger on his right hand. "I'll show you! You'll get the worst of it. I'll cut your fingers off one at a time if you don't cooperate."

Curt avoided his eyes, but the guards forced him to look straight at him. He focused on the ugly black mole on the side of his nose. His face was so close he smelled the kimchi and cigarettes on his breath.

"What was your mission? Confess! Why did you have a metal detector? What were you looking for?"

"My name is Phil Brown, private first class, serial number 0658 913 G131."

The commander's knife plunged into the back of Curt's left shoulder. He snarled. "Maybe I'll just kill you!"

Curt grimaced and breathed through the pain. Tears rolled down his cheeks as a wave of hatred coursed up.

Pissed as hell, the pudgy commander tipped over the chair, kicked him, and stomped to his office.

The men lay in the heat with no food or water until dusk. Tiny birds sang in the forest. A cow mewed loudly as if upset. A woodpecker tapped. A crow landed on his chair and examined him, then hopped down in front of him. Curt stared into its intelligent eyes, willing it to fly for help. He desperately wanted out of here, afraid there was more to come.

Near dark, the guards pulled everyone out of the cages, leaving Curt in the yard tied to the chair. His hands and feet were numb from the ropes. As Taylor stumbled by, he put his index finger to his head. He wanted to kill himself.

Sometime in the night, it rained. Although it was cold, Curt felt a little better as he caught water in his dry mouth, wetting his cracked lips. He told himself, "Go numb all over. Stop feeling anything." God, how he longed to be back home.

Around noon the next day, guards carried him in the chair to the commander's office. The commander said, as he lit a cigarette, "I've changed my strategy. Instead of torturing your men, I'll make you the example. Maybe one of them has enough compassion for you, he will talk." He flashed a hunting knife. Holding it to Curt's nose, he nicked the end, enough that blood ran. "You're a handsome man. You look like that American rock star, Elvis. I bet you have girls falling over themselves." He put the point to Curt's cheek. "Wonder if they will still like your face scarred like fish scales. Ever heard of 'Death by a Thousand Cuts?' I can fillet you without killing you." He smiled cruelly, showing rotten teeth and exhaling smoke. "Tell me one thing.

One simple thing, and I will give you food and water." He waited, but Curt kept his lips closed and clenched his jaws.

He looked at Curt's high school ring on his left hand. Seeing the green skin underneath it, he dismissed the cheap thing. If it were gold or silver, he would have taken the ring finger. "So, how about your fingers? You like being able to do things with your hands, right?" He had the guards untie one arm, and then they held Curt's right hand on his desk, spreading his fingers.

He smiled. "I keep my knife very sharp." He ordered a young guard. "Bring me a dry bamboo rod about the size of a finger."

He returned with one. The commander held the rod next to Curt's hand. He sliced through it. "See, it will cut through your finger bones." He waited a long minute, black and yellow teeth showing through his twisted smile. "One little thing, something simple like where you grew up." He lit another cigarette, blowing the smoke in Curt's face.

Curt didn't speak. He fought against overwhelming fear and tried to keep his eyes steady.

The knife point slammed into the desk a millimeter from the end of his middle finger. "Talk!"

"My name is Phil Brown, private first class, serial number 0658 913 G131."

The commander put the sharp knife back into his sheath. He said to a guard, "Bring me my special knife."

It was a rusty, ragged-edged bread knife. He held it to Curt's face. "You'll enjoy this one more." He placed the knife edge on Curt's little finger. "Last chance to talk." Looking up into his eyes, he gradually sliced deeper, back and forth, sawing into the bone. Blood spurted. He watched Curt's contorted face, slowly applying more pressure. "This is too bad. You could have plenty to eat and drink. I'd let you and your men walk around the compound if you cooperate."

Curt gritted his teeth and looked away. *God give me strength.*

The commander yelled, "Send me more guards!" He held the old knife in the wound as blood pooled on the desktop.

When they arrived, he said, "Hold his head so he must watch me cut through his finger. If he closes his eyes, pinch his ears and nose." He smiled at Curt. "I don't want to do this. I'm a very kind man. You are forcing me. I will take every one of your fingers, your toes, and then your pecker unless you talk. Say something simple, anything, like your girlfriend's name or your hometown, and I'll stop."

Curt just stared at him. The sucker clearly enjoyed this. Something diabolical in his eyes. He had never hated anyone in his life, until…

The commander moved the knife a fraction at a time, watching Curt's face. Long minutes passed as he got to the bone. More pressure. The rusty knife broke through the top of the bone.

Pain sent its ragged blue edges and flooded his brain. It made him furious. Curt couldn't control the tears running down his cheeks. He exploded, "Cut it off! Just cut it off!"

The commander stopped. "So you can speak. Such a shame, your finger is nearly destroyed." He sat back and wiped the blood from the blade. He lit a fresh cigarette. "But I can have my medic sew it back together." He cleared his throat. "Where did you grow up?"

Curt closed his eyes and took a breath, wrestling with anger and fear. Warm tears ran down his cheeks. A guard pinched his ear. He looked at the cruel commander. "My name is Phil Brown, private first class, serial number 0658 913 G131."

Pissed, the commander put out his cigarette on the back of Curt's hand, then twisted off the rest of his little finger. He held it to Curt's eyes. "See! You're stupid GI. You better trust what I say. I'm very honest. You will lose all your fingers, toes, and your pecker if you don't tell me what your mission was." He jumped to his feet and ordered the guards to hold Curt's head. He stuffed the bleeding finger up one of Curt's nostrils.

He choked. The stub hung, dripping blood from his nose. Shock turned into *rage*. He tried to bolt from the chair, and it tipped over. The guards hit and kicked him until he quit fighting, then they tied both arms behind his head. They left him lying for half an hour.

Commander Cruel returned, telling the guards to untie his legs. He pushed Curt's little finger further up his nose, then forced him to march as he called cadence, "Hut-2-3-4."

He paraded him in front of the other men in their cells; the commander called out, "You don't talk, you lose fingers, toes, and pecker. See what happened to your brave leader!" His translator made sure they understood.

"If any one of you confesses what your mission was, I won't take the rest of his fingers and toes off." He snarled, "Have some compassion on your leader. Talk and he will live or end up as an armless, legless torso."

The other men huddled far back in their cells, shock on their faces.

They punched Curt in the groin and threw him into the cell where he lay curled in a ball. He wiggled the finger from his nose and dropped it. He pressed tightly on the finger stub, trying to stop the bleeding. He was weak from blood loss, dehydration, and lack of food. He heard the other men's murmurs of fear and sympathy.

Late at night, he got to his knees. He was too weak and exhausted to ask for the latrine. Curt worked his way to the back of the cell. Laying on his side, he unzipped his pants and peed on his finger stub. He didn't have much urine since he had nothing to drink for more than a night and day. He got some dirt off the stub. Zipping up, he fell sideways, smelling urine, his little finger smarting with pain and tingling as if it was still there. He was frightened and angry. He spent the night trying to come up with a plan to kill the SOB and escape. It was fruitless.

In the morning, the commander paced up and down in front of the cells. "Why are you acting sick and tired? I'm ordering you to be well. If you aren't well tomorrow, I will send you back to the cages."

They were so hungry and thirsty, they simply sat and stared out at the yard. The cherry trees magically exploded into full bloom with marvelous pink and white flowers. Birds sang in their branches as bees worked for nectar. A young guard waved his hand in front of their eyes. They didn't see him. To get their attention, he hit the bamboo bars with his rifle butt. They tried to ignore him, intent on whatever fantasy distracted them from the pain, hunger, and thirst. Curt played football at CU in his mind. He worried if he'd be able to hold onto the ball, especially if the cruel commander took more of his fingers.

Much later, the North Koreans gave them thin rice soup and a cup of water, and then marched them outside to stand at attention. The afternoon communism lecture was that the U.S. was completely corrupt: government, businesses, and religion were corrupt because capitalism makes people into crooks. The rich stole from the poor and planted false beliefs through the media and educational system. The working classes were exploited and suffered, but believed they were free. The United States was the aggressor that started the war with an attack on North Korea. The lecture listed every act of aggression perpetrated by the US throughout history, starting with the Native Americans, then blacks, against Mexicans, the Spanish, the Philippines, and even the Japanese. He compared this to peaceful communism, where the masses shared equally in the state-run economy. The state controlled every facet of life and provided for everyone's welfare from cradle to grave. It would benefit all mankind. "Truman's running dogs and Wall Street warmongers are using you. They're making money while disrupting your peaceful chances for real freedom and knowledge."

After the lecture, the men were questioned about what they learned and asked why they hadn't paid attention when they couldn't remember. The Americans gave their name, rank, and serial number, incurring the commander's wrath. "I will torture you until you confess!"

No one spoke, so it was back into the horizontal cages. Curt caught a whiff of the blooming cherry trees. Warblers sang. The sun grew hotter and hotter as the day wore on. At least he wasn't in the commander's office getting another finger cut off. Black flies bit everywhere, especially on the hole where the little finger once sat. Made him angry, and he gritted his teeth. He sweated and dirt ran into his eyes.

A woodpecker hammered at trees. He remembered the one that made a hole in the cottonwood tree in their front yard. The babies were cute. He felt sad and depressed.

They dragged him back to the cell at nightfall, right through that damned concrete divot. His eyebrow bleed. In the cell, he wiped his face with his arm. They hadn't given their uniforms back. Exhaustion brought frightening dreams. He doubted the others slept, but heard occasional snoring from the other cells. He wished they could talk. Wishing only made the lonely emptiness worse.

On the horizon, Curt saw the faint streaks of light and smelled the dawn scent of the cherry trees. He had survived another day and night. Would he make it through this one? He thought, *That commander is not only cruel, he's also crazy.*

Two days passed with similar interrogations after the communist lecture. They were beaten and kicked, but no one lost any appendages. Curt overheard rumors among the guards that the Chinese and North Koreans launched a massive offensive against the South. Guards announced, "We're winning. The war will soon be over!"

Curt was beyond caring and was losing his mother's faith. He just wanted to die or go home. He remembered why he joined the Navy. To please his father and grandfather. They would be ashamed he was captured. Maybe he'd never get home, and they wouldn't know.

Chapter 6
Imjin Battle Survivors

April 25, 1951

There was a putrid smell in his cell from when he pissed on his chopped-off finger stub. His body was rank with sweat and dirt. Lice made him itch. He nearly caught a mouse, intent on eating it. Guards returned their uniforms and encouraged the Americans to cover their wounds. They wondered what was up.

Later in the morning, the Chinese brought eleven Australian and British prisoners captured at the recent battles near the Imjin River. The Americans were crowded into one cell and were not told they couldn't talk.

The U.N. troops were split into the other five primitive cells while his team was in one. They were allowed to talk, and they did so loudly. It gave the Americans a chance to whisper as long as a guard wasn't watching closely.

His men were deeply concerned about Curt's missing finger and worried it would get infected, but they had nothing, not even water to wash it out. It was filthy with dirt from the cell floor and festered. Flies kept landing on it. They were so hungry they whispered about eating the little finger.

Carl made puking motions and threw it at a boy guard who recoiled and kicked it away. It was the nice kid, the one with warm eyes.

Curt felt bad for him.

Jack whispered, "You guys stink like an outhouse."

"Smell yourself, idiot," Carl growled under his breath.

Each man carried welts, bruises, and punctures where he was stabbed with bamboo spikes and whipped with green bamboo rods. It was clear no one confessed.

"We should start playing roles," Spooker suggested. They should pretend they had brain injuries, acting slow, stupid, and spacy. "Next time they sock or kick you in the head, pretend you're knocked out and when you come to, act as if you have a concussion. Repeat some phrases like, 'Where am I? How did I get here?' Say it over and over."

Taylor was depressed and suicidal. He wanted the commies to kill him. "I'll keep saying, just kill me. It will make my ex-wife happy."

"You love her that much, man?" Spooker was shocked.

"No, I hate the bitch, but I have a feeling I'm going to lose my foot before this is over. I won't be able to walk normally."

Curt patted his shoulder. "Guy, we're going to escape, and I'll carry you out of here on my back."

Taylor looked into his eyes. "Thank you, Curt, you're a good man."

They agreed to become passively resistant, feigning exhaustion, confusion, and weakness. Carl said, "That won't be hard,"

It almost elicited a laugh.

Curt reminded them of the cover story: they were to tell U.N. allies, "We're just privates. There are no officers among us. We're lowly expendables who know nothing. We are marines who were sweeping minefields with the metal detector. During a battle somewhere around the 38th parallel, we got separated from our unit and walked the wrong way into North Korea. Say Taylor fell off a boulder and broke his ankle." He cleared his throat, speaking quietly, "The commander will interrogate the Brits and Aussies and show them the parachutes and gear they recovered. When they come back and ask us, say, "The commander's crazy and cruel. He's trying to get a promotion by claiming he captured spies. None of us know how to parachute." He caught their eyes. "Hopefully, the word will get back to him."

Carl's jaw tightened. "Yes, and don't tell them any other details. The commander will ask them lots of questions about us. Don't give him any ammunition through the other prisoners."

Spooker added, "They will try to divide and conquer us like they forced Curt to watch us get tortured to build resentment against him. They will create suspicion that one of us has talked and is cooperating. They may offer extra food, sweets, or cigarettes. Take it and if you can, share."

Carl patted Curt on the shoulder. "They think you're the team leader because you're so tall and strong." He turned to the other men. "We need to strategize how to protect Curt. It's obvious this commander is obsessed and hates Curt—probably because when he punched him in the gut, he just stood there." He tapped Curt's cheek. "My friend, next time, fall to the ground if he hits or kicks you. I know you won't make a sound, but this is acting school at its most real. We have to pretend we're wimpy minesweepers who are uneducated, dumb, and don't have a clue about anything."

Brows bumped together in a scowl, Spooker said, "Everyone act as if you have a head injury. Talk slow, stutter, and look confused."

It was the first time they felt hope. They had a plan.

They heard the new prisoners talking about how they got captured. Several were wounded, and a British lieutenant hollered at the guard. "Bring a doctor. I've got men who are bleeding!"

The guard didn't understand.

Curt fought to keep from translating.

They lifted a man with a nasty hole in his thigh, pointing. "Bring us a medic. He needs antibiotics and stitches."

The guard yelled, and someone took his place.

An Australian spoke up, "The Chinese attacked without warning on the 22nd. The South Korean 6th Division was shattered by their offensive, and we were ordered, along with the Canadians, to take hilltop positions. We took the brunt of the fighting but inflicted heavy casualties on the Chinese. A second full-strength regiment appeared on our right flank, threatening our entire position with encirclement. We rushed them with guns blasting. That's when the five of us got surrounded and captured."

An English officer said, "On the 23rd and 24th, the Glosters' B Company was isolated on Hill 235. We were outnumbered eighteen to one. They assaulted the hill six times and the only way we repulsed them was to call our artillery on our position. It was during the barrage that a Chinese platoon got the drop on us."

They had several wounded men, possibly from their own shells.

The new prisoners were curious about the Americans. Spooker told their cover story and when asked where they were from, each man motioned with his hands that he could not speak.

A North Korean orderly showed up with a medical kit and began treating the wounded men. Guards brought decent rations and to the surprise of the Americans, they were also given enough to eat and drink for the first time. It made them feel more human.

Curt used the latrine and picked the festering scab clean, then peed on his finger stub. The guard yelled he was taking too much time. He subtly flipped the guard the bird when he came out.

When he returned, Jack whispered, "Maybe having these other men here the North Koreans will lighten up on the torture and treat us according to the rules of the Geneva Convention."

Spooker twisted his mouth. "Don't count on it. They'll be moved to a Chinese POW camp up north. We should try to get them to take us. The Chinese treat prisoners better."

When the orderly finished treating the Aussies and Brits, Curt tried to get him to do something for his weeping finger stub and his eyebrow. He held his right hand out of the cage as he walked past.

The orderly glanced at him and shook his head, saying, "No. I can't treat you." He hurried away.

Curt almost called after him in Korean but the last time he spoke it, his chin took a rifle butt. The briefing officer said the Chinese treated prisoners better if they said a few Chinese terms. He didn't know about the North Koreans. Curt figured they used any excuse to attack those they viewed as invaders. Better to keep his mouth shut than find out.

They lay crowded against each other in the small cell that night, smelling each other's rancid sweat, but for the first time, they slept soundly. They had a plan and each other, feeling like orphaned brothers.

In the morning, they received food and water, including weak green tea. Curt smelled azaleas and wondered where they were growing. Must be fairly close. It reminded him of his mother's flower garden. He could see her in it, weeding, talking to her flowers, and praying. Moisture came into his eyes. He felt like she was praying for him since he didn't write. She would cry when she saw his missing finger. Breaking and tearing it off left a ragged, infected flap of skin the flies kept lighting on. Friggin' lice itched and left tiny red marks. Would they ever escape?

The men felt optimistic. Seemed the North Korean commander wanted to please the Chinese who brought the prisoners. There was no torture that day since the commander was preoccupied with interviewing the Brits and Aussies one by one. They slept and only woke to eat and drink again. When Taylor begged the boy guard for more tea, he brought it.

The other prisoners continued with their battle stories and, during breaks, peered through the bars, asking how the Americans were captured. "Were you in combat?"

Spooker retold their cover story. He refused to elaborate when they asked questions. Individuals pointedly asked different men where they were from, when they joined up, and all that, but the team always pointed at Spooker who told the same story. By afternoon, the new prisoners ignored them. Shaking their heads, they'd smile and wink, saying, "We're on the same side. You can trust us."

That evening, a tremendous commotion broke out among the North Koreans. One of their guards had disappeared when the Chinese brought in their prisoners. Curt figured out the escapee was a conscript from South Korea.

The North Koreans were extremely upset because he was probably trying to get back home.

Carl whispered, "If he makes it back, maybe he will inform his superiors about us. I know they will question him. It might take several weeks, but men, there's hope."

The commander went into a total meltdown. Several guards were whipped in front of the prisoners, and he threatened to toss them in the horizontal bamboo cages for the night. "You idiots! Why didn't you immediately report him missing?"

They were his bunkmates. They didn't know he was gone, saying he was on guard duty.

"It's impossible you didn't see him." In a rage, he pistol-whipped three guards in succession. The men lay on the ground, hurt and humiliated.

An Aussie with beads of sweat on his forehead said, "That man is nuts. Let's hope the Chinese transfer us to the north."

Curt overhead the North Koreans talking. One said, "The Chinese and Koreans are like the lips and teeth, we are very close. We help each other. You cannot eat if you have only lips or only teeth, you must have both. Together, we are driving off the UN forces. They are running away like drowning rats. The war will soon be over and our country will be liberated from foreign invaders."

After breakfast, they took everyone out to the compound yard to stand at attention. It was time for re-education to correct their wrong thinking. The sky was blue and cloudless. The cherry trees waved their scent in the soft breeze, in full bloom, although some petals were starting to fall. A warbler sang beautifully, making Curt feel mournful to be free and walking down the rows of apple trees. Their blooms were likely outrageously beautiful right now. He saw his dog walking behind him, a smile on its face.

An English-speaking Korean lectured that communism was the key to a more equal future for all. He claimed capitalism made life miserable for workers and soldiers like them. They said Great Britain, Australia, and the U.S. were not democracies but were imperialist nations using them for cannon fodder.

Curt carefully glanced around the camp. It was roughly circular with twelve-foot-high barbed wire. The gate was a six-string set of barbed wires pulled tight to throw a loop of wire over a post like a farm field fence. That was the best place to attempt an escape but a guard tower sat next to it and was never empty. A machine gun poked from the side. He imagined there was a continuation of the circular twelve-foot-high fence behind their cells. A guard slapped his face as he pointed at the speaker, snarling, "Pay attention."

The commander glared at him.

As time passed, men with wounds started falling. Taylor was already on the ground, but they expected him to watch the speaker. They made those who fell keep their head directed at the lecturer. Curt winked at Carl and dropped, grinning to himself.

The commander walked over and damned near kicked him but saw the British officer watching. He ordered Curt to prop himself up. Flies attacked his weeping finger stub and the seeping wound on his eyebrow.

At the end of the lecture, they tied their legs together with just enough room to waddle, and their arms were tied in a fashion they could handle a shovel. They were to dig a defensive trench around the compound. They reluctantly started digging. Surprisingly, the North Korean guards didn't whip or beat anyone. But they slapped and pinched the ears and noses of anyone not working to their satisfaction. They were herded inside the compound for lunch and received tea with bamboo soup. Back to work.

Curt struggled to hold the shovel with his right hand, yet guards forced him to dig. "I need a bandage."

At last, the orderly came. He cleaned and bandaged the stub, and then the commander snarled, "You! Shovel—now!"

Damn, it hurt. Felt like the finger was still there, tingling and bawling like a momma cow that missed her calf.

Evening came and everyone bitched about how sore their blistered hands were. It was a gift when dinner came and the guards brought tea. The Americans didn't complain. Working was much better than being interrogated and tortured.

The next day was more of the same. The sun was fierce and the guards reluctantly provided water. Biting flies attacked. Sweat washed dust into their eyes.

At noon, the British officer complained bitterly, saying he would inform the Chinese of their treatment. "I know they will come back and transfer us to the North. They will inform your superiors of the slave labor you are forcing on us."

The commander's face turned purple. He raised his bamboo cane as if to strike him, but thought twice. He ordered them to the cells.

The Americans dug the trench without help. He made Taylor lay on his side, digging with a pit shovel. That evening, in a change of strategy, the commander mixed Americans in with the new prisoners. It was an obvious ploy in the hope they would talk with them. Curt whispered, "You know the story."

Initially, the Brits and Aussies tried to make conversation, but the Americans only repeated their cover story. A private held his nose. "You guys smell like shit."

Spooker scowled. "If you are here for weeks, you will too."

The British officer threw up his hands. "I give up. Seems you have orders not to talk."

Spooker caught his eyes. Tilting his head, he opened his uniform shirt and then dropped his pants to reveal the bruises and punctures on his backside.

The other men on the team surreptitiously showed what they did to them. Curt held up his right hand and pointed at the socket where his little finger once was.

They were angry and murmured they'd get the commander. Curt shook his head no. He whispered it was likely they would be transferred, and the Americans would be stuck here with commander psycho. He motioned at a guard and turned his back to him, mouthing, "He understands some English and will tell everything."

The British officer clenched his jaws. "We'll see about this." He ordered all the men to stop asking the Americans questions. "We will be interrogated again soon."

A Chinese doctor showed up with an orderly and treated the wounded POWs, including Taylor and Curt. He rubbed sulfanilamide powder into the men's wounds. Taylor's foot and ankle were plaster cast, and Curt's hand and eyebrow were cleaned and bandaged. As he examined Curt's hand, he asked how it happened. Curt dropped his eyes, then flicked his chin at the commander's office. The doctor's face darkened, but he said nothing.

The doctor gave the men with wounds a supply of morphine and aspirin. Curt whispered, "Xiè xiè." Thank you in Chinese.

The doctor asked if he spoke Chinese. He almost explained he learned some in language school, then remembered if they were left with the crazy commander, he'd use it to probe and torture him worse.

He kept his face neutral.

The physician seemed to understand.

It felt strange to sleep in the cramped cells with unknown men, shoulder to shoulder but there was safety in numbers and the Americans slept. They felt better from having food and water.

Chapter 7
Blindfolded

At first light, they blindfolded the Americans and marched them out in their straw slippers. There were no clouds, and they walked in the hot sun for hours without food or water, thinking they were being marched north to another POW camp. The men kept tripping and falling, but the guards wouldn't remove the blindfolds.

Birds chirped in the surroundings. The warning call of a squirrel. Magpies squawked and gossiped then it was quiet for over an hour. They heard mooing and kicking stones as cows moved out of the way.

At noon, they were given a sip of water but nothing to eat. Men started falling from heat prostration, and the guards kicked and yelled until the other Americans felt around to help them stand. By afternoon, they stumbled along arm in arm, trying to help one another.

After sundown, they were returned to the same primitive camp, and their blindfolds were removed. The other prisoners were gone. They were again split into separate cells and ordered not to speak.

Listening closely to the guards, Curt learned the Chinese took the Brits and Aussies to POW camps near the Yalu River. The commander told the Chinese the Americans tried to escape and were killed. He blamed the Chinese for the South Korean conscript's escape and asked them to bring more POWs, saying he would take good care of their prisoners. He wanted the supplies the Chinese provided.

Overhearing the guards' muted conversations, Curt learned the Chinese were angry when the commander said the Americans were killed during an attempted escape. The psycho commander believed they were his ticket to a promotion if he could break them.

They received a thin soup without nourishment that evening. Curt forced himself not to gulp it down so he wouldn't lose it. Dizzy, he was incredibly thirsty and dehydrated. He lay alone in the cell and tried to catch the scent of the cherry blossoms. His nose refused to allow it. He woke when a rat nibbled at his finger and yelled at it.

A young guard told him to be quiet. He was the nicest one.

Curt showed with his hands that a rat tried to bite him.

The guard smiled and winked. It was the first act of kindness.

He lay back, wondering if there might be others like him.

Early morning, the commander pulled Curt in for questioning. "So you told the British and Australians you're a mine sweeping crew. Where was your unit deployed?"

Curt spoke very slowly, acting as if he couldn't think. "My name is…Phil Brown…private first-class…"

The commander slapped a green bamboo rod across Curt's face. "Enough! That's probably not your real name. You're smart, conniving special agents, I just know it!"

Curt stumbled from the cane strike and acted dazed. It wasn't hard to act stupid and exhausted. He felt the heat of a cigarette hovering above his forearm.

"From now on, you will call me Commander Park! Be respectful." He pressed the cigarette into Curt's skin, sending the pungent odor of burning hair and skin into the office. He smiled. "I will make you regret being born."

He crushed the smoke out on Curt's forearm, leaving a round burn mark. "Get him out of my sight!"

Oddly, that evening, they gave the Americans food and tea. Curt overheard there'd be May 1st celebrations tomorrow. They'd be lectured for hours. Fine with him. It was better than being tortured.

Commander Park celebrated International Communist Day by sipping soju. A full jug sat at the foot of his chair in the shade. He had his men make a log swing suspended from a tree branch. It was twelve feet long and hung three feet off the ground.

The guards swung on it as the Americans watched from their cells. The North Koreans pushed each other back and forth and laughed. Having a competition, they tried to knock the other guys off and the winner's prize was a shot of soju. The party went on for an hour, then the commander fired an American .45. "Enough. Bring the prisoners out."

Time for re-education. The English speaker read to them from Marx. BLAH BLAH BLAH, he droned on and on, saying they weren't POWs. They were brother soldiers liberated from the oppression of the capitalists. "This is Camp Freedom where you will learn the truth and join us in this great war against capitalist warmongers. One day, the peace-loving peoples of the world will liberate the earth from capitalism and there will be peace."

It sounded like a Christian utopian dream, their religion. "You are a tool of the warmonger capitalists. Aren't you ashamed of yourselves?"

They feigned attention. Jaws hanging open, Taylor and Jack drooled as if looking at a grilling steak. Spooker and Carl kept their eyes wide open as if hypnotized while Curt sat twitching and pulling at his lips.

Commandeer Psycho stood, weaving and wobbling. "I'm proud of you hard-working minesweepers. You dug me a fine trench. As a reward, I'm letting you play on the swing." He ordered them to get up on it, straddling the log with hands tied in the back. He told the guards to swing them back and forth, slowly at first, then faster and higher until they nearly fell.

Curt didn't trust him. It was a trick. He'd make them fight to force each other off, then he'd whip the losers and do something cruel to the winner.

At Commander Park's order, they jostled each other as guards swung the log back and forth. Taylor soon rolled off and received only a tap from the commander's bamboo whip.

Jack and Spooker fell and again, only a mild tap. It was between Curt and Carl. The commander stopped the log from swinging. "Let's make this more interesting." He ordered the guards to raise the log to ten feet and untied their arms.

They jostled each other and put on a show, bumping into each other and shifting back and forth, banged shoulders. Leaning, Carl whispered, "One of us has to fall off. I'm not sure if it's better to win or lose."

Curt said, "It's better to lose." He unbalanced Carl, and he tumbled off, smacking the ground. He pretended to be cold-cocked. Wasn't hard since it knocked out his breath.

The guards clapped and whistled at the commander's signal. He announced. "So the tough guy is back in fighting condition. Great. Let's make this more interesting."

The guards raised the log to fifteen feet. "I want to see you stand and walk the log from one end to the other. If you make it without falling, none of your men will be whipped. If you don't, they will get a lash for every step you're short of twelve feet." He took a shot of soju and lit a cigarette. Sitting back in the shade, he grinned. "Okay, tough guy, walk the log."

Curt hesitated. If he walked the log all the way, he'd blow his act that he was incompetent. If he fell, the men would get whipped. He knew he could do it if the guards didn't jerk the ropes since he walked narrow logs across streams many times in the mountains of Colorado. They'd make him fall, probably midway.

Standing, he grabbed the rope hanging from the tree. Momentarily, he was back at Hart's Basin, climbing the rope to swing off into the lake. He glanced around. If he was fast, he might make it to the other end before the intoxicated commander realized what was happening. Could he shimmy across it and get his arms around the trunk before he shot him? His finger stub started bleeding, and he knew he didn't have the strength in his right hand.

"Start walking!" Park stood to watch, drink in one hand, a cigarette in the other.

Curt looked down. Fifteen feet was enough to break your neck or leg. He knew they'd jerk the ropes to make him fall. He decided.

Acting clumsy, he took a step. His leg swung out, and he made it appear he would fall. Righting himself, he took three quick long steps and balanced at the midpoint, pretending to nearly fall. He saw the commander raise a thumb to signal his guards. Curt sprinted and caught the other rope as they jerked.

They snapped it up and down, and he fell with his legs spread. The log crushed his nuts. *"Argh!"* He latched onto the log like a baby to its mother's breast.

They kept shaking the log up and down.

The commander was enraged. Wobbling on his feet, he pulled the .45 and shot at Curt, emptying the clip. A bullet took out the rope and the log swung down directly at the commander.

His lips twisted into a wacky question mark as he realized what was happening. It took him out with a loud thump. Curt flew head down on the wildly swinging log. Peaking, it swung back over the compound.

The guards stood as if hypnotized.

The log swung back over the commander who was out cold. It reached its peak and started back. As he came over the top of the commander, Curt let go and speared the commander's fat gut with his head.

The Americans roared with laughter and started to applaud but saw the guards and clamped it off.

Several guards laughed, then quickly suppressed it.

The second in command jumped on Curt, hitting and kicking. He ordered the guards to take him to a bamboo cage. He sent the other Americans to their cells while the orderly worked to resuscitate the commander. When he sat up, he puked alcohol all over himself.

Curt suppressed laughter from a bamboo cage as did the men in their cells. There would be hell to pay, but it was worth it.

That evening, the guards dragged Curt across the compound with his hands tied behind his back straight through the pothole. They did it again. Three times. His eyebrow bled like a river. He didn't mind not getting supper. He won a round, even if by accident.

As he lay silently aching, he hummed to himself. It distracted him from the pain. "Amazing grace, how sweet the sound."

Other men picked it up.

Curt realized they could communicate through songs if they kept it short. They hadn't been told they could not hum. He stopped abruptly. The other men understood. They had a tiny tool in this battle.

Chapter 8
Going Numb

They got nothing for breakfast, then sat waiting for whatever the crazy commander might come up with today. The guards were quiet. There was an ominous feeling. Curt had humiliated the commander and knew he was cooking up something.

It was hot and muggy as if it might rain when Curt was pulled from the cell and led to the log that still hung from one rope. They untied it and ordered him to lift the log. "Higher," the guards yelled.

When Curt got it above his head in a military press, the guard nodded, then ordered him to march around the compound. The commander watched from the door of his office. After what felt like hours, Curt started to lower his arms but the guard immediately gestured he was to put the log above his head. He kept it up for another few minutes, then let it drop.

It hit one of the guard's toes.

He yelled and cussed. The guard hopped around while another screamed to pick it up again.

Curt was too weak to stand and dropped to his knees.

The guard looked at the commander, who nodded. He yelled again.

Curt stayed on his knees, hands on his thighs and his head down.

The guard swiftly struck his back with his rifle butt and sent him sprawling.

"You learn lesson, no?" The guard asked.

Curt shook his head, yes, and the guard shoved him toward the office.

They tied his legs with barbed wire to a chair in front of the commander's desk. His wrists lay flat on the desk while guards hammered in staples to hold the wire tight so his fingers spread.

Curt knew what was coming. He suppressed fear and anger. He'd look that sucker in the face with defiance.

Hours later, the commander walked in. He sat down across from Curt. "Why have you ruined my desk by hammering staples into it?"

He looked hungover with dark bags and red eyes. His face was badly bruised and a black eye. He lit a cigarette and smoked the entire thing, staring at Curt and blowing smoke in his face. The translator anxiously stood nearby.

Taking out his sharp knife, he felt the edge with his thumb. An evil smile. He scraped the scab from Curt's little finger. Blood ran.

He smoked another cigarette. "Hold his head," he said to a guard. He scraped the scab from Curt's eyebrow, slowly, methodically, making sure blood ran into Curt's eye. He nodded to a guard.

The guard set a can of kerosene on the desk.

He put his cigarette out on the back of Curt's hand, then drizzled kerosene over his little finger stub. "You got the Chinese doctor to take care of you, didn't you?" He poured kerosene into a cup and dumped it over the scab on Curt's eye as he smiled. "I hope you enjoy this and the resulting infection."

Curt's eyes burned and watered from the kerosene. The fumes assaulted his nose making breathing difficult. He tried to hold his breath as long as possible while blinking the nasty fluid from his eyes. His feelings tumbled as anger and fear tangled into one another. His chest felt tight.

The commander told a guard to get his soju bottle and sat back, waiting for the kerosene to evaporate. When the guard returned, he poured himself a shot. "Bet you'd like a hit of this before we proceed." He held the shot glass under Curt's nose.

Curt didn't drink alcohol. The one time he tried it, he threw up. He wrinkled his nose.

"You don't like soju? You're a pig." He sucked it down and sat back, lighting a cigarette since the kerosene evaporated. "You're a crazy American, you know that. Loyal to a country that uses you for cannon fodder. You've been brainwashed, you understand? There are people in your country so rich they could feed all the Korean people for a year and not notice. You're a slave to your capitalist system. What do they pay you? Not much, I'm sure. Not worth losing more fingers. Am I right?" He glared into Curt's eyes, who made no sound.

Clouds gathered and the sunlight dimmed.

His voice became soft, almost pleading. "Why not consider joining us? With your skills and intelligence, you would go far. What is your real rank? Are you a lieutenant like me? I should be a captain by now, you know. They keep saying I'm unstable. I'm stable. I'm a genius. If you'd only cooperate, I'd be promoted. I'd become the best interrogator in North Korea." He poured himself another drink. "Yes, I can see it. Stalin would want me in the KBG. Why not join me? Help me and I'll help you. We'll be famous together. You, an American spy, join with Lieutenant—no make that Colonel Park, top North Korean interrogator. Together, we'd impress Chairman Mao and Stalin. They will want us as a team."

He smiled. "I'm a very kind man. I'm only doing this because I believe in our cause. Communism makes us equal, we share, we take care of everyone, unlike you American capitalists that let the poor starve while the rich party on their yachts." He put his smoke out on the back of Curt's hand and lit another cigarette.

Curt suppressed a grimace. *This man is delusional.* He tried to think of something, anything. An image of his 1935 Lincoln convertible flashed in his thoughts. *I'll imagine I'm taking it for a ride on Grand Mesa with the top down.*

Commander Cruel's voice became tight and louder. "You know you damned near killed me yesterday. I should have you shot. You made that log hit me square in the face, then my men say you dove right into me." He rubbed his flabby stomach for a moment and grimaced like it was sore. He put the flame of the cigarette near the skin on the inside of Curt's wrist. "Is this hot? I don't like burning you, but you burned me yesterday. You made me look like a fool!"

Suddenly he stood. "You son-of-bitch, you dirty capitalist pig! I should poke your eyes out!" He held his knife to Curt's eyes. He turned and paced. Thunder cracked nearby and the wind blew. He glanced out the window at the compound as he paced, his voice even. "You know, you're something. I admire you. You're strong and smart. If you'd only take pity on me and talk. My parents were very poor. Your American bombs killed them. You? Are you a farm boy? You have big, powerful hands. I bet you were an athlete in high school. I've heard about your sports programs. You have too much wealth in America." His face went red. He stabbed the knife blade into the desk between Curt's fingers. "Your government sponsors big international corporations to rob and rape poor countries. They make big money on war. You're invaders. Why are you here? Talk, damn it!"

Rain fell, drops at first, then it gradually turned into pounding sheets of water. Fierce drumming on the tin roof, so loud it was difficult to hear.

Commander Park sat down, sipped soju, and smoked as he stared at Curt. Something empty and demonic sparked in his eyes.

As the rain squall eased, he smiled. "Be a pal, huh? We can work together. Tell me why you parachuted into North Korea and I'll make you my partner. We'll become a team, you and me, buddies in this fight against capitalism."

Curt stared at the man's rotten teeth or the stubble on his chin to avoid looking into his eyes. The asshole had a deformed mole on the left side of his nose. It was brown and lumpy. He hoped it was cancerous. *Forgive me, Mom, I'm losing your faith.*

The commander's knife flashed and severed Curt's right ring finger. It bled profusely. He smiled evilly, a blank, bizarre evil. "Oops. Sorry about that."

Shock. He expected another grueling session with a finger being slowly sawed off. He stared at his finger, bleeding as it lay separated from his hand. It took seconds before the pain hit his brain. He gritted his teeth as he gazed into the black, sadistic eyes in front of him. Anger rose in his chest.

The commander stood. "I'd enjoy having you as my partner." He did another shot and wobbled out, carrying his bottle. Outside, he fired the .45 into the still weeping sky and cussed a blue streak.

It took the guards long minutes to pull the staples from the desk to release the barbed wire. They held him down and forced his finger up a nostril, then marched him back and forth in front of the other Americans.

Back in the cell, his finger throbbed with an agonizing hot flame. He jerked the stub from his nostril and started to throw it at the guard, but he was the nice one. He dropped it. Maybe he'd save it as a souvenir if he ever got out of this. His eyebrow still bled, leaking into his eyes. He was enraged, afraid, and helpless.

Over the prison camp, a full moon hung in the velvet sky, reflected in the pools of water left by the rainstorm. His grandfather was there, talking to him, telling him about the Battle of the Argonne when he was shot in the ass. "You have to focus on something else, something beautiful. Think of the orchards this time of year or imagine us going trout fishing up on Grand Mesa."

He had to be like him, he must be brave. He prayed for the courage to face one more day. That's what the men whispered to each other, "One day, just one day, then we'll escape." It was impossible. He put pressure on his finger stubs and resigned to losing all his fingers and toes. Are the apples still blooming on his father's farm? He hoped there wasn't a freeze. His heart ached to be home. Taking a deep breath, he gathered his courage and hummed, "Gonna take a sentimental journey. Gonna take a journey home."

His team members hummed along. Made him feel less empty.

Chapter 9
The Ball Game

At dawn with nothing to eat or drink, they were marched out and forced to kneel in the trench they just dug. The guards wrapped barbed wire around their ankles and wrists, making sure the barbs cut into their skin.

The English-speaking Korean lectured: "Before the war, the Communists were rebuilding North Korea while the Americans exploited the South. We divided the land among farmers. We made our factories productive and built new ones. We do not have American skyscrapers or automobiles, but we also do not have any unemployed. In America, you have no soul, only horrible inequality and filth. Religion and your preachers are imperialist tools for the oppression of the Korean people. You are bloodstained, murderous insects."

The men adopted a facade of feigned ignorance, feebly attempting to mask their true capabilities. Their words slurred and stumbled, a deliberate act to appear 'mentally deficient,' a desperate ploy for survival. As they recited their name, rank, and serial number, the air filled thickly with tension, the ruse, a precarious shield against their tormentor.

The commander whipped Jack across the face with a thin, green bamboo rod. He didn't scream or whimper like usual, instead, he said stupidly, his words slurred, "You hurt me." He looked around as if he didn't know where he was, saying slowly, "Why… you hurt me? I didn't hurt you." He shook his head and let it loll to the side, his mouth hanging open as if mentally challenged.

The commander looked confused for a moment. "At least you spoke, so I'm letting you off light."

He stepped to Curt. "You're next, tough guy. You even lied to your allies, claiming you got separated from a marine unit. We found your buried compasses, no way you got confused and walked north into my country." He struck Curt's neck with a bamboo whip. "You're tough, and you're smart. You've told your men to act stupid. I'll make you stupid if you don't talk." He struck the other side of his neck. "Tell me the truth, or I'll whip you until you bleed and let you get infected."

Curt reached a pain saturation point. He felt the bamboo rod but it wasn't as shocking as when Park first started. "My name is…Phil… Brown…"

The whip struck across the front and back of his neck rapidly, ten times in succession. His face purple with anger, the commander yelled, "I want to hear the story from your mouth. How you were mine sweepers with a marine unit. I want to know what battles you fought in. I want to hear how you somehow got separated and walked the wrong way into North Korea, and I want to hear it from your lips. Tell me!"

Curt let himself fall over into the trench, acting unconscious. It wasn't difficult. The whip struck his throat again, and he lost his breath. His eyebrow bled, blinding his left eye.

"You can't be knocked out from that. I've hit you harder with my fists, and you just stood there. Now sit up!" The whip sprang from side to side across Curt's shoulders and chest, but he didn't move. "Get up and look at me, commando. I know you're faking it!" He smacked Curt's neck with the bamboo rod.

He told himself, *Go numb, go away—beat him at his own game.*

The commander stood with his hands on his hips. He lit a cigarette and puffed madly, looking up and down the trench at the Americans.

He turned to his next victim.

Curt suppressed a slight smile as a tear ran down his cheek. Anger made him just a little braver.

The commander followed suit with Carl and Spooker, whipping them, screaming, and calling them American dogs. "I'll chop every limb off your body. They'll carry your legless torsos out of here."

Each man played stupid, mentally deficit, or drunk—slurring words as they said their name, rank, and serial number. Taylor looked up at Psycho Park with dull eyes, his voice weak as if he was dying. "Just… kill me. It will… make my ex-wife happy."

The commander stared at him. He swung the whip like a baseball bat with two hands and it struck Taylor's ear. He keeled over and spasmed as if having an epileptic fit. His tongue came out. Foam floated on his lips.

Curt hoped he was acting.

Panting hard, the fat commander turned to his guards. "What did you do to them? Did you beat them stupid?"

They shrugged. A young boy said, "We haven't given them food or water. Maybe they're dehydrated."

The commander attacked him with the bamboo whip. He ducked and ran. The other guards scattered. The commander chased the guard around the compound for a minute, then ordered, "Stop this instant, or I'll have you shot."

Curt wondered if this was their chance to escape. They were outside the compound fence. He scanned the guards. They were in disarray but one looked right at him and pointed his gun.

The young guard screeched to a halt and stood at attention. The commander whipped him from head to toe. He stood there, his jaw firm, blinking at each strike.

"Why can you take it when these Americans fell over like I beat them with a bat?"

The boy kept his expression stern.

He strode back to the trench where the Americans lay as he left them. He went down the row, striking with the bamboo cane. They didn't move. When he got to Taylor, he stopped. "You want me to kill you?"

Taylor nodded. "Yeah…" slurring his words. "Kill me."

"I won't give you the satisfaction."

Frustrated, the commander stomped to his office. He ordered the guard he whipped brought to him, along with the other three who guarded the Americans when they were on the march.

Curt and his men lay where they were, hearing Commander Park yelling, sometimes screaming, at the top of his lungs. The other guards stood over them in the trench with rifles pointed.

Curt dared a glance. Some grinned, others with worried expressions. He closed his eyes and looked at the red inside his eyelids. *He wanted to divide and conquer us, but we won this round.* A tiny grin spread on his lips.

They returned the other men to the prison cages, but the commander ordered Curt dragged face down across the concrete compound twice. He knew they'd take him right through that pothole. *Here it comes.* Boom! His eyebrow squirted blood. Up the other side, they lifted his legs to scrape off the rest of the scab. He thought to himself, *Fuk 'em, I'll just get dumber and dumber with everything they do to me.*

The morning skies were blue without a cloud, the rain storm was long gone and the light was bright. After a two-hour lecture on the virtues of communism and the horrors of capitalism, Curt, Spooker, and Carl were shoved into the bamboo cages. Curt wasn't sure what happened to Taylor and Jack. Maybe they were being interrogated. They hummed tunes to each other.

Carl went with, "I'll never smile again until I smile with you."

Spooker hummed, "I'm looking over a four-leaf clover that I overlooked before."

"Some enchanted evening…" Curt remembered the night he won the talent show. He wished he had gone to CU instead of the Navy. He lay in the blistering sun, thinking about how his life would have been different. He'd be playing football. They'd be in spring training right now. He shook his head. Darlene would have fooled around with Bud Hamilton on weekends when he wasn't home. He was glad he broke it off.

Surprisingly, the commander let them out of the bamboo cages. They were allowed to wander the compound with Taylor and Jack. It was the first time allowed out. Crazy commander was playing a new game with them.

Curt started dragging his feet to create a baseball diamond. The other men caught on, and they began scuffing their feet until they made a rough baseball diamond traced on the grounds.

They pretended they were playing a baseball game.

The guards watched as one man stood on the 'mound' and threw an imaginary ball at another man who pretended to be at bat. Several guys crossed home before Park came out screaming and put them back into the horizontal cages. They never figured out what his strategy was.

Chapter 10
The Photographic Plane

The compound was suffused with sunlight so ripe and wonderful Curt felt a tiny spark of hope. The cherry trees dropped their blossoms. Life went on, oblivious to their plight.

They were forced back into the horizontal cages that morning. He thought of his mother's pies. His stomach ached with hunger, despite the thin soup for breakfast. He gazed down at his emaciated body under his torn uniform, wondering if he would ever eat her cherry pies again. She would be working in the garden. Maybe the daffodils and crocus were blooming. He hoped she prayed for him.

Late in the afternoon, Curt heard a single-engine, prop-driven plane in the sky. It looped around, and he recognized it. A photographic plane, a Mustang fighter from World War II. As it came closer, the guards were distracted by watching the plane, and Curt stuck his arms out to wave. He hummed the Army bugle attack song, and the other men waved from their cages.

The North Koreans fired at the Mustang as the Americans waved. A few seconds and he passed overhead. He looped around. When he came over the second time, the pilot waggled the wings. The guards blew through all their ammunition and got a few holes into the plane. They were agitated and commander crazy came out, yelling, "Why didn't you shoot it down? What's wrong with you?" He slapped the guards.

He grilled Curt. "What was your mission? Tell me, dog face!" He had the guards stab the men with bamboo stakes for waving at the plane. It ripped their uniforms into more holes.

As usual that evening, they dragged Curt across the compound through the pothole. He lay exhausted, dehydrated, and bleeding on the dirt of his cell. The starvation diet without protein made his skin dry and hard. His hands were the consistency of parchment. He heard Carl hum, "Old buttermilk sky. I'm keeping my eye peeled on you."

They had been seen and photographed!

The line between living and dying blurred. He thought, *There is nothing that could be worse than this.* He promised if he was ever free again, he'd go to college and play football.

Taylor and Jack were treated differently. They passed a few peanuts to the other men when the guard wasn't looking. Jack showed a cigarette. He made a circular motion with his finger at the side of his head to indicate the commander was nuts. He asked the guard for a light and surprisingly, the boy lit a match. It was the nice one, maybe a South Korean conscript. Jack passed the smoke to the next man and so on down the line. Curt got the last puff. He never smoked, and he coughed, then flicked it from his cell.

Taylor's ankle slowly improved. The commander hadn't crushed or broken off his cast the Chinese doctor had put on. He could put a little weight on it, and they gave him a couple of sticks to use as crutches.

Divide and conquer. Create distrust. Make them wonder about each other.

They'd play the commander's game.

Curt hummed, "Comin' in on a wing and a prayer with our full crew on board."

Hope in their thoughts, the guys slept.

The morning brought more lessons on the wonder of communism. "Join us and you'll be treated well." Blah, blah, blah.

The Americans pretended rapt interest.

Afterward, they were led to the trench and forced to kneel. The guards blindfolded them and paced back.

The commander said, "You won't talk, so I'll put you out of my misery." He cleared his throat. "Last chance. Anyone ready to confess?"

No one spoke.

The commander said, "Ready." Shells slid into the weapons. "Aim." He waited long seconds. "Fire!"

Bullets skimmed their hair and shirts. They waited for the burning pain. The guards reloaded and aimed again.

It was a feint, a fake-out. Jack collapsed into the trench.

The commander laughed. "You idiots! You must talk. You must tell me about your mission or the next time, I'll order them to shoot your arms and legs. I'll let you bleed to death."

Taylor and Jack became compliant and appeared to be cooperating. When they returned to the jail after interrogation sessions, they winked at the other men. Carl, Spooker, and Curt were kept in horizontal cages throughout the day, but the other two stayed in their cells.

Curt got it the worst since they thought he was the leader as the tallest. He wasn't. They were all leaders. The guards always dragged him across the compound, skinning the scab off his eyebrow. He tried to imagine he was a sword being forged, the strikes and kicks were the blacksmith's hammer, pounding carbon into the steel. He would become stronger, more flexible, and bend without breaking.

He worried Jack may say something impulsively when frustrated or in pain. The briefing officer said the North Koreans would ask them to admit the United States wasn't perfect. Commander Park probed, asking for examples. Curt knew he would create a list and demand the men sign the document or lose fingers. The men stated their names, ranks, and serial numbers loudly each time they were back in the prison. It was a way to communicate they didn't cooperate.

Crickets sang with their legs sawing together. One crawled up near the cells to share its song. It was irritatingly loud.

Towards dawn, they came for him, Carl, and Spooker. They forced them into the bamboo cages. The English-speaking translator paced in front of them, reading the Communist Manifesto, and explaining it from a North Korean perspective. He said, "People all over America are rioting in the streets against your government's involvement in this war. People are starving because the capitalists are taking everything to feed the war machine." He cleared his throat. "Your buddies are cooperating. We have their signed confessions. There is no point in resisting further."

In the afternoon, they came for Curt. He was so weak and dehydrated, he couldn't stand so the guards half dragged, half pushed him into the office.

Psycho Park held a sheet of paper to Curt's face. "See, your buddies are talking. I've got private Benson's signed confession." He slapped it on the desk so Curt could read it.

Initially, Curt was scared, but then he realized Jack wrote their cover story of being minesweepers separated from their unit when North Koreans attacked. It looked like a second-grader wrote it. It was a confusing tale with terrible grammar, heavy cross-outs, and misspellings about getting lost. It went on for several pages about how confused they all were. They didn't know north from south and were shocked to find themselves in North Korea surrounded by the platoon. He signed it, Private James Benson, his phony name.

Curt fought a smile.

The commander slapped a signed confession by Taylor in front of him. It was the same cover story adding he fell from a large boulder and broke his ankle. He signed it Private Fred Stanford, his assigned name.

They had nothing.

"You won't talk, so write. I want details. I want to know the name of your unit, where they were based, how many men were in it, and what battles they fought." He put a pencil in Curt's hand and sat back, smoking.

Curt hadn't tried to write since losing two fingers. He debated about simply refusing. He stared at the paper.

The commander took out his sharp knife and began casually cleaning his fingernails as he looked at him with a cocky expression. "Write."

Curt started slowly. The letters were wobbly and illegible. Blood from his finger stubs dripped on the paper. He splattered blood on the other two letters.

"You capitalist pig, you're ruining those on purpose." He grabbed Curt's hand and scraped the scabs with his knife. "Go ahead, bleed, bleed all you want. I've got two signed confessions, and your other teammate will give me his. I'll make you talk yet!"

In a quick move, Curt smeared blood all over the letters.

Purple veins sprouted from the commander's forehead. "I'll kill you!" His face changed. "No, first, I'll cut off every one of your fingers and toes." He turned to the guard, "Stick him in the cage and don't give him any water. Leave him there all night."

The guards dragged him out to a bamboo cage to sweat in the hot sun.

Curt had lost so much weight, they didn't have to force him into it. He lay with his eyes open because if he let them close, they stabbed him with bamboo stakes. He heard the commander trying to force Carl to write a confession. Maybe he'll bleed all over the papers too since he had lost his little finger. He'd be out here soon.

He focused on a tree branch to go away. He imagined he was a kid again, climbing the big cottonwood in their yard. Dad helped him build a treehouse out of used plywood and boards. Before he was big enough to drive a tractor, he spent most summer days climbing up into it, imagining he was a frontiersman guarding a log fort. Eyes open so he wouldn't get punctured, he went into that world.

That was the pattern: the morning communist education lecture, interrogated, stuck in the bamboo cages, then dragged across the compound. The commander went from pleading and pleasant to violent within seconds. He scraped off the men's scabs and doused them with kerosene. Their wounds were infected, seeping yellow stuff and attracting flies. Spooker's little finger was sawed off with the rusty knife.

The days faded into night and the only reality was in the moment. Each moment hung over the Americans like death. The stench of infections, lice, and mosquitos in their cells was enough to make them want to puke, but there was nothing in their stomachs to throw up. Commander Park hooked up a 12-volt battery and enjoyed shocking the men's balls. It didn't work.

Curt hoped they'd get more prisoners to distract the commander. He dreamed of food, of having enough water. He hummed, "Smoke, smoke, smoke that cigarette. Smoke, smoke, smoke yourself to death." Maybe the commander would die of lung cancer.

The commander became increasingly agitated with the refusal of the Americans to say anything other than their cover story and name, rank, and serial number. He pulled Curt into his office for another round.

Helpless fear and anger. He knew what was coming.

Two guards held his head still, forcing him to watch the commander maliciously, slowly, sadistically, saw through the middle finger on his right hand with the old bread knife. When it broke through the upper bone, he stopped and smoked a cigarette, staring at Curt.

Red-hot intense pain. Curt clenched his jaws as tears ran down his face.

"I could stop now. It's a clean cut. I could have my orderly sew it back together." He took a shot of soju. "I'm quite serious. I'd make you my partner if you come to our side. You Americans are extremely tough and courageous, especially you." He blew smoke in his face. "What do you think?" He took hold of Curt's middle finger and wiggled it.

He wanted to explode with hysterical laughter but sat silently watching the smoke curl from the commander's cigarette. Curt closed his eyes to fight through the pain. He imagined himself at home. He was at the lake, swinging off the rope.

Guards pinched his ears and nose, closing off the air.

Curt opened his eyes again. Tears tumbled down his face from the blistering pain.

The commander twisted and pulled the middle finger, gradually applying pressure and bending it to break the lower part of the bone but the underside skin was still attached. He sat back and lit a smoke. "There's still a chance my medic could sew it back together." His voice was calm, eyes calculating. "Tell me one thing, just one simple thing other than your story of being a minesweeper and I'll stop." He waited.

Curt said his name, rank, and serial number.

Lieutenant Park put out his cigarette on the back of Curt's hand, then pulled the index finger until the skin snapped, tearing raggedly. He nodded at a guard. The boy sat a kerosene can on the desk. The fiendish commander used his bread knife to peel the scabs from the other two stubs and shaved the scar on Curt's eyebrow, then poured kerosene over the wounds.

Weak from lack of food and the hours in the bamboo cage, he passed out. When he came to, he was back in the cell, shivering with pain, dehydration, and lack of food. He just wanted this to end.

Chapter 11
Spread-eagled

The luminous dawn edged blue shadows down the pines and into the cherry trees and compound. Small green buds formed with the promise of delicious fruit. The air was brushed with a whisper of flower fragrance. Above the prison, the blue sky was open and wide. It was bright after the gloom of the cells.

They ate breakfast in silence since they weren't allowed to talk. He heard the faint kiss of spoons on bowls empty of nutrition.

The morning brought another interrogation round with the commander. After the communism lecture, they dragged Curt to the side of the concrete pad. They spread-eagled and staked his arms and legs as wide apart as possible.

He suffered staggering muscle and joint pain as everything was stretched beyond his limits. Imagining he was home, he hummed a tune to himself, "I'm sorry, so sorry." He thought of singing at the Delta County talent show to focus away from the pain. When he won, Darlene mushed her breasts into his chest and kissed him like he was a movie star.

They assigned the nice young guard to watch him. He began humming along.

Surprised, Curt smiled at him. If the commander heard, they'd both get beaten.

Typically, guards took no initiative without an order from the commander. This kid was different. Very slowly, one at a time, the boy cautiously pushed the stakes holding his wrists and ankles toward his body, giving a little relief.

Curt whispered, "Kamsahamnida." Thank you.

The boy's eyes went wide. He smiled and winked, making it clear he wouldn't say anything.

Curt asked in Korean, "What is your name?"

The boy checked to ensure the coast was clear. "Bitgaram Kwog." He shyly smiled. "I'm sixteen and from Seoul." A hesitation. "What's yours? How old are you?"

"Curt Conrad. I'm eighteen."

Afraid to say more, the kid paced in a circle, occasionally giving a slight smile.

He lay spread-eagled for over twenty-four hours without food or water. During the day, the sun's savage glare bounced into the compound like rocks hitting his face. His tears were a dry creek. He felt totally, utterly defeated.

He woke to gaze at the shimmering silver moon, thinking nothing could or should be that beautifully luminous. Strange, it was the same moon he had always seen, but that was before he was tortured. Now, when he saw the man on the moon, he felt threatened. His joints began to give out.

He was unconscious when they moved him back to the cell. He must have been close to death because the next day, he received plenty of food and water, and they let him lay in the cell. He realized the North Koreans had no regard for human suffering. The commander wanted him to recover so he could continue torturing him.

The commander brutally continued torturing them, sometimes, even Taylor and Jack, his favorites. To fight and thrash invited defeat and the only way to survive was to bear it without crying out. For days, the pattern remained much the same: bamboo cages or spread-eagled for Curt, Carl, and Spooker, while they often kept Taylor and Jack in the prison cells.

The commander pulled different men and cajoled, begged, and then sliced them with one of his knives. Spooker and Carl both got another finger chopped off. It surprised Curt he didn't lose another.

The English translator said, "You Americans do not care that Korean people bleed. You started this war against the peaceful people of North Korea, then cry when you lost a little blood. What is the loss of a little blood? You're wrong thinkers!"

Ribbons of pink, orange, and violet lit up the eastern sky when Commander Park ordered his guards to rig up a barrel with a hose hanging from it. Around noon, they forced Curt's mouth open and unkinked the hose. Water flooded down his throat as they held his nose. His stomach filled to the point of bursting.

"Talk. Tell me what you were doing in North Korea!" Psycho Park choked with anger.

Hell, he couldn't talk. Water bubbled from his nose and mouth.

The commander punched him in the gut.

He blew water all over Commander Park; it spewed in his face and soaked the front of his uniform. Curt wanted to laugh but heaved more liquid.

The commander was so shocked that he just stood in the shower provided by Curt's mouth. He screamed. "I'll kill you!" He reached for Curt's neck, but his arms were too short. He kept jumping, trying to grab his neck. Curt blew more water because the stupid guards kept trying to force it down his throat.

Livid and raging, the commander threw himself to the ground and shook his fists like a child throwing a tantrum, his face purple as he screamed.

Curt vomited water.

The guards tried to keep from laughing. They came to their senses and kinked the hose, shutting off the water.

Curt involuntarily regurgitated more water that finished soaking Commander Crazy – mud was on his back, his pants and shirt. He rolled side to side, flailing his arms and screaming.

The guards let go of Curt and helped the commander stand. Swinging his fists wildly, he came at Curt to slug his gut. One of the young guards warned him, "Remember what happened the last time."

He slugged the boy, stomped his feet, cursed Curt, and cursed the sky, then fired a whole clip wildly around the compound. He rumbled off to his office.

Curt figured he got drunk that night. It was funny, and he wanted to tell the other prisoners what happened.

Carl was staked to the ground during the event and as Curt marched past, he mouthed, "Great job."

Curt enjoyed the small victory. Dusk settled like a cooling blanket over the prison compound as the fading sun fell to the west and the atmosphere lost its vigor. All around, the forest sighed with the rustle of leaves and animals foraging in the night. The clicking and chirping of insects put him on edge. He'd have to deal with whatever Commander Cruel came up with tomorrow.

That night, he hummed, "Bell bottom trousers, coats of Navy blue." The other men picked it up.

Surprisingly, the young guards did nothing.

It helped keep up the men's morale by humming songs and it distracted from the misery. They held onto the hope that the photographic plane saw them waving from their cages. Maybe they would be rescued. They got weaker and sicker as infections ravaged their bodies.

Chapter 12
ROK Prisoners

A platoon of South Koreans from the ROK 1st Division was marched into the prison camp after being captured when they chased withdrawing communist troops. The soldiers were so exhausted, they were asleep on their feet. They were forced into the back of trucks and rode through the night. They squeezed into the cells with the Americans but weren't forbidden to talk. Thirty-one men in six tiny cells meant they crouched side by side at night.

The South Koreans complained, "You salams smell bad. Why don't you take a shower?"

"Sorry," Carl whispered in Korean, "We haven't been allowed to clean up."

Seeing their wounds and missing fingers, the ROK soldiers shuddered, knowing they would also be tortured. "They will try to convert us." They hoped their men would try to rescue them.

Oddly, they could talk. Curt whispered to the South Korean lieutenant, "The commander hopes we'll talk about how we got here. Please don't let them know I understand your language."

He learned it was May 24th. They bailed out on April 9 and were captured on the 19th, so they had been captive for 35 days. During that time, he'd lost around sixty pounds, along with three fingers. His wounds festered with yellow puss. He woke that night feeling cockroaches nibbling his finger stubs. Lice were everywhere. The ROKs complained about the American's smell, the lice, and the crowded cells.

The new prisoners dropped to sleep and snored as the Americans dreamed of being rescued.

Listening to them talk about the many battles they were in, Curt admired them. The South Koreans were not only brave and tough but were determined to save their country from communism. They admired their commander who they said was a brilliant and fearless leader, by the name of Captain Kim Chin-mae. They were sure he would organize a rescue mission before they were transferred to the northern POW prisons run by the Chinese. It gave him hope, and he let the other men know.

Restless clouds beckoned with fingers as if to warn of a waiting doom. It started raining and water sizzled on the tin roofs like grease in a frying pan. Without warning, a great slithering sheet of rain mixed with hail dropped like shells all around, making the tin roofs rattle so loudly it hurt their ears. It felt like the sky collapsed into the earth, and the atmosphere brooded over the camp. In it came the crack of lightning and the rumbling of thunder as if artillery batteries fired. No one slept.

In the morning, thin, ghostly trails of mist rose from the prison compound after last night's rain. The drizzle stopped as cloud banks began to break apart, allowing cracks of sunlight to pierce through with dazzling rays. A smattering of partial rainbows scattered. Raindrops clung to every leaf, glistening like tiny fairies.

The humidity rose, despite a breeze carrying the scent of flowers sweeping over the sodden atmosphere. Sunlight burst across the camp, splashing the dirt and ragged concrete with orange and yellow as if someone hit a theater light switch.

Curt learned from the ROKs that the UN had launched a massive counter-offense, and the communists were routed. The South Koreans entered Munsan-ni three days earlier, and their platoon made the mistake of crossing the Imijin River without sufficient support. The young lieutenant estimated the prison camp was about 60 kilometers northeast of Seoul by road. "Maybe half that to the new battle lines."

Curt shared the news with his men. "The battle lines are only about 20 miles south."

They were excited.

He whispered, "My mom always said to not count the chicks before the eggs hatch, and remember the rugged terrain with horrible roads. It could be a very long 20 miles."

The commander lost interest in them when the new prisoners came in. He was in hog-heaven, marching South Koreans to his office, interrogating and cajoling them to join the North.

The South Koreans occupied the bamboo cages, and the Americans felt lucky to be ignored, although it was hot and sweaty to be crowded in with them. The South Koreans complained so loudly about their smell, that the guards took the Americans out to stand under a water barrel.

Curt saw a red fox outside the fence. It stood watching for a moment, then moved on. He wished they would let it in near the cells. Maybe it would take care of the mice and rats that walked over his chest at night.

After they washed the men off, they sprayed them with pesticides to delouse them. Although they coughed, it gave the men renewed hope. Maybe soon they could hear NATO artillery booming. They hoped the photographic plane gave the coordinates of the prison camp so they wouldn't get shelled.

Energized, the crazy commander interrogated and tortured the new arrivals. He forced everyone to stand at attention for hours in the scorching sun for the daily communism lecture. Curt whispered to the South Koreans, "Pretend to pay attention."

They reoriented it toward the South Koreans with many offers that if they confessed and joined the communists, they would be treated as heroes and brothers who saw the truth that the UN forces were invaders. They only wanted a peaceful and united Korea where everyone was equal. "You must confess and accept the truth."

He put those who didn't pay attention in the bamboo cells and, when they were filled, ordered men staked spread-eagled in the yard.

They learned that combined American and ROK forces reached the Imjin River and entered Uijongbu and Sinp'al-li. The communists were withdrawing, fighting a defensive action.

He and Carl quietly acted as translators in the cells. They felt somewhat optimistic.

Carl said hopefully, "If we're lucky, they'll overrun this prison camp."

Taylor challenged the commander to kill him, staring straight in his face. "Just finish me off. It will make me happy."

It was unintended reverse psychology. The commander said, "No way. You'll be the last to die."

Curt worked on Taylor. "When you lose hope, you will die. Hang in there, man. We're working on an escape plan. I have the guards' schedules and habits down. Many are young teens. There are only fifteen guards, and they're as afraid of us as we are of them. With all these South Koreans in here, they're distracted and nervous. Now, we've got the numbers, and we just need to figure out how to disarm them. Some night, we'll make a break." Escape seemed impossible. They had no plan that made sense.

In the morning communism lecture, they preached, "The community is everything and the individual is nothing. A single life has no more value than a feather."

The commander beseeched the South Koreans, "We are on the same side. We are brothers who desire a peaceful, united Korea. It was the Americans and British who divided our country. Please, just confess and learn the truth of communism that we are all equals. Come to our side, and you'll have plenty to eat and will be treated with respect. Help us fight these money-hungry invaders. They are worse than the Japanese and only want to make us a colony of their Wall Street Corporations."

They made the prisoners sit on their knees and chant, repeating over and over, "Loyalty to communism, to Stalin and Chairman Mao."

The commander said, "You should show gratitude for the food and water we give you. We are your liberators, your friends."

They gave anyone who showed the slightest inclination to collaborate cigarettes and extra food. Those who resisted were labeled reactionaries and punished.

Being a guard in a prison camp was not an honorable duty. They reserved it for those with discipline issues, or who were too young to fight. Some guards appeared to be fifteen or younger. A young guard was particularly curious and when he was on duty, he stood close to the cells and stared at the Americans. It was the kid who pushed the stakes in for Curt.

He whispered to the boy in Korean, "We're not your enemies. I'll remember you when I'm released. I'll find you and send you help."

The boy whispered back, "Remember, I'm from Seoul and my name is Kwog Bitgaram." He was afraid to say more.

They got a cup of boiled rice, millet, or barley and a cup of water every day. It was more nourishment than they ever received. They never knew what the commander was going to do. They got more nervous the longer nothing happened.

The commander focused on the South Koreans for the next few days, intent on turning them to his side. Fine with Curt. They weren't being tortured or pushed into the cages or spread-eagled and were receiving more food and water. Things were looking up.

The morning sun rose quickly as if excited about the coming day's events and it heated everything to near boiling. Seeing a few dark clouds gathering, Curt thought it might hail. He wondered about his father's orchards. If they made it past the freeze, hail could still damage the crop. It cost them more than if they were frozen out since they paid the picking bill.

He sweated as if he had just taken a hot shower. Dust nestled into the creases of his forehead and turned to mud, running down his face. He wiped his eyes. The storm clouds withered away, leaving interesting figures.

Jack imagined he saw a ship and said it was a sign they'd be rescued. The other men shook their heads, but inside, they felt a sense of hope with the South Koreans there and the front so near.

One of the captured South Koreans went over to their side. He showered and received a new North Korean uniform. He sat in front of the prisoners and ate soup with meat and vegetables while drinking a beer. He tried to convince his comrades to join the communists with him. "Look, I have plenty of food. They will treat us well. They only want a peaceful, united country. We must evict the foreigners." He lit a cigarette and blew the smoke at the cells.

His former platoon members called him a traitor and every disgusting name they could think of. After two days, he refused to have any contact with them and disappeared. The men figured they sent him to join a North Korean fighting unit.

They had been in captivity for 41 days. The Americans' bodies were covered with infected sores, were sixty percent of their former weight, and lice covered them. They stunk so badly, they couldn't stand themselves. The cells were hot and crowded. They slept in shifts or kneeled against each other. The South Koreans were respectful to the Americans and whispered with Curt and Carl, telling them where they were from, what happened to their families, and the battles they fought. They seemed to like these tough Americans.

Death would end the suffering. "No," Curt told himself, "Be mentally strong, don't give up. You did this for your country. You will be treated as a hero. You've survived in North Korea for over forty days. Give it one more."

The magpies had a party outside the compound, calling out, and gossiping as they foraged.

Chapter 13
The Rescue

Not long after nightfall, a tremendous commotion broke out, startling everyone awake. The guard tower's machine gun spurted fire. Koreans yelled and shots rang out all over the place. Flares lit the entire camp.

Against the backdrop of a quarter moon, bullets soared and showered the compound with magnificent flashes of lights as if they were fireworks, only deadly. Like a million candles burned, they spewed color across the fences and turned the night into day. The straw-roofed huts caught fire. Screams, orders, a machine gun rat-tat-tat, rat-tat-tat.

An Asian in a North Korean uniform shot off the locks of the cells. He yelled in Korean, "Get out!"

Curt hollered at the others, "We're being rescued! Scramble." He sprinted out with Carl right in front of him. Prisoners scattered like a flock of sparrows taking off. The young guards fell to the ground, some shooting, others trembling in fear. The Korean boy who talked to Curt sprinted beside him.

They ran for the gate. It was pushed down and some military men crouched near it firing. They didn't aim at the prisoners.

Just outside the gate, rifle fire knocked Carl down. Enemy machine guns were on full automatic. Slugs slammed all around. Carl was still alive.

Curt leaned to pick him up.

He groaned. "No man, I'm gut shot."

"Fuck you, bro, I'm carrying you to Seoul if I need to." Curt ran as fast as he could with the straw slippers slipping and sliding into the pine forest, trees spit past as he carried Carl. The ground was rocky and uneven. He smelled blood and gunnite as he dodged left and right, trying to keep trees between himself and the prison camp.

Taylor came by, limping with his homemade crutches, being half-carried by Spooker. Curt was amazed they hadn't been killed as slowly as they went.

A husky Korean threw Taylor over his shoulder and took off running through the forest. Spooker caught up and jogged beside him. "Curt, I can see his guts hanging out, they're hanging down the back of your leg."

Curt couldn't put Carl down, he was his best friend. He ran, just ran. He ran like a rabbit from a wolf. He had no idea where to run. Slugs hit Carl in his back. Curt lost his bamboo slippers and lost track of Spooker. Rocks and sticks cut his feet as he ran as hard as possible. He was out of shape and emaciated. Weak, he couldn't sprint as like in high school. Warm blood ran down the back of his right leg. Didn't know if it was his or Carl's. He just kept running. Out of breath and weak, it turned into a slow jog. Men dropped all around. He wondered why he didn't get killed. The South Koreans fought back fiercely. Curt was an athlete but other prisoners passed him since Carl was heavy, almost as big as him.

Jack yelled as he passed, "He's dead! Drop him, save your own life."

Rounds rang off rocks and thumped into trees. Bullets smashed into Carl. Curt felt a sharp pain in his left shoulder. Carl's body was saving his life. Splintering guilt, but he couldn't stop and wouldn't drop his buddy.

He stumbled and nearly fell but fear kept him going. A bright burning pain hit his butt. Hurt like a mother. He stumbled and his ass went numb. He stopped to rest. He leaned against a coniferous tree. He was lost and didn't know which way to go. The enemy was coming up behind him. A Korean yelled and pointed. He ran in the direction he pointed. Other Koreans opened up on the pursuers. He was scared shitless.

He didn't know how long or how far he ran. Korean soldiers kept trying to get him to drop the body in the forest. Carl was dead but they promised to haul out each other. He couldn't believe he still ran. His butt hurt like hell. He was too scared to stop. He ran for what seemed like miles over the rough terrain. He got weaker and weaker with blood loss. Didn't know how far. He didn't know how he kept running. His shoulder hurt like a bullet hit him. His ass was numb on one side.

He stopped to rest against a tree. A Korean soldier yelled to put Carl down, making slashing motions at his throat. That got him running again. He didn't know how he kept going. Just fear and adrenaline, running, stumbling.

He stubbed his toe on a rock or tree root, and fell, dropping Carl. It was a swirling dream, a Maytag washer of emotions, everything at once. The rapid-fire shots pinged off rocks and bullets thumped into trees. He panted, trying to get oriented as terror painted his body red.

A Korean soldier tried to get him to leave Carl, wrapping his hands around his neck to show he was dead.

Curt picked up Carl and trotted again.

Spooker came back and jogged next to him, urging him on. "You can do it, Curt, keep going."

Finally, he saw a duce and a half military truck with a canvas top. The engine was running. Upset and anxious soldiers waved him in. Some trucks were pulling out, loaded with South Korean POWs. The other American prisoners were already in the back. He was the last one. The soldiers were upset he was so slow. The tailgate was down. He dropped Carl in the back and collapsed.

Book II
Arirang Hill

Chapter 14
The Wounded American

June 2, 1951

It was breaking dawn, yet still dark when Misun heard a big truck rumble to a stop outside of their tin-roofed home. Neighboring dogs barked in a chorus of howls. "Stay quiet," her mother said with a frightened whisper. With no man in the home, they must defend themselves. She picked up a broom and handed a kitchen knife to Misun. It drizzled softly so the windows were closed.

Abrupt, very loud pounding on the door. A man's urgent voice, "We have a wounded man for you to take care of. Open up!"

Momma crept to the door. "Who are you?"

"Captain Kim Chin-mae, your daughter's uncle, said you take wounded men since our hospitals have been destroyed. Let us in, this salam (American) is heavy." Hammering on the door again. "Come on," he said, "You've nursed other men that he sent. We're tired, and we've been through hell."

"Misun, light the kerosene lamp," Momma ordered. She opened the door and the scent of blooming lilacs and soft rain floated into the one-roomed house. Sleeping mats were at one end of the hard-packed dirt floor, and at the other, three wooden chairs, a rickety table, and a small charcoal stove.

Dirt-covered, bloody, and sweating South Korean soldiers carried in a wounded, unconscious American and laid him on her sleeping mat. The rank odor of perspiring men overwhelmed the lilac smell.

The sergeant said, "We just rescued this salam and his buddies along with our soldiers from a POW camp." He lit a cigarette. "We don't know why Americans were in the prison camp with our men, but we brought them since they're our allies."

The young man leaned against the door as if his legs would no longer support him. "We had a hell of a time getting out. We lost men." He took a drag on the cigarette and then noticed Misun. His gaze rolled down her lithe body dressed in bedclothes, appraising her beauty.

Eyes down, she backed away, holding the knife pointed at him.

One of his men said, "Let's go, we have to deliver the salams to other homes, and we have to stop at the morgue." They opened the door and tramped out.

Jimin asked, "You said Captain Kim Chin-mae sent you?"

"Yes. He's our company commander."

"Is he alive? Is he well?" Her eyes betrayed anxiety. She and Chin-mae were seeing each other.

He snorted, "Yes, of course. How could he order us to bring a wounded man here otherwise? He was on the mission but reported to headquarters."

She squealed with excitement and looked at Misun.

The sergeant shrugged. "He'll be promoted. Because of the captain, we were able to locate and rescue an entire platoon of our men held in a North Korean POW camp."

Jimin wasn't the type to show affection, but she almost hugged him. She stopped herself. "Thank you for the good news." She stared into his eyes, "Please tell Captain Kim we love him."

"Sure. I'll see him in the morning." The sergeant said, "A doctor will come tomorrow." He started to leave.

Jimin looked at the huge man lying on the floor. "I didn't volunteer to take care of Salams." Her voice was stressed.

Irritation in his tone, he raised to his full height and nearly yelled, "Take him, or we'll have to move him to another home." He mumbled a profanity. "Captain Kim is used to getting his way. What do you want?" He took a drag off his cigarette. "Come on, we're exhausted, and we've got others to deliver."

"Don't worry, we'll take care of him. Tell Captain Kim we miss him."

He saluted. "Will do." He left several oranges and a bag of medicine, then disappeared into the dark. The military truck restarted and ground away to the barking of village dogs and the lighting of lamps.

Misun stared longingly. She hadn't tasted an orange since the communists invaded South Korea last year, and she was hungry.

The man moaned.

She cautiously peeked at him. His bare feet were bloody and a big toe hung by the skin. The soldiers hadn't cleaned him, and he stunk of sweat, blood, and infections. Heavily sedated, he was dressed in a blood-smeared, tattered camouflage uniform. He was missing three fingers on his right hand and a nasty yellowing scab festered on his eyebrow. There were no whiskers on his washed-out cheeks. He was hard to look at. She shrank into a corner without putting down the knife.

"There's nothing to be afraid of. He just smells," Momma said, "Chin-mae didn't say only Koreans. This man is on our side. Get water boiling."

Misun gathered coals for the small charcoal stove as her mother carefully began cutting off the man's camo uniform. "He is certainly stinky!" She opened both windows to let the salty breeze wash the smell. The wind blew in rain, causing mud to form on the dirt floor. Ganghwa Island was subject to heavy rain.

After setting a pan of water on the small stove, Misun helped cut and remove the sticky, blood-soaked, and sweaty uniform. Bruised and lacerated skin stretched over his emaciated ribs. The man was pallid and disgusting. Curly black hair with a bleeding bullet graze down the middle of his scalp and no whiskers, he looked young, but it was hard to tell how old he was. His feet dangled off the sleeping mat, and his shoulders hung over its sides.

He seemed to fade in and out of consciousness. He didn't cry out from the festering cuts as they cleaned. *Must be a tough man.*

"There's lice everywhere on him. We need alcohol." After cutting off his clothes, Jimin grumbled, "We have to do this even if it's disgusting. We need to find something to kill them." She tossed the ragged uniform outside, and after brushing off her clothes, went through the bag the soldiers left. She found alcohol and hydrogen peroxide.

Misun stared. She hadn't seen a naked man before and his torn-up body spooked her. Momma gave her a grumpy stare so she cautiously dabbed his bloody scalp. "Eomma! He has lice all through his hair."

"Use alcohol. I hope there's enough." Her tone was irritated. "We'll need to shave his head."

It looked like the man would lose some hair where a bullet's path made a straight furrow, leaving inches in the front and back. *He must have ducked.*

Soapy water helped untangle his hair. After cleaning his face and neck, she gently combed his overgrown curly locks, pulling lice nits. He was as handsome as John Wayne. *Such a shame he's hurt.* One eyebrow seeped yellow and red stuff from heavily crusted skin. It was hairless like the graze on top of his head. His forearms and the backs of his hands had round burns: some encrusted, others scarred, a number recent and swollen with infection. *He is so pitiful.*

His left big toe flopped off to the side.

Jimin gently squeezed, feeling gravel where there should have been bones. "He might lose this one, it's crushed." Muttering, she cleaned between his cut and bleeding toes, picking out slivers of rocks and wood splinters.

Misun used a wet cloth to wipe his hideously bruised chest and belly but stopped above his groin. She hadn't seen a man's penis before. It was thick and long, surrounded by curly black hair. Scary. His big balls hung in a sack under it. She wanted to puke. She looked at her mother. "I can't do this."

"I'll take care of it tonight but you must learn. It's time you grew up."

Misun gagged at the thought. The school strictly forbade relationships with the other sex. She stopped hugging her brother long before Poppa was killed during the communist suppressions. In Korea, men dominated women, and she resented being treated like a servant girl. She was smarter than most boys.

Without a man in the house, her mother became independent and determined to raise her to compete in this man's world. Misun could do the expected aegyo, the cutesy Korean girl giggle—widening her eyes and putting her hands to her cheeks coyly—but she never did. She kept her hair cut short like a young schoolgirl instead of the traditional mid-waist for her sixteen years of age. She didn't want men looking at her that way.

They managed to turn him over, and he groaned.

She gasped. There were lacerations and puncture wounds all over his buttocks, thighs, and shoulders. His body oozed with yellowish-red, infected sores. Every muscle was a deep purple with some bruises older and yellowing. His body was like a gravel quarry: shattered and blasted granite with pools of blood. There was a bullet wound in his right buttocks seeping fresh blood through a hurriedly applied bandage. The soldiers hadn't taken the time to bandage other wounds that bled or wept puss. His left shoulder looked like he was recently shot or stabbed, but it had sealed itself.

"It's a wonder this man is alive." Jimin shook her head. "We must disinfect his whole body." She jerked back. "Look at the lice crawling around his body. We'll have to disinfect the whole place."

The hydrogen peroxide foamed madly as Misun wiped his skin.

Her mother had a grim look. "One of us must constantly be with him. Most of it will fall on you while I work at the fish market." Distress on her face, Jimin's voice squeaked. "I didn't expect to have one this bad."

Suddenly brave, Misun said, "Don't worry, I'll take care of him." She wished she was away from this war-torn country, away from the communists that could attack at any time, away from a land where violent men raped girls and slaughtered each other for politics. She sang softly, "Arirang, arirang, arariyo, you are going over Arirang hill."

Chapter 15
To Pluck a Star

On Mondays, Misun's mother didn't work at the chaotic fish market where people yelled and tossed fish to each other in preparation to sell. The catch varied depending on what was running. Some days they brought in croaker, mackerel, tuna, or octopus; other days, they caught shrimp or squid.

Hoses pumped saltwater, and women constantly sprayed to keep the fish from drying out. Sometimes they had a poor run, coming in downhearted. South Korean military trucks waited for the boats and took everything—leaving merely fins, guts, and little else for the locals.

Jimin ordered, "Get the bike you found fixed and go back to that traditional healer for more sterrella. I'll feed and clean him today." Like most Korean women, no matter what, she complained. "Men! I don't know why they smell so bad even when they're healthy. He is worse than the fish market."

Misun went around the small thatched-roofed village and traded a hwamunseok mat to an old man who patched the tubes on the bike she had found. He worked on it until it was ridable. She felt a new sense of freedom. Now, she just needed to keep someone from stealing it.

She rode to Ganghwa town in an hour and talked again to the traditional healer who traded her sterrella and ssanghwacha, a slightly bitter tea known to cure fatigue, weakness, and cold sweats.

He spent a great deal of time talking about how to heal using the traditional ways. He suggested feeding the wounded man kimchi and their local turnip since they are rich in vitamins and can help cure skin diseases, and digestive ailments and also have an antibacterial effect. "Ganghwa turnip has anticancer effects. Give him as much as he will eat." He grinned. "He will have gas."

Misun heard the military lines were stabilizing near the thirty-eighth parallel just north of Ganghwa Island across the Han River. The United States and North Korea started negotiations for POW exchanges. She felt a slight optimism. Maybe the war would end soon.

In the morning with her mother back at work, Misun managed to get his penis in a jar just as it started leaking. She kept an eye on it and reacted quickly, or it would stream all over and then she'd have to rinse the urine spots. He wet the mattress a couple of times, and their little home smelled like an outhouse.

Despite periodic rain, she kept the windows open, hoping the blooming lilacs would dampen the odor. She learned if she left it hanging in the jar and then ran to hold the jar, it would keep him from spraying the pad. It was a curious thing, this organ. She wondered how it worked to make babies. She mentally detached to cleanse him where it stunk. She rolled his sack away to clean under it. It was gross yet fascinating. She gagged.

He muttered, "Mianhaeyo." Sorry.

She looked at him with surprise. "Hangug-eohaseyo?" Do you speak Korean?

He nodded weakly then drifted out.

She sang softly as she worked. "Arirang, Arirang, Arariyo, you're not crossing over Arirang Hill, please get well." The song had thousands of variations, and she made up her own, depending on the occasion.

The school segregated boys and girls, and she knew nothing about sex. It didn't matter. She imagined herself as a nurse, a strong brave young woman, healing this man. She read and reread the first aid manual, committing it to memory, telling herself, *I'm a nurse. I will approach this scientifically.*

Constantly beside the American, she talked softly and sang folk songs. "Arirang, Arirang, Arariyo, if you cross over Arirang Hill, please take me with you if you will." She watched intently as her mother used a straight razor to cut off his curly locks so lice had nothing to cling to. She stared at his face. She started to view his facial features as desirable, his big nose and huge brown eyes were kind when he looked at her. He was young to be in this war, a war of horror, rape, and burning.

She remembered the one movie she got to see, *Fighting Seabees,* in which John Wayne fell in love with a nurse, but he was killed fighting the Japanese. Her John Wayne wasn't going to die.

Misun vowed to herself. *I'll do everything possible. I will save his life. It will be perfect.*

When she finished, Jimin said, "He looks like a teenager."

His eyes were closed, but he whispered, "Kamsahamnida." Thank you.

Jimin sat back in surprise.

"He understands Korean, but his pronunciation is bad."

"Maybe when he is better, the two of you can talk," her mother said. "You know some English, maybe you can teach each other."

Entertaining herself while preparing food, Misun sang, "Arirang, Arirang, Arariyo, you're going over Arirang Hill, and you'll love me before you will," watching his eyelids. Sometimes they fluttered as if he dreamed or responded to her songs.

She knew he was having nightmares when he thrashed his hands muttering, "My name is Phil Brown, private first class, serial number 0658 913 G131."

She ran to hold his rough, scabbed-over hands. "No bad dreams. You're safe with me. I'll protect you." Somehow, she felt strong in his presence, forgetting how tiny she was.

A smile came over his lips, and he squeezed her hand.

When Doctor Lee returned, although the American was still out of it, he was pleased with the color of his face. "He smells better. He might make it." He nodded to Misun.

"Where is your mother?"

"Cleaning fish at the market."

"You're doing a good job, keep it up." He left more oranges and flat noodles along with five pounds of rice, and more cartons of saline, morphine, and antibiotics. "If he keeps improving, I'll cut back the morphine, then you can talk to him."

"Can you please send some clothes and blankets?"

"That boy! I've told him twice." He nodded at the man. "Maybe he'll fall in love with you and take you to America where it's safe and there's plenty to eat." Everyone knew Americans were rich. They all drove cars and smoked cigarettes.

Some villagers told her mother the same thing. Misun replied, "Haneureui byeol ttagi." To pluck a star in the sky.

Doctor Lee smiled. "You never know." He left a bag of oranges and more medicine.

In my dreams, she peeled an orange and put the skins into the soup. She crushed one slice at a time, then slipped it into the American's mouth with an aspirin. She detected his throat moving as he swallowed. Initially, she pried his lips open to smash them in. The smell of chocolate kisses helped. She held a piece to his nose until his jaw relaxed. She spoke in mixed Korean and English, "Want a kiss?" Crushing slices, she fed him all the oranges, knowing they were rich in vitamin C, a cell builder.

She changed his wound dressings, gently rubbing antifungal and antibacterial salves before replacing them with fresh bandages. Whenever his eyes fluttered slightly open, she used chocolate to get him to take a spoonful of soup. She rewarded him with a taste of chocolate when he took three spoonfuls.

He murmured, "Thank you, kamsahamnida."

"You welcome."

Grandpa made a toothbrush for him, and Grandmother brushed his teeth using mint herbs. Much better.

One afternoon as he slept, she took a bath in the galvanized tub, singing to herself and taking her time. Standing to dry herself, she glanced at the American and realized his eyes were slightly open. Misun looked down at her chopstick body. Her breasts were swelling. Her face grew hot. *He is becoming aware. I must be careful from now on.* One of the South Korean soldiers she nursed back to health had tried to rape her. Her grandfather ran him off with a pitchfork. She was very careful around the American, ready to jump away if he tried to touch her.

As his bodily functions returned, she recruited her grandparents to help get him over the bucket to relieve himself. It took all they had to lift him since he was over 196 centimeters. The doctor's errand boy eventually brought a hospital gown but it was far too small and the back was open. She cut the armpits and neck to get it over his broad shoulders. Her grandparents were stunned at the whip scars on his back.

Harabeoji shook his head with admiration. "He must be a very brave and tough man like our son."

The American was huge and his hips were too sore. It turned into an ordeal as they propped him between two chairs. "Ouch, oh!" Swaying, he faded in and out of consciousness. "I'm sorry, kamsahamnida."

It took a moment for Misun to compose a response. "My pleasure." Truthfully, it wasn't. He still smelled from infections.

She did their washing and hung it out to dry on a line where it snapped and flapped like gossiping tongues. Everyone in the village talked about the wounded salam. People asked her mother if she would allow him to take Misun with him when he left. She didn't want to get her hopes up. It would be the best thing that could happen since she didn't have a dowry. Marriages were arranged based on social and financial standing. Misun would be lucky to marry a fisherman or factory worker.

Doctor Lee continued to reduce the morphine each visit until one day, he said, "Next week, I'll take out the IVs. Give him pain pills if needed." He teased her, "You are a beautiful young woman. Maybe he'll take you home with him."

Her walnut-faced grandfather also suggested it. Misun shook her head. "I'm only sixteen." She didn't know this man or much about America, but it might be better than marrying a Korean since she would have to move in with his family and become their servant.

"So what? You're gorgeous, if badly undernourished. Americans are so rich they eat meat every meal, not just little chunks in soup but a great hunk for each person. It's a paradise where you could live like a princess compared to Korea." He pointed at the man. "He must have been in combat to have been captured and tortured. I think he was a commando. Look at him. He was likely very strong before the North Koreans nearly starved him to death."

She looked him over. Yes, at one time, he was an athlete. She wondered what it would feel like to have his body pressed against hers once he healed. Her groin warmed. It surprised her to have such thoughts.

The old doctor said, "I've been asking around. The American military has no record of a Phil Brown with that serial number. They won't accept responsibility for him."

"That is strange. Why would they refuse to take care of their own?"

"I don't know."

Alone again, the man's eyes were slightly open, and she pointed at herself. "Misun, you understand?" She pointed to her chest. "Misun."

A weak reply, "Me son."

She corrected, "Me soon."

"Misun."

"Good!" She pointed at his chest. "Your name Phi Brown?"

His eyes closed as if seeking energy. When he reopened them, she pointed to her chest, "Misun," then she pointed at his chest. "You?"

"Curt."

"Curt?"

He nodded ,and his head dropped as cute as a puppy.

She checked his dog tag, wondering why it said Phil Brown. She would ask the next time he was conscious.

Momma told her to lay close to him in the darkness to keep him warm against the ocean breezes. There was so little room in the house that with his large size, she couldn't help it. She was careful because his wounds seeped. If she wasn't, she'd have to wash her bedclothes in the morning.

An island, Ganghwa has moderate weather but got occasional light snow in winter. June temperatures were hot and nights cool with more frequent rains. They kept the windows open because of his smell, the antiseptic, and his terrible gas. He often woke her and Jimin with explosions. They fed him kimchi and turnips every chance as they had probiotics to help the colon but flatulence was a side effect. Seemed he farted all the time.

Doctor Lee disconnected the IVs and gave her morphine pills on his next visit, saying to give them only when needed since they are addictive and cause constipation. He brought a case of canned Spam so the American would have more protein. She didn't know how to prepare it or that the meat was already cooked.

Curt was more alert now. He said in a mixture of English and Korean, making motions with his hands, "Try frying the Spam."

It smelled so delicious the neighborhood dogs came to the door and whined. Misun fried slices for her mother when she came home. She was stunned at the flavor, saying, "Next time you see the doctor, ask him for more of this."

Several weeks in, the infection began to leave his wounds, and she could rest her palm against his chest. It was wonderful to be close to a man. She hadn't been held in one's arms since she was a child. Misun remembered her father carrying her on his back because he didn't want her feet to touch the muddy ground. It made her brother jealous like when Uncle Chin-mae came to the house and sat her on his knees. She wondered about him. Was he still alive? Was he directing a great battle? She missed him terribly, perhaps as much as her mother did.

When the American was awake, she read him her favorite folk tale, *The Weeping Princess.*

Princess Pyeonggang chronically wept like a child and it grated on her father. He warned that if she didn't shape up, he'd marry her off to Ondal the Fool. The poor young man was said to be so stupid even the king heard of him.

When she turned 16, Pyeonggang got into an argument with her father. The king wanted to marry her to the son of a nobleman named Go in the Sang province, but she refused because he was reputed to be mean. She said the king constantly threatened to marry her to Ondal, so she would do so.

The king shook his head. "Those were empty threats to make you stop weeping."

She replied, "A king should never break his word."

This infuriated her father. "If you're going to be impossible, then leave!"

So she did.

When Pyeonggang showed up at Ondal's door and informed him of her intentions, Ondal was wary. His mother didn't think a princess should marry below her station, and he also didn't believe Pyeonggang was serious. After some time, Pyeonggang convinced them, and, to the shock of everyone, she and Ondal married.

Their marriage did not go smoothly at first, but Pyeonggang held it together by being all but perfect. Before leaving the palace, she gathered her jewelry and sold it to provide a solid foundation for her new household. She worked tirelessly to grow the family's fortune. Her efforts paid off: not only did they become financially stable, but Ondal, due to his wife's training in archery and horsemanship, worked his way up to become a brilliant general since she consulted him on battle strategy.

Ondal cemented his reputation when the Han Chinese invaded. Grabbing the armor and sword his wife gave him, Ondal rallied the people to confront the invaders. Upon meeting the Chinese on the field of battle, his soldiers were so intimidated no one made a move. No one except Ondal: He leaped forward in a surprise attack and killed their general with one blow. The Chinese soldiers fled. Ondal was the victor.

Upon hearing of this unexpected win, King Pyeongwon summoned this unknown provincial hero to thank him personally. When he arrived with the King's daughter in tow, the king asked his name.

"My name is Ondal."

"What? Are you serious?"

"Yes. It's me."

The king was dumbfounded and impressed. He showered his newly introduced son-in-law with gifts.

Ondal continued defending the country against both China and the neighboring Korean kingdom of Silla, his perfect wife advising him. In one battle, Ondal was killed on Mount Arirang. According to legend, when they tried to move his body for burial no one could budge it.

Pyeonggang knelt beside his body. Putting her arms around it, she whispered to her late husband, "The question of life and death has been decided. So why don't we go back home together, my dear?"

The body came free and General Ondal was buried soon thereafter, where his perfect wife came every day to leave flowers.

Uncle Chin-mae said, "You are like this princess. You will marry a man no one expects. You will help him and love him forever. He also will love you with all his heart." He whispered, "You're my perfect little princess."

"I love you too."

She missed him when he was gone. She often dreamed of marrying a man no one expected, someone she helped who sacrificed for his country. He would love her forever with all of his heart just as Chin-mae said. They would honor one another. It would be perfect.

Curt chuckled with delight. "Maybe I'm Ondal and you are the princess. You'll take me from being a stupid fool to a famous man."

They laughed together. "Yes, I'm Princess Pyeonggang. I'll marry you and make you my prince."

"That's a nice book. It must have cost a lot."

"My uncle gave it to me when I was a child. It's my favorite book." She explained, "He's the officer who led the men who rescued you."

"I owe him. I'd like to meet him."

"Maybe you will. You are two of a kind." She looked into his eyes. "Do you believe in fate?"

"I do now."

Her cheeks warmed. She put down the book and stood. "I need to check if the laundry is dry." She went outside and looked up at the sky, wondering. In America, they say 'Ladies first.' Here it is men first. This man was like the Statue of Liberty, beckoning freedom. She knew it was premature but couldn't help wondering.

Chapter 16
Kamsahamnida

Misun made dumplings with kimchi from a large pot buried in Halmeoni's yard. Rich in minerals, vitamins, and probiotics, kimchi is good for digestion and the immune system. Halmeoni added to the cabbage Ganghwa radishes, hot red peppers, turnips, carrots, scallions, ginger, onions, and garlic.

She thinned it because she didn't know if Americans liked spicy food. She minced fish fins for protein left over after the military took the day's catch. She brewed the ssanghwacha tea used for centuries to promote healing and knelt beside him on the mat.

Opening his brown eyes, he said, "Kamsahamnida, thank you, My Son."

Smiling, she corrected, "Soon, Me soon." Using chopsticks, she put kimchi into his mouth, giggling when he squinted his nose. He wasn't used to its sour spicy flavor.

"Misun, thank you for feeding me."

"Chonmahnehyo, you're welcome." She spoke slowly, "You say, chon-mah-neh-yo."

His pronunciation was bad. "Come ma need you."

"Close enough." By propping his head on a thick hwabangseok cushion Grandmother made for him, she could feed him without help and also taught him more Korean. She was surprised he already knew so much, but his pronunciation was terrible. Each time he opened his mouth, she made him correctly say, "Kamsahamnida," thank you, or, "Jwesonghajimahn," meaning, please.

It turned into a little game, and she giggled as he tried to pronounce the multisyllabic words. To Koreans, English was very challenging, and she assumed Korean was equally hard for Americans.

She gradually fed him and knew he was full when he turned his head away. When done, he always said, "Kamsahamnida, thank you, Misun."

"Honor to help you." She bowed with hands steepled. "My full name is Kim Misun, what yours?"

"Conrad. Curt Conrad."

She repeated it several times until he nodded. She asked, "Why dog tags say, Phil Brown?"

His face turned dark. "They say Phil Brown so the North Koreans wouldn't know my real name if we were captured."

"You brave man."

"You are a kind and gentle girl."

"We friends?"

"Yeah, we're friends." His eyes sparkled, then he dropped into sleep. Soon a fart erupted.

She sang, "Arirang, Arirang, Arariyo, crossing over Arirang Hill take me with you if you will." She dreamed of having food, so much food she put on weight and could lift big, heavy things. She'd be stronger than Momma and Harabeoji. She wouldn't be afraid of anything if she had enough food and a big man like Curt to take care of her. In her culture, marriage was practical and love had nothing to do with it.

As the days and nights traveled on, the American strengthened and could sit propped against the wall if she balanced him on his left bum. His hip hurt terribly and tears scurried down his cheeks. He'd say, "Joesonghabnida, sorry," over and over until she gave him morphine pills, then he'd sleep.

When he was awake, they often sat side by side, trying to communicate. He was appreciative of everything and his face turned red when she washed him down there. "I can do it."

He insisted on holding the jar to urinate and asked her to hold up a blanket. She giggled, pointing at his crotch. "I help many times." His eyes articulated something warm and kind.

She reached intuitively for his thoughts and a tingle ran up her spine.

Curt's face went bright red at needing help to sit on the bucket with three of them holding him up. He repeated, "Joesonghabnida, sorry, kamsahamnida, thank you."

Her grandparents didn't mind helping because he was so appreciative. Harabeoji started coming to talk with him every day and they laughed as they pantomimed. Curt had a wonderful sense of humor and his brown eyes sparkled.

Grandfather said, "If I had another son, I'd want him to be kind and gentle like this man." He winked at Misun. "He is also brave and very smart."

She had his permission.

Grandpa was skinny as a rail like her while Grandma was rectangular with a big head like her mom. Before the war, she was chunky, but now she was thin like everyone else. She was a great cook and often helped Misun prepare meals. Grandma tweaked Curt's cheek. "You are handsome like Elvis Presley." She looked at Misun. "You're a lucky girl."

Curt's ears turned red and he smiled. "Kamsahamnida." In bad Korean, he said, "I like you too."

She started to tell him her name, then smiled. "You can call me grandmother."

Misun knew the family had agreed that if he wanted to marry her, she had permission.

Grandpa talked and gestured, telling stories while Misun translated in broken English. They laughed and pantomimed, pointing and picking up things to demonstrate.

Doctor Lee reported that no American military branch had a record of a Phil Brown. "Don't worry. Someone will take responsibility. In the meantime, our government will pay you and send food since he was rescued with our soldiers."

Curt said, "I'm in the U.S. Navy." He hesitated. "Can you keep this confidential?"

Doc Lee nodded.

"My real name is Curtis Conrad. I was sent on a top-secret mission, and they gave us fake dog tags. They said there would be no record of our mission and if we didn't make it out within a few weeks, they would report us as lost at sea." He shook his head, as if worried. "That's why the Navy isn't taking responsibility for me."

The old doctor warned Misun, "There are communist sympathizers all over the country. Someone could kidnap him. It's your responsibility to keep him safe."

All the villagers knew. Some thought it was a scandal they kept a salam in their home, saying Misun would be polluted if she got involved with him. Only the dregs of society were military camp followers with no other hope to survive. Others thought it would be wonderful if he fell in love with her. "Her future would be great. She'd send us things from the land of plenty."

Jimin tried to put a stop to their talk. "My daughter will not marry the salam!" However, it would be fantastic if Curt fell in love with Misun and took her away from the war.

Chin-mae came home and was very interested in the American. "We rescued him with one of my platoons. They say the five Americans were horribly tortured. One was killed during the rescue and this man refused to put him down. He carried his friend for miles despite being shot. I have to admire him."

He sat down in a lotus position to talk with Curt. "Annyeong-haseyo. I'm Captain Kim Chin-mae. We rescued you with our platoon from a North Korean POW camp not long ago. I'm happy you survived."

"Bangap-sumnida." Nice to meet you. "I'm U.S. Navy Seaman third-class Curt Conrad. Thank you so much for rescuing us." He extended his hand, and they shook.

Chin-mae didn't flinch at the missing fingers. "I should thank you. Because of the success of our raid, I am being promoted to Major." He smiled.

Curt gave a slight chuckle. "Glad to be of help."

"And here you are being taken care of by my wife and daughter."

Misun's mouth fell open. She wondered if they were married and Uncle had adopted her.

"They are very good to me. You have a fine family." Curt glanced at Misun, his eyes admiring and warm. There were tiny sparkles of gold in his brown eyes.

They talked for a long time about the war, various battles, and strategies.

Chin-mae turned to Misun. "Curt is very intelligent. He's given me some tactical ideas I may implement." He coughed slightly and cleared his throat. "I'm sure he will rise in rank and become an important Naval officer when he is well."

He and Jimin left and her grandparents came over to visit. When her mother and uncle returned, they were relaxed and laughed together.

Jimin proudly said, "So you've been promoted again by General Park and will have your own brigade. You must be very smart and very brave." She took his hand. The grandparents looked at each other and smiled.

Misun focused on Curt. Warmth was in their tiny home. She

touched his cheek, wondering if he might fall in love with her. She could see compassion in his heart. She slipped into his deep brown eyes becoming one of the gold flecks. She was his if he wanted her.

Before leaving, Chin-mae shook Curt's hand, being careful not to hurt it. "I admire your courage for not talking to the North Koreans. You are a hero to us. I don't know what your mission was, but I will do everything I can to help you when you are ready to go home."

Curt saluted. "Thank you, sir. You ROKS are the toughest men in the world. Also, thank you and your men for rescuing us. Someday, if at all possible, I will pay you back."

They looked into each other's eyes as only warriors could.

Jimin asked the villagers to keep quiet, explaining there could be an attempt to kidnap the salam. "We don't know why the U.S. is refusing to acknowledge he is one of theirs."

They held a town meeting and all swore to keep it secret. It was a blessing to have an American POW being cared for here because when the doctor came, his helper brought a lot of food that Jimin traded.

One by one, they came to visit, offering small handmade gifts. Fishermen brought some of the catch they kept back from the military and interesting things they fetched floating on the sea. They were amazed he knew Korean. Oohing and ahhing, they gave respect to Misun.

On Jimin's day off, taking her bicycle, Misun rode to Ganghwa and traded handmade mats, cushions, and baskets for cotton cloth from the textile mill. She'd make him pants and a shirt while Jimin worked.

Although he was off the IVs, Curt still needed pain medicine and was often droopy. Misun had little experience and had trouble getting his measurements.

Halmeoni took charge of measuring him. They sat watching him and sang folk songs as they worked. He'd come to, then Misun fed him, cleaned his wounds, and rebandaged them. Curt never tried to touch her arm, never reached for her.

Halmeoni wondered if he was one of those who don't like women. She told of Japanese men trying to molest her and how Korean men had little respect for a woman's body. "I hear Americans are better, but they are still men." She nodded at Curt. "He is a good one. His parents raised him well." She smiled at Misun. "Perhaps you'll be lucky and he'll take you to America."

Misun explained Momma warned how poorly she would be treated by everyone if she got involved with a foreigner.

Halmeoni nodded. "But if you are in America would it matter?" Some villagers already had them married and imagined Misun sent them money and gifts from the United States where there was more than enough to go around.

Misun shook her head. "He will leave and forget me."

Halmeoni said, "I was fourteen when I married." She caught her eyes. "You will be seventeen in September. You're over the legal age to marry. One can dream." She grew quiet and shook her head. "It is only an old woman's thoughts. I would love to go see you in America but your mother is right, he might forget you."

Misun let herself fantasize a little. She imagined riding in a car to see American movies with Curt. They'd see all of John Wayne's films. He would put his arm around her shoulders, and they would eat popcorn. She heard it was tasty.

The doctor came. He was pleased Curt was recovering. He recommended giving morphine pills only when in distress. "Use the herbs and teas, they're better for him." He said, "I'm guessing the American military will come to get him when he can walk on his own."

"How long?" Misun worried. *Had she made enough of an impact he would come back for her?*

Doctor Lee shook his head. "The bullet probably fractured his pelvis and may have damaged his hip. I don't know without an X-ray but such injuries take between two and three months to heal, plus he's missing a big toe. You have a lot of work to do. In the meantime, you'll have food and money while he's here." He mentioned, "The U.S. Navy says they have no record of him."

Curt raised his head. "Like I told you. I volunteered for a top-secret mission so there is no record of a Phil Brown. Ask the Navy to search the records for my complete name, it's Curtis Alan Conrad, Seaman third class." He had recited his fake serial number so often that he only recalled the first part of his actual one.

"Sure, I'll send a message. I'll see if they will take responsibility for you but don't worry, our government will pay your costs as long as needed." He grinned. "It's your government's money."

He left three feather pillows as a gift for their work. What a luxury! Misun used them to prop his hips, and he gratefully said, "Kamsahamnida. Read me another story from your book."

"Okay." She flipped through it and began reading.

Deep in the mountains, there was a small, quiet village, and on the mountain behind this village, lived an enormous tiger, a terrible beast whose roar made every creature tremble for miles around. One snowy winter evening, the tiger was hungry, and he crept down into the village to get something to eat.

By and by, the tiger came to a house and paused outside the window where a baby was crying inside. "Aaang! Aaang! Aaang!" The child sounded exhausted, as if he had been crying for a long time, and yet he went on and on without pause.

"What an annoying brat," thought the tiger. "By eating him, I'll put an end to this racket." He peeked into the room and was just about to leap inside when he heard the baby's mother.

"Look! A fox!" she said. "Stop crying or he'll hear you and come eat you up!"

The baby was hardly distracted—he cried just as loudly. The mother tried to comfort the child, then to cajole him, but he would not stop. So she tried again. "Look! It's a bear! He's opening his huge jaws to eat you up!"

But the baby wasn't frightened at all. He kept right on crying without even the smallest interruption.

Crouching outside the window, the tiger pondered this. "What sort of baby is not afraid of foxes or bears?" he thought. "Surely, this is a brave child." He was full of admiration, but the rumble in his belly reminded him why he had come down into the village, and he prepared to pounce into the room.

"Look!" cried the mother, "The big tiger from the mountain is here, right outside the window!"

The tiger paused. "Let's see how terrified he is before I eat him," he thought, and he peeked into the room to gloat. But the baby was still crying without the slightest sign of fear.

The tiger had never in his long years, come across a human or an animal that did not fear him. Even the trees and stones trembled at his approach. But this boy—what manner of child was he that he did not fear a tiger? The tiger was troubled by this question, but in the end he was a tiger, and he decided to resolve the issue by eating the child.

But just as he was about to pounce, the mother cried, "Look! A persimmon!" And the baby stopped in mid-cry. Just like that! Not a peep.

In the sudden silence, a terrible idea occurred to the tiger. "A persimmon!" he thought. "More fearsome than a fox or a bear! Even more terrible than me! What a horrible monster it must be!" He quickly glanced left and right, his heart pounding with fear. "I'm done for if the Persimmon sees me," he thought, and in a single leap he left the village and ran away back up into the mountain.

Misun giggled softly as he smiled. She produced a persimmon from under her skirt and held it to him.

He felt tears run from his eyes. "Misun, you are a persimmon, so sweet, beautiful, and tasty. I could just eat you."

She sighed. "Someday, I'll let you."

Chapter 17
Take Me with You

One night, the South Korean police arrested a village couple for suspicion of collaboration with the communists. It frightened everyone. People became quiet, wondering who to trust and who else might disappear.

Jimin talked about how Misun's father was falsely accused as a communist sympathizer by the corrupt government. "It was because his partner wanted to steal his share of the business. He was the communist sympathizer!" She stood for a few minutes, then said, "You must always be prepared to take care of yourself. As soon as possible, I want you back in school. You must study hard and get into college."

Misun felt conflicted. She wanted Curt to fall in love with her and take her where there was no war, no starving, and no heartless killing. Another part thought it impossible and he would forget her. She must learn to take care of herself. She had to be perfect to compete in this man's world.

Glancing at his face, she realized Curt understood they talked about the arrest of communist collaborators because he was agitated. She went to his side and took his hand. "Don't worry. I protect you."

He seemed to feel better when she put a large kitchen knife by his side. "We will fight to the death together." Something inside her solidified. She would make this man remember her. Someday they would marry.

Misun collected persimmons and chestnuts from the forest to make a hot pot that bubbled over the charcoal with steamed millet and barley rice.

Curt smacked his lips and burped loudly in the Korean way to show appreciation. That night he didn't fart since she didn't give him kimchi or turnips.

To celebrate that peace talks started on July 10, Misun began the morning by giving Curt a bowl of tteokguk, a tasty soup of disc-shaped rice cakes in a clear broth. The white rice cakes symbolize purity and bring good fortune for the upcoming year.

He had trouble chewing them. His jaws were still sore from the beatings. She chopped it for him so he could swallow small bites. He had developed a taste for Halmeoni's kimchi, and she taught him how to use chopsticks with his left hand. It took another week before he could sit up by himself, leaning against the wall if she propped him on his left bum using the pillows.

Speaking better Korean, he said, "Misun, I'm so grateful for your help. You are very kind and hardworking. How can I pay you back?"

She smiled. "Just get well." Looking into his kind eyes, she asked, "Will you remember me after you leave?"

"Yes. How could I forget?" He searched her face. "Will you wait for me until you are eighteen so we can get to know each other?"

Her face went hot, and she turned away. Rushing outside, she walked to Halmeoni's house to talk with her. "He asked if I would wait for him until I'm eighteen."

"He's falling for you!"

Strange feelings shot around her chest. It was exciting and terrifying. Before it was a fantasy but with his request, it was becoming real. She didn't know how to handle it.

When she returned to the house, she carefully avoided looking directly into his eyes. She caught a glimpse: his face was sad and his lips were pinched together. She knew he was sorry for asking. He was such a good man. She wanted him to take her to America. She knew he would treat her respectfully, unlike most Korean men who treated their wives like servants and often hit them.

He sang a verse of the song he composed in his head.

Misun said, "You're writing a song for me? Sing it, please."

He shyly sang with a baritone voice. "The way across forever, stretching 'tween me and you. Our hearts laced together, pledging our love is true."

She knew he wanted her.

When Misun gave him kimchi with turnips, she teased, "Want some more gas?"

He smiled, "Sure, if you don't mind."

Curt watched as she and Halmeoni worked on his new pants and shirt. They sang, *Arirang*. Amazed, Misun heard his baritone voice singing along. She sang it so frequently, that he knew all the words.

She ran to his side as she sang. They sang it through once more, harmonizing.

> "Arirang, Arirang, Arariyo,
> you must pass over Arirang Hill
> My love, please take me if you will.
> Wondrous time, happy time, let us delay,
> 'Till night is over, do not go away.
> When you leave through the pass, please take me and go.
> Let us hold hands so together we know.
> Arirang, Arirang, Arariyo
> Our hearts will be one as we grow."

She asked if he understood the song's meaning.

He shyly put out his left palm, and she took it. "I'd take you with me."

There was something in his eyes, more than she could understand.

"I'd go with you."

They stared into each other's eyes, and it was like stardust sprinkled between them. She remembered Lao Tzu taught, "From caring comes courage." She became braver to love this man because she knew he cared about her.

Halmeoni shook her head when Misun returned to their work. "Be careful. They never come back. Americans think we are inferior. Keep your heart in your chest."

Curt raised his head. "No Halmeoni, don't say that. I will come back when she is eighteen."

Halmeoni laughed at him. "You are a tease. You will forget once you are back home."

They argued back and forth, laughing.

He said, "I'm like MacArthur, I shall return."

"No, you won't. MacArthur got fired."

Misun couldn't keep from wondering what it was like for wives in the United States. If she married a Korean, she would have to move in with his parents. The son's wife was little more than a servant—expected to clean, cook and do everyone's laundry. Under those conditions, she'd rather not marry, but a Korean woman without a man was a half-person and few respected a widow or an unmarried woman. Misun's only hope was to get an education and never marry or convince Curt to return for her. Things were in such chaos that neither might happen. She worked hard to show him how valuable and smart she was.

Grandmother chuckled pleasantly. "You two are fun to watch. It makes me wish I was young again."

When they finished his pants and shirt, Curt tried helping get them on, but his hips and pelvis were painfully stiff and sore. The two women wiggled up the pants. Still no underwear for him. Their fingers struggled to get the pants over his hips.

Misun tried to look away but was fascinated with his penis. The pants were loose and baggy and the shirt sleeves short, but having dyed the material a deep blue, it had a vague semblance of an American navy uniform.

Grandfather came to help get him standing for the first time.

They had no buttons, and it needed to be tied closed with a strip of material. His right hand didn't work so Misun did it for him by reaching around his waist. She wanted to hug him and have him put his arms around her. She stepped back and looked up into his eyes.

He looked down at her as if he wanted to take her in his arms. He was very pleased. "Kamsahamnida." His brown eyes twinkled as if little stars were in them.

Misun said, "When you can walk, your military will take you away."

Momentarily, his face appeared hopeful, then turned sad.

"Take your time, I like having you here."

"I like being here with you." He looked like he wanted to say more.

She needed to find a way for him to remember her. He was her best hope for a decent future, and he was very gentle. He said they would share everything. She began thinking, *What can I do?* She decided she would make love with him.

It was very hot in late July and frequent rainstorms made it humid. She was pleased Curt never demanded anything or ordered her around like a Korean man. And he never tried to touch her body or pull her to him. She was entranced by this handsome man. She overheard villagers talking about how the salam would take her with him: saying how beautiful she was, how wonderful her voice was, and how a man could not help but fall in love with her. "She is so smart, surely he will take her with him."

She tried to teach him the Korean game, Yutnori, a board game with four wooden sticks. She drew the board on the hard dirt floor using white and black stones for pieces. Pointing, she showed you were to try to get all four of your pieces back to the start before the other player. You move the pieces so many spaces according to how the four sticks fell. She tossed them in the air and moved her first piece two spaces, then gave him the sticks.

He threw them, thinking he needed to read the Korean signs on the sticks. He didn't understand how many spaces to move.

She didn't know the English equivalents and kept pointing at the sticks and counting.

Curt understood numbers in Korean but couldn't connect counting the sticks.

Sitting on the floor propped against the wall, he started squinting and sweating. He closed his eyes and tried to stay upright but wobbled and toppled onto her. She tried to keep him upright but he was so much bigger, she collapsed and he fell across her.

"Mianhaeyo." I'm sorry.

It was exciting to have him on top of her. She felt his chest muscles and wanted to rub against him but full of energy, she wiggled out from under him and got on her knees, saying, "Munje eopseoyo," No problem. She sweated from the exertion. She saw moisture in his eyes. It was strong feelings for her. No, he was in horrible pain. Sitting on the floor was a bad idea because of his pelvis. "Sillyamnida, chway-seong-ham-ni-da," I apologize, I'm sorry. She helped him roll onto his back and was surprised he laughed as he wiped tears from his eyes.

"I understand. You move around the board based on the sticks as if they're dice. If they land on the side without the signs, it means you can move a space. It's like the American game, *Sorry*."

They had a great laugh but didn't play Yutnori anymore since he couldn't sit on the floor due to pelvic pain.

Her grandfather loved playing the flower card game with the American at the rickety table. Curt could communicate with her help and their little home was filled with laughter. It was so much fun, he asked her to invite him over every day. They laughed and gestured wildly.

Curt joked, "What do Koreans eat in America?"

Misun translated, and Harabeoji grinned, putting up his hands.

Curt smiled widely. "Seoul food."

They didn't get it and stared at Curt. His lips were twisted up like a watermelon slice. They laughed at his expression.

He laughed with them, not realizing they didn't get the joke.

Everything was fun with him. He was very gentle and sweet.

She made boonguh bbang, a fish-shaped, pancake-like snack filled with sweet red bean paste.

Harabeoji ate noisily, smacking his lips and burping to show appreciation.

Curt imitated him; smacking his lips and burping, he nodded at Misun, his eyes sparkling.

When Harabeoji readied to leave, they patted each other's backs. Very unusual. She knew Grandfather truly liked this man.

One afternoon, Grandfather looked at her. "You should marry this American. They're all rich, and he is a good one. I like him." He lifted a small cup of rice wine, toasting her and Curt. "I can tell he likes you a lot."

Curt smiled, and she averted her eyes, saying, "Others' rice cakes always look bigger."

Harabeoji answered, "Even the straw shoe has a mate."

She glanced at Curt. His eyes were on her face. Her feelings burned in her heart like a torch as she met his shining eyes. She took a deep breath. *Maybe, just maybe, he will come back for me.*

Chapter 18
Thank You

Because of Curt, Misun asked her mother about sex, wondering how a man and a woman made babies. She was sure if she was pregnant with his child, he would return for her.

Jimin's eyes narrowed. She took her outside and explained everything.

On July 30 Misun lay two fingers on his forehead and felt a normal temperature.

Looking shy, he asked her, "Can I use the outhouse?" He pointed outside. "Eo-di-ye-yo…" Where?

She didn't understand what he wanted, and it took long minutes with both of them gesturing. Misun said, "Oh, hwajangsil, poo place."
One of the village fishermen had carved him a cane from driftwood, marking delicate signs for health and happiness. Misun gave it to him and supported his side so he could make his way to the shack. She nervously scanned the area, worrying. Children played in the streets. Nothing out of the ordinary.

He sat in there a long time making explosions. She started worrying when he stayed long after it went quiet.

Unlocking the door, he called out, "Can you help me, please?" He couldn't stand up.

She opened the door. Sweat dripped down his red face. She giggled. She started in but the atrocious smell made her back out. She laughed and held her nose. "Leave door open," she ordered.

After the odor cleared, she entered and tried to get him standing. She realized the dyed clothes made his skin blue. Misun was embarrassed, but he didn't mind the blue stains. Helping him pull up his pants, the plain cotton underwear she made for him pleased her. The embroidered crossed fingers meant affection. She knew he had no idea what it meant. Someday, he might figure it out and remember her.

He couldn't lift his buttocks to get his underwear and pants up. Thin as a wand, she leveraged her feet against the wooden bench and leaned back as far as she could, helping him stand. "Hwa-it-ting!" You can do it!

When he came up, he caught the edge of the door with his good hand, keeping her from falling by pulling her to his chest with his free hand. His pants dropped to his feet. They laughed. He was becoming erect, and it excited her. She kneeled to pull them up again, watching his member stand.

She got wet. As her head came to his chest, he looked down, and their eyes went into each other's. They almost kissed but laughed. It wasn't romantic in an outhouse.

"You're stronger than you look."

"I surprise you?"

"Yes." He joked as they hobbled back to the straw roof home, his arm pressing heavily on her shoulders. "You don't mind hanging out with a big-nosed, smelly man?"

She flashed her teeth. "No. I like you, even though you make big farts." She wondered if this was the right time to make love with him, but he wanted to sit on the wooden chair at the table.

After getting him arranged on a pillow, Misun made green tea with ginseng and honey. They sat together like old friends and she asked, "Why POW? How you captured?"

Curt frowned and shook his head. "It's not a pleasant story."

She made him hoeddeok, a sweet syrupy pancake. Not one to concede defeat, she probed, pointing at herself. "Friends, I care you and tell no one."

Slowly, he told her about parachuting into North Korea on a top-secret mission to defuse a nuclear bomb and how they were captured and tortured by the North Korean commander. It took all afternoon. He finished at the rescue and closed his eyes, moisture at the corners. "I tried to save Carl's life, but he saved mine."

Her heart could not hold back; standing, she pulled his head to her chest and cried. "My Curt, very brave man. You hero. Hurt all over." She realized tears also trickled down his face, and she moved closer with her arms around his waist. She kissed his cheek softly, wiping his tears with her fingers.

He kissed her forehead and his big arms folded around her. They sat together, vibrating and sharing feelings as they talked in a mixture of English and Korean.

The encounter changed her feelings like the communist invasion solidified South Korea into an ally of America. She could never think of marrying a Korean. Something in her committed to becoming a strong and modern American woman. It would be perfect. They would be perfect together. Everything would be perfect just like in the Weeping Princess fairytale.

When Jimin came home that evening, she sensed something different between them and asked Misun what happened.

She briefly told what he went through.

Jimin kneeled near his sleeping pad where he stared at the ceiling. It wasn't Korean to be affectionate even with family, but she placed both hands on his cheeks, looked into his tormented eyes, then touched each cheek with her fingers, saying, "You are a very brave man."

His face brightened. "Thank you." He caught her eyes and said again, "Thank you."

Misun bowed with steepled hands. "You're welcome."

Their relationship made a right turn. They often sat close to each other, playing Godori, the flower game where you match months with flowers on cards. He never tried to touch her intimately.

Jimin said he must have been raised by honorable parents. "You might be happy with them." In Korea, the wife was expected to move in with the husband's parents where she served the family and kowtowed to his parents, keeping her eyes down. She hoped her daughter would have a better life.

While Momma was at work, and she was sure her grandparents wouldn't come visit, she crawled onto him. They began kissing. She had never kissed a man, and it felt strangely wonderful. She felt him become erect, and she was wet. She was ready; she wanted to make love with him.

He stopped her. His face was flushed. "Misun, I'm falling in love with you, but are you sure?"

"Yes, I want to be your wife."

"I want you to. If there's any way in the world, I'd love to marry you and raise a family with you."

She wiggled against his erection, and he put his hand over it.

"I'm afraid the Navy won't allow me to marry you. I've heard they make it almost impossible. It could take years before I can take you to the States."

"I can wait."

"What if you get pregnant?"

She thought for a few moments. "My family will help me raise it until you can come for me."

He kissed her gently. "Let's give this some time. We need to think it through."

She was disappointed but knew he was being honorable. He loved her.

Misun helped him hobble around outside the small house and one evening, she took him for a short walk to her grandparents' home. Villagers stared from their windows but ducked when Misun shook her head.

Her grandmother welcomed them and heated water for tea on the charcoal stove.

Harabeoji excitedly grabbed the flower cards and sat them on their table, pointing to a chair.

"No, he's tired. This is the first time he's walked any distance."

Curt nodded his head and pointed, indicating he wanted to play.

Halmeoni brought tea and a sweet red bean snack while Harabeoji shuffled the deck. He offered a cup of rice wine but Curt waved it away, making a face to show he didn't drink.

Halmeoni was impressed. "Misun, you are very fortunate. He doesn't drink and he will be kind to you when you are married."

Curt understood what Halmeoni said, and he grinned, saying in Korean, "You're right. I will treat her honorably."

Misun's face felt very hot.

He looked at her seriously and she glanced down shyly.

After one game, Curt gestured he was tired so they all walked him home, supporting him under the shoulders. Everyone was proud and thrilled. Misun tried to sew her heart back together. He would be leaving soon.

During the next week, she asked him about his home and Curt said he grew up in a small Colorado town. "Cedaredge? Where Colorado?

He used a stick to outline a map of the U.S. on the dirt floor and near the center of the country, pointed to the west on the rectangle.

"No ocean?"

"No ocean. It's dry." He told her how irrigation water came down from a big flat-top mountain called Grand Mesa and described apple farming with his father. "It's a lot of hard work and there's always the risk of getting frozen or hailed out."

She was entranced and tried to imagine what it would be like living in a quiet, peaceful place. She asked how children were schooled.

He told her about his high school and how he played sports and sang in the choir. He wrote down his address, including his parents' phone number. "My folks will love you as their own. We'll write. I'll come to get you in three years. We'll marry, and you can return with me to America."

"Okay, but I must finish high school."

"I'm eighteen. After you finish high school, we will marry, then you can go to college if you want and I'll pay for it."

It felt like pepper juice made her face hot.

She snuggled into him that night, and he pulled her close, nuzzling into her hair, saying something she didn't understand but she felt his love. She brushed the back of her hand to his underwear and felt his massive erection. They couldn't make love with Momma sleeping next to them.

He whispered in English, "We'll make love tomorrow."

They kissed quietly and with a deep sigh, she relaxed into his arms.

During the next weeks, they made love. They couldn't get enough of each other. Misun's face glowed.

Her mother frowned at them suspiciously.

They didn't care. They were completely, totally in love.

Curt grew stronger the more she took him for walks to her grandparents' house. He tried to help her cook and wanted to help wash clothes but she refused. She couldn't believe it. Korean men thought such work was a woman's job. They often beat and treated their wives like slaves.

She imagined living in America with plenty to eat and a car to drive to the market. And Curt would love her like Ondal loved his princess.

Chapter 19
The Ring

One night after dark in early August, Misun led him hobbling with his carved cane along a path to an overlook above the market and fishing boats. The air filled with little particles of light. At low tide, the coast of the island had long exposed mudflats, home to Blackfaced spoonbills. Tonight, the twenty-six-foot tide was in, and Curt pulled her close, resting his arm over her shoulders. A perfect night with romantic stars in the velvet sky inspired her to wrap her arms around his waist, enjoying the view of moonlight on the slow waves.

They stopped near the jangseung, a totem pole made of wood placed at the edge of the village to frighten away demons. Although they could hear American bombers streaming north and saw an occasional flash beyond the Han River, the war seemed far, far away. She sang, "Arirang, Arirang, Arariyo, you must pass over Arirang Hill. My love please hang in there and be well."

His baritone joined.

When the song finished, she asked, "Do you know what it means?"

"It's about a man leaving and the woman wanting him to take her with him." She sighed.

"I wish I could take you with me immediately."

She looked up and saw the moon reflected in his eyes as he cautiously leaned to look into her eyes.

High clouds drifted above ocean currents and Misun saw herself flying to America. A sudden fear coursed through her body and she stepped back. "No, you must leave and I'm afraid you'll forget me."

He looked down at her as if taking stock.

"Please don't tease me."

Pulling off his high school class ring, he offered it to her. "I'm not teasing. It's good this isn't gold or the communists would have cut off this finger. Please accept it. It will mean we are going steady, and we're committed to marriage. I will come back for you."

She stared at the huge ring. She wanted it but refused, hoping he would insist.

He didn't. Curt was too polite, too respectful. His face became sad and she saw moisture in the corners of his eyes.

It was tense but tender until after Gwangbokjeo Liberation Day on August 15 when Korea freed itself from the Japanese empire. Although only eight, she remembered Japanese emperor Hirohito's unconditional surrender to the Allied forces on August 15, 1945. To celebrate, she made Curt a special kimchi dinner with a sweet red bean dessert.

"If you can handle being a Navy wife, our future is assured. I'm sure I'll get promoted because they promised if we went on the mission to defuse the bomb, our navy careers would take off."

"I can handle being a Navy wife. Please, I don't want to dream of you for years, and then for some reason, you aren't able to return for me."

A percussive swarm of sparrows woke her on the first of September in 1951 when a jeep came for him. He was with her for three months. She made him a special Korean calligraphy:

고생 끝에 낙이 온다

He asked her to translate it.

"At the end of hardship comes happiness."

He bent down. "Will you take my class ring? It will mean we're promised."

She wanted it but shook her head, "No, you will forget me and it will make my heart ache."

He rolled her calligraphy up tightly and shook his head. Curt looked back at the house, saying, "I want one last look." She started to support him but he motioned her away. He limped into the house. When he came back, they kissed and kissed.

"Kamsahamnida, I owe you my life."

"Go in peace and get home safely."

His eyes were warm. "Please wait if you can."

Weeping, she hastened into the house and sadly looked at his empty sleeping pad, then froze: his class ring sat on their rickety wooden table. She picked it up and stared at the blue and silver ring engraved with Cedaredge High School 1950.

Will he return from over Arirang Hill and take me with him? She was very sad to see him leave. She had fallen for him headlong with the absorption and obsessive hope of first love. She thought it was fate; the gods brought together from opposite sides of the world. She knew Curt intimately. She had cleaned every inch of his body like a baby and his ears turned pink from embarrassment. She knew the shape of his mouth and the way he smiled with warmth and a natural reserve. They had made wonderful, passionate love.

The jeep driver who had picked up Curt kept coming to see her. She told him repeatedly that she was engaged. He was persistent and she said, "Please, stop coming to see me." He came every time he had the chance.

Two months after Curt left, she realized she was pregnant. She hoped he would return for her. She didn't have any good choices.

Book III
Deprogrammed

Chapter 20
Unbelievable

Curt saluted the jeep driver who was staring at Misun.

The corporal demanded, "Let me see your dog tags. We have no record of you in the Army."

"I wasn't in the Army. I'm Navy."

He slapped the steering wheel. "Well, crap. I just made a two-hour trip out here for nothing." He started the jeep.

"Wait a minute, can't you at least give me a lift to a Navy port?"

"I'm based near Seoul. I hear there's a U.S. naval hospital ship in Incheon, but the main naval base is in Busan at the southern tip of Korea."

"Come on man, we're on the same team." Momentarily, he thought about just staying with Misun. He loved her in the deepest regions of his soul. They probably reported him as lost at sea, and if he stayed, he'd never be missed. But if they ever caught him, they would arrest him as a deserter and court-martial him. H could end up in Fort Leavenworth, Kansas, the federal prison.

The corporal debated. He kept staring at Misun, lust in his face.

"Listen, I was a POW." He held up his right hand. "They chopped off my fingers. Please give me a lift."

"Get in. It's weird you're way out here in this little fishing village. I had a hell of a time finding it. My captain thinks you went AWOL (absent without leave) and were living with some sweet thing. That girl is a looker." He grinned, then shrugged, saying seriously, "I have to take you to the Army base. They'll decide what to do with you."

Curt struggled to get in the front seat. He lifted his right leg with his hands.

"They got you pretty bad, huh?"

"You could say that."

"Strange clothes."

"They cut off my uniform since I was badly wounded. Misun and her grandmother made them."

The soldier laughed. "I'd burn them first chance." He glanced at Curt. "You said her name is Misun, right?"

Curt stared at the road, thinking of her. He didn't answer.

A rough ride. He hurt from the bouncing and limped into the Army headquarters. A captain interviewed him. Curt told how he ended up a POW and at the South Korean woman's house.

Captain Finger ordered a physician to examine him. He confirmed Curt's injuries, saying, "Well, there's no doubt you were tortured, but your wild story of being on a top-secret mission to defuse a nuclear bomb and getting nursed back to health in a Korean fishing village is bizarre. You better do some serious thinking, or the Navy will think you're a fruitcake."

They placed him in a secure room and took the clothes Misun made, giving him an army uniform. The next day, the captain said, "Conrad, there's no record of you in the Army and since you claim you're Navy, we're transferring you to the naval hospital ship in Incheon harbor." As they escorted him out, Captain Finger advised, "If I were you, I wouldn't be talking about a top-secret mission to defuse a nuclear bomb. The U.S. never dropped any nukes on North Korea. It makes you sound like you have a screw loose."

At the hospital ship, a psychiatrist examined him, then they kept him in a secure room under guard. He wasn't allowed to talk to the other patients. A guard brought food and watched him constantly as if he were some criminal. After a week, the Navy located his records. "You were on a spy ship and reported missing at sea on April 28."

"That's what I've been trying to tell you."

They transferred him to a troopship where a naval intelligence agent interviewed him. The first thing out of his mouth was, "You should be dead. You were washed overboard in rough seas with a sailor named Carl Brooks."

It wasn't rough the night they catapulted off the carrier. Curt wondered what kind of problems he'd have establishing that he hadn't gone AWOL. There were no records and would be no acknowledgment of their secret mission.

Rather than flying men home, the military took its sweet time by shipping troops to the States. It surprised Curt that they separated him from the other men on the ship. One section was specifically for POWs, and they weren't allowed to mix with the other troops. The former POWs didn't talk much. They didn't know how to make friends and didn't trust anyone. Some stayed in their bunks with a blanket pulled over their heads. POWs called it, "The give up-itis."

Curt was in a good place compared to the other former POWs. He was well-nourished and optimistic about his future in the Navy. He planned to look up his spy ship captain and ask for help to get the promised promotion.

Then it started: the Navy prepared for extensive interrogations of POWs by installing four-by-four booths with a small field desk, two chairs, and a tape recorder. It lasted all day, sometimes eight hours, with different Navy intelligence agents asking the same questions over and over.

"The records show you were lost at sea. Tell us again how you were captured."

"We had just located the bomb and were starting to defuse it when we heard a North Korean patrol. We reburied it and hid in the brush all night."

The interrogator's face was serious. "You keep talking about a nuclear bomb dropped in North Korea. There was no such thing. Where did you get that idea? Did the North Koreans brainwash you to use you for propaganda?"

"I'm not making up anything. It's a fact: five of us parachuted in with the mission to save America from international condemnation. I never told the communists anything. I only said my assigned name, rank, and serial number. That is why I was tortured." He held up his right hand with the missing fingers.

"We don't doubt you were tortured, but this idea of being on some secret mission is a product of your imagination. It's bizarre. How in the world did you come up with that story?"

"I'm telling you the truth. I have nothing to hide. I know there is no record of our mission. They said if we didn't make it back within three weeks, we'd be reported as lost at sea."

"So, temporarily, we'll go with your story. Did your team put up a fight when you were captured?"

"No, I woke up in the morning with a rifle barrel to my head."

"So they got the drop on you. Why didn't you have someone standing watch?"

"We did. They snuck up and surrounded us before we realized the commies were there."

"Who was on watch?"

"Jack Honeycutt and Adam Spoker."

"Were either of them a collaborator?"

"I don't think so."

"Were they tortured along with you?"

"Yes, but not to the degree I was. The communists think the biggest man is the leader, so I got it the worst."

"Did any other men lose fingers?"

"Adam and Carl each lost fingers."

"What about this Honeycutt and the man you call Taylor?"

"It's Taylor Hawkins. He's from Billings, Montana. Taylor broke an ankle and kept asking the commander to kill him. Jack started acting like he was retarded after the commander knocked him out with a bamboo shaft."

"So those two collaborated to avoid losing appendages."

"I didn't say that. They had their fingernails pulled out like the rest of us." Curt asked, "Where are they? Where are Jack, Taylor, and Adam? You should bring us all together, and you'd hear the same facts."

"I know nothing about those men you keep talking about. We're only concerned about you." He lit a cigarette and blew smoke into the room. "Want a cigarette?"

"No, I don't smoke. I'm an athlete."

"Did you or any of the other men on your team sign any statements?"

It felt like he was back in the crazy commander's office being interrogated. He fought the heat rising in his chest. "No, I did not."

"Did any others?"

"The North Korean commander handed me a signed sheet of our cover story with a fake signature on it."

"Whose name was signed?"

He didn't want to rat anyone out. "I don't remember. You shouldn't worry. I bled all over them and got beaten unconscious for it."

"How did you bleed all over the signed statements?"

"As I told the guy yesterday, the commander cut off my fingers, and he scraped the scabs so they bled." He held his hand to the agent's face. "You think I didn't bleed when he did this?" The scars were ragged and ugly since they hadn't been stitched and had been badly infected.

The agent's face was drenched with disbelief. "What was this cover story you mentioned?"

"I've already told your agents. Do I need to tell it all over again?"

"Yes, please."

"Man, you've already got hours of recordings. Why do I need to tell you again?"

"Proceed or I'll have you locked in the brig for the duration of the journey."

Initially, he wanted to cooperate—these were Americans and he had nothing to hide. The agents were polite but extremely skeptical. He told the truth as accurately as possible, yet they asked the same questions over and over, trying to trip him up. They didn't believe anything about the secret mission. The agents got progressively more frustrated and aggressive.

Curt felt betrayed by his country.

He asked the new interrogator, "How did they know to rescue us since there's no record of our mission? Someone has to know."

"You were rescued quite by accident. The South Koreans were after their captured platoon."

"Call the captain of the spy ship I was on. He's the one who asked Carl and me to volunteer."

"We have contacted him. He knows nothing about any secret mission. He said they lost you at sea in a heavy storm along with a man named Carl Brooks."

"It was calm the night we catapulted off the carrier in a bomber. What about the briefing officer on the carrier?"

"We have no idea who you're talking about. There was no briefing, no secret mission based from any carrier in the U.S. Navy during the period you went missing. Guy, the North Koreans brainwashed you."

Curt realized no one would admit they knew – not even the admiral who promised to promote them. It was challenging to write with his missing fingers, so he carefully dictated a very long statement into a tape recorder, detailing everything he could remember. They typed it, and he signed with a scribble.

"This isn't anything like your signature on your records. Are you sure you're Curt Alan Conrad?"

"Geez, you've got my photograph pasted right there. Of course, my signature doesn't look the same. I'm trying to write with three missing fingers."

They firmly believed he was brainwashed.

Curt said, "Ok, let's say I was lost at sea. Logically, I must have managed to swim to North Korea where I was captured. Do you agree?"

"Yes, it is obvious they tortured you, and the South Koreans confirmed they rescued you when they got their men out."

"It doesn't explain why I was in a POW camp so far inland, but at least we agree I was a POW, right?"

"We aren't contending that. But you need to give up your crazy story of trying to locate and defuse a nuclear bomb. We're sure they brainwashed you, and the communists planted the story of a nuclear bomb in your head." He took a puff from his cigarette. "We're guessing they tortured you to get a signed statement of this so-called secret mission, and they planned to broadcast it to show General MacArthur was a psychopath, and the U.S. was barbaric."

After seven days of eight-hour-long recorded interviews, he just said, "My name is Curt Allen Conrad, seaman third class."

They didn't stop. Sometimes three interrogators sat in the small boarded-off room questioning him with a recorder running. He was interrogated along with the other POWs for seventeen days while they crossed the ocean. Curt realized repatriation marked a turning point, not the end. Like the others, he was expected to tell everything about his experiences as a POW. They demanded chronological details and names of anyone who collaborated, strongly implying he and his men went along with the communists since some POWs had refused to return. It was a hot political issue.

"You've become quite uncooperative, Seaman Conrad. We can have you thrown in the brig and court-martialed as a traitor." The agent blew smoke in his face. "Compared to the other POWs, you're quite healthy and well-nourished. That makes you highly suspect."

"As I've told you dozens of times, the soldiers took me to a South Korean home since all their hospitals were destroyed, and a woman nursed me back to health. I was there for three months because I took a bullet in my ass. The Korean doctor said my pelvis was fractured. I had infections all over my body and nearly died. They saved my life."

"Why weren't you taken to a hospital? It doesn't make sense."

"As I just told you, the South Korean hospitals were destroyed in the fighting so they placed their wounded in homes. I'm guessing they didn't make the trip to Incheon to the naval hospital ship because they were exhausted, or maybe they didn't know about it. They figured I was Army or a Marine. Hell if I know, ask Major Kim Chin-mae. He's directly under General Park. He knows my story." Curt went on, "I was dressed in a commando uniform, and they assumed I was Army." He had a terrible headache and rubbed his forehead.

"Conrad, we're getting fed up with you. You keep telling the same story over and over without adding any new information. Tell the whole truth."

"I have. I've told you and the other agents dozens of times, and I've signed a detailed report: We were sent to remove the nuclear trigger from a bomb that MacArthur ordered dropped on the south fork of the Taedong River. He wanted to poison the riparian system to P'yŏngyang, hoping it would end the war. They wanted us to get the trigger out so they could deny it was a live bomb and also prevent the North Koreans from reverse-engineering it. The bomb was defective, or it would have gone off and poisoned half the country. That's why Truman relieved General MacArthur." He took a breath. "They said all knowledge of our mission would be disavowed. I doubt the bomb has ever reported."

The agent laughed. "You're delusional. The U.S. never dropped a nuclear bomb on North Korea. MacArthur was recalled because of his big mouth. He kept threatening to take the war to Chinese soil."

"Bullshit. The nuclear bomb is why we parachuted in. We were told there would be no record of our mission and no records that MacArthur ordered it dropped, but it's the real reason Truman recalled him." He swallowed. "Why would my dog tags say I was Phil Brown, private first class? Why?"

"You must have gotten those dog tags from the North Koreans. They wanted to confuse you."

"Have you located Major Kim Chin-mae? He may be a colonel now."

The agent looked at him like he was nuts. "Do you know how many Kims there are in Korea? It's like Smith, Brown, or Jones in the United States."

Curt couldn't speak. He sat staring at the man.

The agent shook his head. "We're going to have a psychiatrist exam you."

"You have hours of recordings in which I've consistently reported the same facts. I understand that no one believes me, but I'm telling the truth."

They left him alone, then a few days later, they helicoptered a psychiatrist to the troopship out of Hawaii. He interviewed Curt all day, gave him several tests, and provided a report to the agents.

A day out from San Diego, an intelligence agent called him back to an interrogation room. He started from the beginning. Curt told him every detail recorded in his typed statement. The thing was the size of *War and Peace*. Hours later, the agent said, "You are absolutely sure everything you have reported is the whole truth?"

"Yes, ask me something different, and I'll be happy to answer. You're asking the same questions over and over. I didn't break, and I didn't tell them anything. Why do you think I have scars all over my body? Why would I have this huge scar on my eyebrow and be missing three fingers if I said anything?" I said my phony name, rank, and serial number over and over, that's it."

"What name did you give them?"

"Jesus! As I reported a thousand times, Phil Brown, private first-class—that is what they assigned me so the communists wouldn't know my real identity. The government wanted to deny any knowledge of our mission."

The agent shook his head sadly. "Seaman Conrad, the psychiatrist diagnosed you with severe delusional grandiosity. There was never such a mission. The only thing we can confirm is that you were rescued by accident with a platoon of South Korean soldiers and were nursed back to health in a South Korean woman's home. The psychiatrist thinks you made up the secret mission story as an unconscious way to explain your capture and the subsequent torture." He frowned. "However, we are convinced the North Koreans brainwashed you to believe this wacky story about a nuclear bomb to use you as propaganda. You are an unconscious collaborator. You're lucky we don't court-martial you and throw you in Federal prison." He paused and lite a cigarette. He blew smoke into Curt's face, then went on, "Some of us think you should have turned yourself into the U.S. military immediately after you were rescued, and instead, you went AWOL so you could live with some whore. They're saying you're a chickenshit who didn't want to serve."

"No way!" Calling Misun a whore pissed him off. Curt stood and pushed his chair back. "Don't call the woman who cared for me a whore!" He clenched his fists, ready to fight. "That's nuts! If there was any way to turn myself into the Navy, I would have. Hell, I couldn't walk! I want to make the Navy my career." He shook with anger.

The agent called the MPs. "Take this man to the brig. He's out of his mind."

The ship doctor gave him a shot, and he zonked out.

When the troopship docked in San Diego Harbor, there were no bands, cheering crowds, or dancing girls like greeted the men returning from WWII. Since he was in the brig, he was the last off the ship and walked down the gangplank handcuffed between two MPs as if he were a criminal. They took him to the naval hospital in San Diego, where the doctors would deprogram him.

The new psychiatrist shook his head. "You're badly in need of treatment. The North Koreans brainwashed you and planted false memories of a wild, top-secret mission to defuse a nuclear bomb. They hoped to use you for propaganda to allege the U.S. used nukes on civilians. If they were successful, it may have caused our allies to pull out of the war, and the U.S. would have been condemned." He filled his pipe. "You don't even realize you were a collaborator. It's very sad." He puffed on his pipe, filling the room with smoke. "I'd love to understand how they inserted this into your head so deeply that you still believe it – despite our efforts to help you."

Curt said, "The briefing officer told us the potential ramifications if we weren't able to remove the trigger from the bomb. That's why I volunteered." He took a deep breath. "Hell, I'm probably the most mentally tough and sane man you've ever talked to. We located it. We had the nuclear bomb unearthed, and Taylor just got the plate off the nose when we hid from a North Korean patrol."

The psychiatrist shook his head. "You have the most entrenched delusion I've seen in my twenty years as a psychiatrist. I feel for you." He shook his head with amazement.

They locked him in an empty hospital room. The bed was bolted to the floor. He stared out of the barred window. "Shit, I can't believe this. I'm a prisoner of my own country." He wished he was back at Misun's house. He realized that if he hadn't pushed the Army corporal to take him, he would still be there, he'd still be snuggling with her at night, joking and singing with her.

Chapter 21
Deprogramming

The CIA injected him with LSD. They were researching its use as a "truth drug" for brainwashing or inducing prisoners to talk. It made him hallucinate weird images, rainbow colors that melted onto the floor, floating in space, turning into an orange, being eaten by Misun, kissing her from the inside out. They piped extremely loud classical music into his room. He started hating classical music. He once loved it and sang along with recordings of operas. With a severe headache, he banged on the door until someone came.

The sound went off. The attendant asked, "What's the problem?"

"God, that's a relief. Can you please ask them to turn down the volume? It's making my ears ring, and I have a terrible headache."

The attendant walked into his room. "I don't hear anything."

"Yeah, they turned it off when you came to the door. Dang, my ears hurt from the loud music."

The attendant shrugged. "Sorry man, you must be having auditory hallucinations."

As soon as he left, classical music blasted through the speakers.

Head pounding, Curt tried to find some way to break the speakers. The bare room and the bolted-down bed haunted him. He couldn't reach the grilled speakers embedded high on the wall, and there was nothing he could use to bang on them. He stood at the window, hanging onto the bars, wondering how to get out of the hospital. He tried using toilet paper to dampen the sound. It made him look like a screwball with paper hanging from his ears.

He wanted to write Misun, but they took everything: the clothes she made for him, the calligraphy saying, 'At the end of hardship comes happiness,' the slip of paper with the contact information of the old Korean doctor and Misun's address. The only personal thing they let him have was his original dog tags. It felt good to have the chain around his neck. At least he had his identity back. He padded around the room in slippers and a hospital gown as if he was sick.

At different times, intelligence agents came to interview him. They followed the same line of questioning as aboard the troopship. "You say you were a POW. Where were you held?"

"I'm not sure, but it was at least a day's truck ride from the south fork of the Taedong River."

He drew a map of the compound and told of tracing a baseball diamond to play a pretend game. They sat with stern faces, but smiles arose when he told about the camp commander shooting the ropes off the log and how it swung back and knocked down the commander.

"You certainly have a good imagination, don't you?"

"I didn't make this up." He held his right hand to their faces. "This is proof." It was the first time he was glad to have physical evidence he was tortured.

They wanted information about the other men, and he told them everything he knew.

"So you hauled your buddy's body, this Carl Brooks, all the way to the ROK soldier's truck. What kind of truck was it?"

"A duce and a half from World War II with a ripped canvas top. The tailgate was down, and I got him in, then collapsed."

They took notes.

"Talk about the British and Australians who were brought to the camp. What were their names?"

"I don't remember names, but the highest ranking was a British Lieutenant. Seems his last name was London." He wasn't sure if the name might be from the novelist, Jack London, but didn't elaborate. It would just open another can of worms.

He gave them all the same details he had dictated while on the troopship.

A British intelligence agent interviewed him, wanting to know anything he could remember about their men.

"It's all in the report I dictated shipboard. They have nearly a hundred hours of recordings of what I said. I'm sorry, I can't recall anything else. They weren't with us long before the Chinese took them off in trucks. I'm guessing to one of the POW camps up north."

"Well, you're certainly consistent. We'll keep an eye on you if you're ever released."

"Why would the British monitor me after I'm released?"

The agent didn't smile, but he saluted as he left. "You're one brave man."

Confused, Curt sat on the hospital bed staring at the bars over the window, thinking, *If I'm ever released?* A fly stunk in molasses had better odds.

They always watched him; someone checked on him every hour, twenty-four hours a day. A psychologist interviewed him. "Are you depressed and suicidal?"

"Damn right I'm down, but I'm not suicidal. I didn't expect to be treated like a criminal after what I went through. I wish I never volunteered."

"Volunteered for what?"

"The mission to defuse the nuclear bomb."

"Still fixated on that, huh?" Dr. Bryne shook his head and looked directly into Curt's eyes. "Listen, I want to help you get out of here. I don't know whether you were brainwashed or were on a secret mission to defuse a nuclear bomb, but the reality is you will not be released until the chief psychiatrist, Dr. Blackwell, is convinced you don't remember anything about it." He cupped his chin. "Curt, true or not, you absolutely must stop talking about the mission to defuse a nuclear bomb or they'll have you institutionalized for life and fry your brain with ECT."

After Dr. Bryne left, Curt anxiously paced his hospital cell. He heard a small voice mocking, "So where did all that blind patriotism land you?"

A nurse came in with a tray of pills. "This should help you relax."

"What is it?"

"It's a tranquilizer called meprobamate. It will help you stay calm."

Curt took it.

"It can make you sluggish and sleepy."

He shrugged.

"You're wound up like a spring toy. Man, I feel for you."

It helped. But he still couldn't sleep. He lay on the hospital bed staring at the bars, wishing he was back in Korea with Misun under his arm.

When he was too out of it from lack of sleep, Dr. Blackwell prescribed Nembutal for sleep and anxiety. Curt learned it was a highly addictive barbiturate, so he tried not to use it. He'd rather lay there staring at the blank walls, imagining getting out and returning to South Korea for Misun. She was waiting. He felt it in his heart. He begged them for her address and something to write with.

Dr. Bryne said with compassion, "I'm sorry. Everything on you was destroyed. You should forget everything. You can write your parents."

No way he wanted to inform his father that he was held in a mental ward. Dad would go ballistic for not being mentally tough.

One day, they strapped him to a gurney and wheeled him into a room with machines. They gave him a shot and forced him into a straightjacket. A huge male nurse shoved a heavy rubber guard into his mouth. They put an apparatus over his head and a jolt of lightning. Blackness.

It was days before he could get orientated again. He realized he had been subjected to Electroconvulsive Therapy, ECT. *As Dr. Bryne said, they're trying to eradicate my memory.*

Different psychiatrists, each one shaking his head, more medications. When he refused to take them, they strapped him to the hospital bed and injected him. More extremely loud music, and hallucinations. Another round of ECT.

Curt realized they weren't being intentionally cruel. As Dr. Bryne explained, they sincerely believed that he was brainwashed by the North Koreans to use him as propaganda and were trying to help. *Shit!*

His missing fingers hurt as if the cruel commander cut into them. He had chronic pain in his left shoulder which a doctor said was built-up scar tissue. "Feels like you've developed a calcium deposit under the scar tissue." His pelvis and hip hurt but they did nothing for it other than give him Vicodin. He started stretching and doing pushups, jumping jacks, and sit-ups to get back into shape, thinking that once he got out of here, he'd get into the frogmen. The admiral had promised preferential treatment, and he'd be promoted if he survived the mission. He wanted to be ready when they released him. This was a step up from the North Korean torture. At least they weren't cutting anything off his body, and he had plenty of food and water. At night, sometimes he caught himself weeping as he thought of Misun. *I should have just stayed with her.*

Chapter 22
Fading

They eventually gave him writing paper when he promised he wouldn't use the pencil to hurt himself. He wrote Misun letters, despite not knowing her address. He wished he was back there, talking and laughing with her and her grandparents. He was so happy with her. He'd go back as soon as he could but the memory of her was fading. He wrote, "Dear Misun. I think of you all the time. I'm being held in a Navy hospital. They think I was brainwashed by the North Koreans to believe I was on a secret mission to defuse the nuclear bomb. I hope you'll wait for me. Please. I promise to come for you as soon as I'm able." He hid the letter under the mattress, but when he came back after a round of so-called ECT therapy, it was gone.

He got so he wasn't sure about anything since he had left the spy ship. Those memories stayed clear. It was odd – as if they targeted a beam of energy at a specific period of his memory. God, his head hurt. He kept getting an aura in his field of vision. People talking gibberish in his brain. Stress brought on a migraine. He could only lie with his eyes closed. He ripped a corner from the sheets to plug his ears because the friggin' classical music blasted away.

Strapped to the gurney, they wheeled him into a brightly lit room, preparing for surgery. They were going to stick a pike up his nose to do a frontal lobotomy! He struggled against the straps. They injected him with something and then talked about him as if he was an animal. "Have you seen any improvement with his delusions?"

"Some. However, he is very consistent with his story. Almost makes a guy think he went through all that. Those North Koreans are good. I wonder how they permanently inserted that secret mission tale about a nuclear bomb into his brain?"

Dr. Byne rushed into the operating room. "Please stop this! Don't do a frontal lobotomy. Let me try aversive counter-conditioning like we do with alcoholics. I'll have him recall everything that happened in Korea while taking Antabuse and drinking alcohol. I'm sure it will help. There is no way this man deserves to be subjected to a frontal lobotomy."

Dr. Blackwell reluctantly consented.

Anything was better than a frontal lobotomy. Curt immediately agreed to go through aversive counter-conditioning.

Dr. Byne explained how it worked. "In the treatment of alcoholism, the client sits in a bar with bottles of alcohol, a jukebox, a pool table, and the like. He takes Antabuse which is the brand name of disulfiram. When you drink alcohol, your body metabolizes it into a toxic substance that causes hangovers. Antabuse interferes with this metabolic process. It triggers a very unpleasant physical reaction within ten minutes of drinking and generally lasts an hour. You will experience flushing, nausea, copious vomiting, sweating, and thirst. In addition, you'll likely have throbbing in the head and neck, headaches, respiratory difficulty, and chest pains. You may have heart palpitations, dyspnea, and hyperventilate. You may also pass out, be dizzy, and have blurred vision and confusion."

"Sounds like fun," Curt said sarcastically. "Anything else?"

"You could have a heart attack, convulsions, and even die."

He sighed. "At least it won't fry my brain, right?"

Dr. Byne nodded. "No. Aversive counter-conditioning is much better than ECT and certainly healthier than letting them do a frontal lobotomy on you."

During the next month, each afternoon for three hours, he took Antabuse and drank alcohol while recalling everything possible about the mission, the POW camp, and the girl taking care of him. Dr. Byne probed and probed, digging for memories as if they were gold nuggets.

Curt threw up, had terrible headaches, and heart palpitations. In some sessions, he passed out. Between his alcohol allergy and the Antabuse treatments, anytime he thought about his time in Korea, he felt nauseous, his heart raced, and his throat tightened. At times, he couldn't breathe or focus his eyes.

After four weeks, he doubted what he remembered. Maybe he made it up. His memory went from full-color three dimensions to flat black and white like a TV set that wasn't tuned. Static on the radio, snow on a TV. His thoughts were scattered, and he couldn't concentrate. By the end, he had little idea about what happened in Korea. When they questioned him, he said, "I don't know what you're talking about."

They allowed him to go for walks on the hospital grounds and let him eat with other patients.

A social worker talked to him. She was warm and friendly as they chatted. She offered him a cup of coffee, and he accepted. "We need to talk about your plans for civilian life and how you will adjust."

"I'm planning to make the Navy my career. They promised if we volunteered for the secret mission, we'd rise in rank and get preferential assignments." He was optimistic. "Did anyone talk to the admiral? He promised."

A sad look on her face. "Did you say you volunteered for a secret mission?" She jotted a note. "I have no idea about any admiral." She looked into his eyes. "I'm going to be straight up with you, Curt. You don't have a Navy career given your condition. When you're released, you should have medical and dental care, vocational rehabilitation, life insurance, and a pension. They're talking about another GI Bill, and I'd recommend you consider getting a college degree." She promised to get him on permanent disability.

Upset, he stood and knocked over his coffee cup. Brown liquid spread across the desk, soaking her notes. "I'm so sorry." He used his hospital gown to guide the coffee to the trash can. An odd image of a female spilling a drink across the table made him feel nauseated, but it dissipated.

She sighed. "That's the second time this week." She got a cloth and wiped up everything. "Now, where were we?"

"I don't want disability. I want to finish my career in the Navy."

"You don't know they have discharged you?"

He slumped back in the chair. "No, no one told me."

"Oh dear, I thought you knew." She was very kind and gentle as she talked him through it. As she left, she mentioned, "I don't want to, but I'm required to report you mentioned being on a secret mission."

Another round of ECT was followed by three more weeks of Antabuse and alcohol-aversive counter-conditioning because he mentioned the mission. His brain was already scrambled. Now, when he tried to remember what he went through, it was like a shredded book, and if he thought of Korea, he involuntarily puked. The only thing he knew for sure was being on the spy ship, and one little slice of crawling into a bomber with a heavy pack on his back. He didn't dare mention it. Everything from that point to being on the transport ship turned into a gray fog. It was as if he had been in a coma for the last seven months.

One day, Dr. Bryne said, "Hey guy. You're doing well. You just have to convince Dr. Blackwell you're as sane as the next guy." He winked. "Fake it 'til you make it."

One afternoon, Dr. Blackwell smiled. "What do you think Curt, would you like to get out of here?"

He took a deep breath. "Yes sir. I'm ready to go home."

"Well, you haven't talked about anything strange for several weeks. I think the ECT combined with the aversive counterconditioning and the psychotropic medications have completely deprogrammed you. How about I authorize a weekend pass so you can wander around San Diego, go to the beach, and spend the night in a motel?"

"Sure, that'd be great."

"You have to promise to report back Sunday by five PM. If you don't, I'll send the MPs."

"I can do that." He thought for a moment. "What about money and an I.D.? I don't have anything."

"I'll authorize a draw on your disability payments. It's in an account in your name."

"Disability payments?"

"After they discharged you, the social worker applied for disability. With your missing fingers, head injury, and mental problems, you will receive enough to get by. You have substantial back pay coming and there's additional compensation for having been a POW. I talked them into giving you combat pay since they shot you during the rescue." He smiled. "So you'll receive a purple heart, a POW medal, and a Korean service bar. That should make you feel better."

Curt saw spots before his eyes. It took a few minutes to say, "I wanted to make the Navy my career, I wanted to do at least twenty years, that's why I volunteered for the..." Nausea made him stop. "That's why I volunteered for the Navy."

Blackwell peered at him suspiciously. "I hope you are mentally stable enough to never have delusional thoughts again. Remember to tell yourself: 'Stop it. Think realistic thoughts.'" He went on, "This weekend pass will be a test. If you're successful for two days on your own, I will gradually extend your leaves and eventually, you can go home."

"Sure doc. I'll prove I'm stable. I fell overboard and washed up on a North Korean shore. Being tortured did something bad to my mind."

Chapter 23
Leave

It was strange to be out on the streets of San Diego. He was disoriented walking up and down the boardwalk along Pacific Beach. Beautiful shapely blondes strolled past in two-piece suits, but for some odd reason, he was most attracted to a skinny Asian girl with long black hair. Waves of nausea. "Stop it," he told himself, "Think realistic thoughts. Forget everything that happened in Korea." He felt pretty good because he had his billfold and driver's license. He thought about renting a car to go for a drive somewhere in the mountains. Feeling homesick, he called his parents from a pay phone.

"Hey, Mom. I'm back stateside, I'm in San Diego."

He heard a gasp. It sounded like she dropped the phone.

His dad's voice. "Son! Oh, God, I can't believe you're alive. Tell us what happened. They sent a Navy man who informed us you were lost at sea and presumed dead. I can't believe I'm talking to you."

Curt took a deep breath. "Dad, it's a long, strange story, and my memory is messed up. Think I received a head injury." He told him a few bits and pieces and avoided mentioning he was in a mental ward. "I've been in the hospital. I don't remember where and how, but I've lost three fingers on my right hand, and I took a bullet in my butt."

They talked briefly since the call chewed up his coins. Mom sobbed. "You're alive. I knew it! I prayed and prayed. The whole church prayed. Please come home as soon as you can."

"How's Partner?"

She burst into tears and handed the phone off.

Dad came on. "I'm sorry son, Partner got mauled by that mountain lion again. He lost his other eye, and his nose was nearly torn off. I had to put him down."

Shit! He lost his best friend. They were together for twelve years.

He wanted to find other guys he served with and tried to remember where each one was from. He concentrated deeply. Surprisingly, he remembered some names. Jack Honeycutt was from Sacramento,

Taylor Hawkins was from Montana, and Spooker, that's right, Adam Spoker was from San Diego. Friggin' nausea. They said his best friend, Carl Brooks, on the spy ship, had died during the rescue. "You carried him on your back." He wasn't sure where he served with the other guys. Bootcamp? The spy ship? It was all confusing, mixed up, scattered, and fragmented.

He bought a swimsuit and enjoyed the waves. Loved swimming. When he came back to the beach, he realized he was being followed. The agents were in dark suits and wore sunglasses as they leaned against the seawall. It was irritating.

He took a beach shower and changed into shorts and a T-shirt, then wandered up and down the long, wide boardwalk. At one point, he walked straight at the agents. "You guys are so obvious, you're embarrassing me. How about you change clothes if you're going to follow me around the beach?" He gave them the address of his motel. "You're welcome to knock on the door." He saluted. "Thanks for trying to keep me safe. I'm cool."

The agents disappeared, then showed back up with stupid-looking Hawaiian straw hats with their holsters bulging under bright Hawaiian shirts. They still wore dress pants. Absurd-looking dudes.

He bought a newspaper and read that letters from GIs were sent to stateside newspapers asking, "What is the purpose of the Korean War?" It had ignited a discussion in the House of Representatives on whether those GIs should be investigated as possible participants in a communist plot.

Senator Joe McCarthy alleged he had the names of 205 communists in the government, making everyone a suspect. Rumors circulated that through indoctrination and brainwashing, the communists successfully turned many POWs, leading them to commit various acts of treason such as signing false confessions or denouncing America and its leaders. Editorials claimed this generation of men were weaklings compared to those who fought in World War II.

Curt wandered across the sandy beach, feeling strange. The U.S. had changed in the past year and a half. There was talk of communists infiltrating the U.S. government. Soviet spies were arrested for stealing nuclear secrets. The whole country was paranoid. Some POWs were tried for collaboration with the enemy and sent to Fort Leavenworth, the military prison. It was shocking. He knew he didn't dare try to remember anything that happened after the spy ship.

His pelvis hurt and his finger stubs tingled. The headache and fuzziness wouldn't go away. He took a deep breath of salty air. He looked across the bay – a vague image of a fishing village made him dizzy. He shook his head. *At least I'm out of the mental hospital.*

It took another month with longer times out before Dr. Blackwell released him. "You'll have VA benefits, disability payments and they're talking about passing a GI Bill so you could go to college."

Curt shook his head.

Dr. Blackwell took a quick breath. "I'm trying to help you. I stated in your records that you suffered a severe brain injury when you were washed overboard. You can tell people back home that's why you aren't able to recall things."

Before he was released from the hospital, he attended classes for three days to learn how to act and talk to civilians. They caught him up on who won the World Series and other news people were likely to talk about. They gave him a booklet for former POWs called, "Welcome Back!" And one titled, "What Has Happened Since 1950."

The payroll officer calculated his accumulated pay: Overseas pay: $200. POW pay: $375. Housing allowance: $256.50. Back pay: $668.85. Foreign Duty Pay: $40. Disability pay, two months: $152.88. Total: $1693.23

It was a small fortune. Gas was 19 cents a gallon and a pound of hamburger was 40 cents. Most folks made around $3500 a year. His monthly disability of $76.44 was enough to rent a place, feed himself, and pay for gas. "Wait a minute, I had some savings from when I was on the spy ship. I won a lot of military script playing poker. It should be about $500.00."

The clerk said, "I'll check into it. Often when a man is presumed dead, they send it to his family."

He'd be home for Christmas, but wasn't sure what he would face. Everyone expected he'd be in the Navy for at least four years. They'd think he did something bad to get discharged after only a year and a half. Just before release, he signed a loyalty oath swearing he would protect and defend the United States from communism.

Chapter 24
Returning Home

His dad's face wrinkled with concern when he picked him up at the bus station in Delta. He started to shake Curt's hand but instantly recoiled. The thing was ugly and mangled. "What happened to you? How'd you lose your fingers?"

"I'm not sure. I had a head injury."

"What? You were on a spy ship. Did they take the whole boat? Was there a shootout?"

"Dad, let's talk about this later. I'm tired and hungry, and I can't remember much."

Mom cried and sobbed. "God brought you home to me. I'm so happy you're safe." She hugged him and kissed his cheeks. She took his hand and gently kissed the ragged finger stubs. "Oh, dear, what happened to you?" She wept so hard she couldn't catch her breath.

Even Dad's eyes teared, but he kept probing.

"They say I was washed overboard and received a severe head injury, and apparently, I was captured by the North Koreans. They tortured me, but the Navy deprogrammed me so I wouldn't remember it. My memory of seven months is blank."

Periodically, he got flashes of something but told himself, as a sick feeling hit his stomach, "It's a false memory, a delusion. Be realistic." He was as stressed as a cat surrounded by bulldogs

Over the weeks, Dad kept at it. "Why were you discharged? This doesn't make sense. What did you do? Did you collaborate with the enemy?"

It hurt his feelings. Curt stood. "I had a brain injury, and they said I wasn't fit for service." He went for a walk in the orchards. Branches were on the ground from pruning. They lay in crisscrossed, tangled patterns like his memory of everything since he left the spy ship.

He imagined that when he got home, everything would be the same as when he left. It was, but he was different. People weren't interested in what he went through, except they probed for something to gossip about. "Did you collaborate with the communists? Is that why the Navy kicked you out?"

"No, I had a brain injury so they released me."

It was clear how little the townsfolk and farmers knew or even thought about the Korean War. They simply weren't interested.

Dad said gruffly, "We solve our own problems. It's nobody's business."

Some days, grief washed over him. He felt guilty that he survived while Carl died. He called Oklahoma, and his parents asked him to come to visit. "Maybe someday. I'm just getting adjusted to being home."

He went to the dog pound to find a replacement for Partner. A cute little cocker spaniel came up to him, sniffing and licking. He asked the attendant, "What's wrong with his eyes? Is he blind?"

"Yes, I'm afraid so. I'm guessing that's why they brought him in. No one will take him, but he's very smart and sweet." She shook her head. "We're to euthanize him this week if no one adopts him."

Curt's heart went out to the puppy. "I'll call you Pal. We'll take care of each other." His thinking was so mixed up that had he not found the puppy, he might have gone to Hart's Basin and swam until he drowned from exhaustion.

Pal was cute and a little helpless. He'd bump into things and had trouble finding his way around. "You're like me. Feels like I'm blind." Curt spent hours and hours playing with him, teaching him to listen to commands, and showing him the boundaries of the farm. He took him everywhere but kept him on a leash for his safety. He carried him on his lap while driving the farm tractor that chugged away, disking the fields for crops that would bring food.

Grandpa came to see him and talked about World War I. Just as he was leaving, he said, "Curt, you need to find a woman like your grandmother. She was the sweetest, kindest, and most loving woman a man could wish for. Her love brought me back to life." Tears formed in his eyes, although she had been deceased for years.

Curt wondered if he could find a woman to raise a family with. He felt as if he was already married. It didn't make sense.

He went to the Chocolate Shop where the high school kids hung out, smoking cigarettes and drinking Coca-Cola. Although he was still only 18, he didn't fit. They talked about sports, who was seeing who, and the next party. He felt like an old man. Former acquaintances didn't miss him. "Where've you been? I haven't seen you around."

A guy asked, "So have you been having fun playing football at CU? How is Boulder anyway? It's a weird liberal city, isn't it?"

He tried to make fun of himself. "I never was much of an athlete, I just liked playing."

"What? You set two state records. You're an incredible athlete."

No one wanted to know what he went through, what he felt or saw. When they asked about his hand, he said, "Got it caught in some farm machinery. It's okay now."

One girl gawked and almost fainted. She backed away. "Yew, that is really ugly. You should see a surgeon to get those flaps cut off." She acted like she wanted to puke.

Curt grinned. "Actually, a mountain lion was after our chickens. I stuck my hand in his mouth like those lion tamers and, I'll be darned, he ate three of my fingers."

Everyone laughed.

"No, the truth is, that in the Navy we're around lots of big fish, and one day I was dragging my hand in the ocean, you know how you do in a rowboat, and the next thing I knew, three fingers were gone. Good thing I'm fast or it might have gotten my whole hand."

Although he joked about himself, he wanted to say, "You have no idea what's going on in the world." He had little in common with them.

He and Pal wandered up and down rows of bare apple trees, he helped his father prune. He found himself looking for persimmon trees. Where are they? Then he realized they didn't grow in Colorado. Confused, he didn't know where that idea came from. The cocker spaniel was the only one who understood him. He didn't understand himself.

Curt got his driver's license renewed when he turned nineteen on the first of January. He drove up the Grand Mesa to remember fishing on one of the three hundred trout lakes. Back then as he tossed the fly line, he'd go into a Zen-like state. Now he was in a zombie-like state with only Pal for company. On the way home, he went past the pullout where he used to park with Darlene. He wondered how his life might have turned out if he had taken the football scholarship to CU Boulder instead of joining the Navy. He'd be in weight training and taking classes right now. Probably dating some babe, getting laid, partying, all that.

Although Pal slept on the bed with him, he couldn't sleep since he was nervous. He kept wondering why the Navy was so intent on deprogramming him. Near the end of January 1952, he went to the VA hospital in Grand Junction.

The psychiatrist reviewed his records and when he looked up, Dr. Winker asked. "What have you been thinking about?"

"I feel as sharp as a spoon. I'm confused and it's hard to think clearly. I have an enormous gap in my memory, a black hole like I'm mentally blind. I feel like I did something wrong."

"When you look into that black hole, what do you see?"

"Nothing. It's like a thick night fog."

Dr. Winker nodded. "Well, I suppose that's good. You shouldn't worry about it. You were washed overboard, and the records say you received a severe brain injury. You were a POW and tortured. There is no point in remembering anything painful."

Curt asked, "So that's how I lost my fingers, right?"

"I would presume so."

Curt sighed. "That makes sense." He sat thinking for a few moments, then said, "My left shoulder still hurts and so do my pelvis and hip. Think someone could look?"

After the exam by a physician, Dr. Winker said, "Your records indicate the North Koreans shot you in the buttocks during the rescue." The doctor said, "The results of the physical show that all of your organs are healthy and your blood pressure and lungs are normal, but you have scars all over your body from when you were a POW. There's also a hard lump on your shoulder, but the physician doesn't think it's serious – perhaps a benign calcium deposit or very heavy scar tissue. Much of your pain may be psychosomatic."

"You mean it's all in my head?"

"Not all, but what you focus on enlarges. I'd advise you to learn to ignore it. Get back into shape, get involved in activities, make friends, and keep your mind focused on the future, not the past." He was prescribed an antidepressant and sleep medication along with Vicodin for pain. "Only take the Vicodin when you can't stand it. It's very addictive."

"My hand repulses people. Is there anything that could be done to make it look less offensive?"

The psychiatrist sent him to consult a hand surgeon.

The surgeon shook his head. "You lost these very brutally. We'll need to cut the bones so they are smooth and even. We'll trim the excess skin and when healed, it will look much better."

"When can we schedule the surgery?"

One night at dinner, his father said, "The Navy erased your records and deprogrammed you for a good reason. I'd guess you were on a top-secret mission and were captured." Dad's face wrinkled with worry. "During World War II that's how they handled men's records of secret missions, but they usually got promoted, not discharged."

That ugly sick feeling, Curt didn't want to talk about it. "As I told you, I had a brain injury." His Navy records said delusions of grandeur induced by brain damage. He hoped it wouldn't affect his job prospects.

"Your records say you were POW and got your fingers chopped off. You should have been treated like a hero instead of being discharged." He took a drag on his cigarette. "You've lost all memory of everything that happened about the time MacArthur was recalled by Truman." Dad thought he was a hero. "Hells bells, the general wanted to drop nukes all across North Korea to prevent the Chinese and Soviets from coming into the war and it would have worked. Truman's a son-of-a-bitch! I wonder if you were on a mission with something to do with that? It might explain why you've got intelligence agents following you."

"Dad, don't plant ideas in my head. The Navy deprogrammed me, and I don't want to remember. The last thing I recall, I was crawling into the belly of a plane with a heavy pack, and the next thing, I was in the San Diego Naval Hospital. I've lost seven months of my life."

Polls showed that the majority of the public disapproved of Truman's decision to relieve MacArthur. By February 1952, nine months later, Truman's approval rating was 22 percent. He wondered if Dad was right—he was on a top-secret mission. And, he was supposed to go back and finish something he swore to do. Every time he heard about MacArthur on the news, he got a sick feeling as if he had an unfinished task. "Stop it. Be rational," he told himself.

They did surgery on his hand and when it healed, Curt was pleased that people no longer made faces and turned away. But they always asked, "What happened? How did you lose your fingers?" Then they'd look at his face. "That's a nasty scar. What did you do to your eyebrow?"

"It was a mining accident. I discovered this lode of gold and set dynamite to blow the rocks. Hell, I'm lucky to be alive." He chuckled at their amazed expressions. The next time he saw them, he made up a new story to mess with them. "Lost them to a wild boar. He was a big sucker." He liked watching the stupid expressions on their faces.

He bought store glasses with a heavy black frame and tried to keep his right hand hidden. It was just easier than trying to explain something he couldn't remember. He kept his curly hair longer than most guys because he didn't want the bald bullet graze across the top of his head to show. He wore a ball cap and long sleeves to hide the burn scars on his arms. He let his beard grow. It was simpler.

Curt enjoyed the peace and solitude of working on the apple farm. Pal was always with him, riding on his lap as he disked or marked out the fields. He could look back and see what he accomplished. His migraines faded. He felt pretty good, but people in Cedaredge and his old high school friends kept asking, "Why did they kick you out of the Navy? Weren't you supposed to serve four years? What did you do? Did you punch an officer?"

Curt told someone, "I had a head injury so I have trouble remembering things. I'm fine now, just as dumb as ever."

"You were the salutatorian."

He chuckled slightly. "I used to have a photographic memory so school was easy, but I ran out of film." He couldn't remember the huge gap during the Korean War, and worried he might have trouble if he went to college.

In May, Darlene called. She had married Bud Hamilton and was three months pregnant. She asked if they could meet. He picked her up at the Chocolate Shop, and his internal tach redlined the moment he saw her. She still had curves like the double yellow lines on the highway going up Monarch Pass and her dress clung to her like cellophane on a roast.

Pal instantly didn't like her. He moved to the back seat and stayed on Curt's side. At Hart's Basin, they sat in his Lincoln convertible near the rope swing.

"Curt, I heard you have a cancerous brain tumor. I'm so sorry. What is your prognosis? Will you recover?"

"Sounds like the gossip train around here still runs full speed. I don't have a brain tumor. They said I received a head injury when I washed off the ship. I'm fine now."

Her hand went onto his thigh, rubbing back and forth. Then her fingers tickled his penis. "I'm so sorry you didn't go to CU, we would be married by now."

He felt himself getting erect and pushed her hand away. "You aren't happy with Bud?"

She started weeping. After long minutes, she said, "I didn't realize he was such a heavy drinker, and he smokes one cigarette after the other. When he comes home drunk, he forces me to have sex." Her cheeks went red. "I hate him. I don't want to be married to him anymore."

Curt didn't know what to say. Divorce was unheard of, and she was a rodeo cow who had bucked him off. After some time, he spoke, "Darlene, you're pregnant. You need to work it out for the child."

She unzipped his pants. "How about a BJ?"

Pal jumped over the seat and tried to get onto his lap.

He pushed her hand away and pulled up his zipper. "No, Darlene, I stopped loving you the day you showed up here with Bud in his new pickup. I set you free then and there's no going back."

She cried all the way home, but Curt didn't feel bad. It was her choice, and she just acted like a whore. Made him happy he had broken it off with her. Pal agreed. He didn't like her either.

One morning at breakfast, he announced to his parents, "I can't take it here anymore. People either judge me as if I'm some major screw-up or look at me with pity. The latest rumor of why I was discharged early is that they did a frontal lobotomy, and there's another one going around is I lost my fingers in a fistfight with a naval officer who bit them off. I'm done with this town."

Dad said, "I understand. Just today Bill Cowder asked me if you blew off your fingers to get out of the Navy."

Mom nodded. "Yes, even the women tell stories. Mable Harding said she heard you weren't a POW, instead, you went AWOL and lost your fingers in a bar fight."

That did it. He had to get out of there.

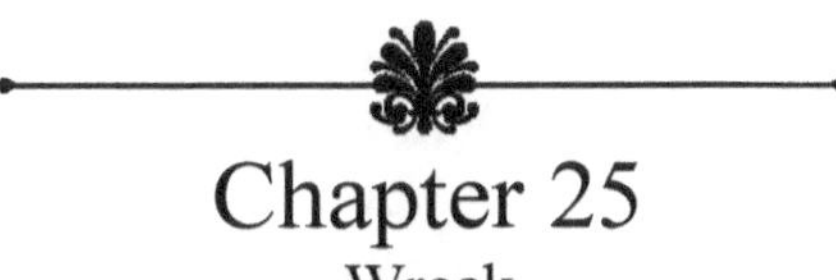

Chapter 25
Wreck

Taking off in his old Lincoln with Pal, he rambled around the country, living on military disability and taking odd jobs. He was looking for a home where he wouldn't be judged, where he wouldn't have to lie. Somewhere peaceful. Maybe he'd buy a farm with a VA loan. Nothing felt like home so he went back to Cedaredge.

He irrigated, sprayed, and worked the apple orchard that summer and only went to town when necessary. Congress passed the GI Bill for Korean Vets in July. He told his parents, "I might as well go to college."

He was only eligible for 25 months of higher education – an associate's degree. Talking it over with his parents, they'd help with his tuition and fees at Mesa Junior College in Grand Junction since the Navy sent his savings to them. Tuition was much cheaper there and $500 would cover it for two years. Dad said, "You can transfer to CU to finish your bachelor's and the GI Bill should pay your expenses at the university."

In the fall of 1952, he enrolled at the junior college and found a room where they allowed his cocker spaniel. Signed another loyalty oath stating he wouldn't associate with communists. The town held around 18,000 people, the most in western Colorado. Cedaredge had 600 inhabitants. The Junction was a big city. Curt walked into the glittering dry heat and felt at home.

An intelligence agent interviewed him the day he moved to town. He asked, "What are your plans?"

"I'll get an associate's, and then transfer to CU Boulder. Why?"

"Don't get involved with any socialists or communists."

Curt laughed. "Here in Grand Junction? You've got to be kidding."

"Some of you POWs have done stupid things. It's my job to check on you."

"Fine. Follow me all you want. Just don't interfere with my life."
That night he dreamed of a reed-thin Asian girl. He woke feeling like

a knife had ripped his guts open. He couldn't call his wandering thoughts together.

On Tuesday, November 4, 1952, Republican Dwight D. Eisenhower won a landslide victory over Democrat Adlai Stevenson, ending a string of Democratic Party wins stretching back to 1932. Curt was happy. He hated Truman since he recalled MacArthur. Had he let the general run the war, America would have driven the communists out of Korea, and he would never have been sent on that mis… *Stop it. You don't dare remember.*

Saturdays, he usually took the Lincoln for a drive over Grand Mesa to Cedaredge to visit the folks. As he braked into a tight turn, the pedal hit the floor. "Shit!" He shifted down but it wasn't enough. A set of aspen trees brought him to a stop. His left front wheel hung off the cliff. Holding his cocker spaniel in his arms, he still shook like the aspen leafs when a Delta County Sheriff's Deputy showed up.

"You been drinking?"

"No, I don't drink. It makes me puke."

He made him do a roadside test anyway. "You have outstanding balance – proves you're sober."

"Thanks."

The accident crushed the Lincoln's front and all along the right side. If the trees wasn't there, he would have died fifty feet below on boulders.

At a shop in Cedaredge, a mechanic looked it over. Joe said, "Your brake fluid is dry as a bone."

"Huh? I check everything at least once a week. Is there a break in the line?"

The mechanic crawled under. He called out, "Man, it has a clean cut through the line. It's not a hole or nick from a rock, it looks like someone used a hacksaw. Every time you stepped on the brake, it pumped out the fluid."

Joe's face was white when he crawled from under the Lincoln. "You have any enemies? Piss off somebody?"

"Not that I know of."

"It's a good thing you were in a Lincoln. If you were in anything less solidly built, you'd be dead."

Curt wondered if Navy Intelligence did it, but couldn't fantom why they'd want to get rid of him. To save money on the surveillance or his disability? Periodically, an agent interviewed him, checking to see if he still had delusions about some mission, or was involved with the communist party. If they simply left him alone, he'd have stopped wondering about it. They kept asking about his political activities. "Have you contacted any Russians, Koreans, or Chinese? Do any of your associates belong to the communist party?"

The only other suspect was Bud. He knew Darlene kept calling, asking Curt to rescue her.

Mom said, "Pray for your enemies."

But Curt stopped believing. He didn't believe in God or country anymore.

Curt located a 1948 Cadillac Series 62 Convertible Coupe. Cool car with lots of power and was safe in a crash. He drove the passes to Denver one weekend to take a stunt driving course, figuring that if something like that happened again, he'd be ready. Loved it. He had the big V-8 motor souped up with tuned exhausts. He practiced driving the Colorado mountain roads until he could do a police-style U-turn and burn rubber away.

In July of 1953, the U.S., China, and North Korea signed the Korean Armistice Agreement, but Synmon Rhee refused to sign it for South Korea. It was a cease-fire, not the end of the war. Skirmishes and assassination attempts continued.

Curt felt let down. He told his Dad, "We would have never fought that war if the Allies hadn't traded the North to the Soviets."

Dad said, "The wealthy make money on war while us poor men fight 'em."

The optimistic bubble in his brain was a chunk of green jade and it wasn't gem quality. When he saw happy couples, he felt jealous. He told Pal, "I guess the best way to get my anxiety to leave is to fall in love with it."

Chapter 26
CU Boulder

He entered as a junior at the University of Colorado in the fall of 1954, declaring a business major with a minor in psychology. Students from all over the world walked the campus. Everyone was required to sign the loyalty oath and avoid any association with communists. He was tempted to watch the CU football team practice but knew it would just make him upset. Had he accepted the scholarship back in 1950, he would have played four years, and pro scouts might have checked him out. He knew if he went to the football games he'd be seething because he'd want to be on the field. "Guess, I'm pretty much within the same time frame. I should have graduated college in the spring of 1954. I had a year and a half in the Navy and traveled the country for half a year. It just makes me more mature."

One dorm held more students than his high school. Professors didn't know the students or care about them. He wrote his student number on everything and learned his test grades when posted outside the professor's door by some teacher's assistant. Had to make an appointment to talk to one, and they kept it short. Publish or perish.

It was a challenge to find a place that accepted his dog, and he didn't want to be without his little Pal. The GI Bill gave him a monthly stipend of $110.00, but he needed to pay tuition and fees upfront. Dad coughed it up since he worked on the farm all summer. Curt was overwhelmed. Boulder was a much bigger city and a part of the Denver Metro area. Whenever he had a chance, he drove up into the mountains and camped to get away from all the people. Always carried a sleeping bag and tent in the trunk of his car. Friends called him 'Camper Curt.' Pal crawled inside the bag to snuggle with him.

CU was a member of the Big Eight Conference with Oklahoma State University. Curt would have played against Carl Brooks. He shook his head. *And now he's dead.*

Curt couldn't go home at the holidays because the CU courses were too challenging. The University had a policy of grading on a strict bell curve to flunk out weak students. This allowed them to keep the state and federal money without educating the dropouts. He didn't have time to date, and didn't want to. Not only couldn't he get it up, it was as if he had promised a girl, but had no idea who she was.

Boulder's weather was much more severe than western Colorado, and the periodic blizzards caught him by surprise. And the wind. Hundred-mile-an-hour winds. He leaned into it to make it to class. The expectations were much higher, and the competition more intense. He was glad to have his general education classes out of the way since CU's were in big lecture halls taught by graduate students.

He got into lifting weights to get back into shape. He learned there was a Krav Maga club on campus, and since it was the fiercest martial art, he joined. They say Krav Maga combines the best of all martial arts. Stressing every part of your body is a weapon to defend yourself if someone threatens your life. They often practiced under extreme stress with multiple men attacking. The founder, Imi Litchenfeld said, "We train in Krav Maga so we may walk in peace."

He took punches and came back stronger. He got images of Asians punching and kicking him, and Curt wailed on the other club members. Everybody in the club took him down. The second time, they threatened, "We're going to kick you out if you don't learn to control yourself."

"Sorry, man, I don't know why. It's like I'm fighting for my life." After a couple of hours with the men, his lonely anxiety dissipated and he could sleep, but he dreamed of fighting Asians. Often the dream evolved into laying on a mat with a gentle girl taking care of him. He woke sweating, with a yearning in his heart, feeling he made a promise he must keep. "Knock it off," he told himself. "Don't let those thoughts take over."

The Army court-martialed fourteen former POWs, charging thirteen of them with collaboration. Suspicion fell on all former POWs, particularly after twenty-one Americans declined repatriation and chose to stay with the Chinese.

Another intelligence agent showed up. "I want to talk to you."

"Fine, talk away."

"I see you're involved with Krav Maga. Why did you join?"

"To defend myself if I'm attacked. Why else?"

The agent acted suspicious. "You also joined a Korean book study. Are any of the participants former members of the communist party?"

"Not that I know of. You're the intelligence agent. Why don't you check them out and let me know?"

"Just trying to keep you safe." The agent said, "Our information is that you had some serious mental problems after the communists brain-washed you."

"From what I've been told, I suffered a brain injury. Get off it." He paused. "And please try to be less obvious when you're tailing me. It's embarrassing to have some guy in a dark suit and sunglasses skulking around. You should at least try to look like other college students."

"Sorry sir, this is how we're required to dress."

"B.S., the agents in San Diego changed to Hawaiian shirts and straw hats. They were just too obvious on the boardwalk."

"I'll talk to my chief."

Chapter 27
A Horrid Memory

Curt pointed at his left shoulder. "This is the worst pain. It aches and at times, it's like something stabs me. When this shoulder gets hit at Krav Maga, it's like a bolt of lightning." He wiggled on the medical table, trying to get comfortable. His pelvis hurt.

The clinic doctor asked him to remove his shirt. She let out a gasp. "My goodness, your whole back and chest are scarred. Where you tortured?"

A wave of nausea hit him. "I was a North Korean POW, but the Navy deprogrammed me so I wouldn't remember."

She lifted his right hand. "How did you lose your fingers?"

"I don't know. I tell people it was a farm accident, but I'm sure lost them in the POW camp. Honestly, I don't remember, and when I get flashes, I feel nauseated."

A tone of disgust. "You were tortured."

She let go of his hand and surveyed his upper body. "Some of these are stab scars, others are like whips." She pointed at the back of Curt's hands. "These look like cigarette burns."

Curt stared at them. "I have them all over my arms. I thought they were from the measles or something."

"Those aren't disease scars. They're cigarette burns."

He pointed at a white scar on his forearm. "Got this one from high school football. I remember when he cleated me."

"What about this terrible scar on your eyebrow?" She pointed. "Looks like the muscle is frozen."

A sharp pain hit above his eye, and his hand snapped to cover it. "Oh, it suddenly hurts." He saw ragged concrete. Blinding pain ground across his eyebrow. Sweat gathered on his forehead. It took moments before he took a breath and shook his head. "Seriously doc, I have no memory of how I got so beat up. I feel like I was in a bad car accident. My body hurts all over, especially my pelvis and my shoulder."

"It appears you were severely tortured by the North Koreans."

She palpitated his back and shoulders. "It feels like you have something very hard under the skin on your left shoulder. Let's get an X-ray."

When Curt returned, she placed the developed X-ray on a viewing screen. "Look at that," she pointed, "It appears you have a hunk of metal lodged near your scapula. It's probably the source of your shoulder pain." She studied Curt. "It's shallow. I could give you a local and remove it."

"Huh! The VA docs said it's a calcium deposit. Go for it doc."

An injection, the smell of antiseptic and Old Spice aftershave, Curt held steady with only a wince.

Metal clinked into a stainless steel dish. "There," she said, "It wasn't deep. I'm surprised the VA never X-rayed your shoulder."

Curt shook his head. "They never do anything unless I demand it. They just keep prescribing more drugs as if the pain is in my head." He opened his palm.

She dropped the bullet into it. Blood shrouded the steel but the shape was clear: an AK-47. It had been a part of him for four years with a chronic, dull ache in his shoulder that periodically hit him with sharp stabs. Something sick roiled inside his guts.

"Do you remember getting shot?"

Slowly shaking his head, he said, "They said we were rescued from the camp by the South Korean marines. " Holding the projectile between two fingers, his stomach felt jittery as if he was preparing for a dangerous mission. He searched his memory of being in the Navy. A sick feeling. "They discharged me after only a year and a half for, quote: 'mental problems.' I wanted to make it a career. I've got disability but there is nothing in my records—no combat missions."

"Your shoulder should feel better since I took out the projectile. It may be sore for several days but you shouldn't get those stabbing pains."

Holding it between thumb and index finger, Curt stared at the blood-tinged bullet: flashes, images, running through the forest.

"Do you recall anything?"

He stared at the slug for a long time, then as if in a trance, spoke, "Wait a minute, shit! I just remembered parachuting into North Korea. It was early April in 1951." He looked up at the doctor. "How much time do you have?"

"You're the last patient. Please tell me what you remember."

"It's coming back. Crap. I was in a POW camp. That's where I got my fingers chopped off. The commander was a sadist. He thought I was the leader because I was the tallest man." He rubbed his left eyebrow. "They kept putting us in these horizontal cages and when we only gave our name rank and serial number, they'd stab us with sharpened bamboo stakes." He took a breath. "Phil Brown. That's the name they put on my dog tags in case we got captured. We were supposed to defuse a nuclear bomb that MacArthur ordered dropped. That's the real reason he was recalled by Truman."

The doctor took a breath. "Go on."

He sat thinking as memories coalesced and images popped into his mind. He fought through nausea. "We located the bomb and Taylor had the nose plate off when we heard a North Korean patrol coming up the river. We got it covered up and hid in the brush." He shook his head as he breathed through waves of nausea.

"Are you okay with telling me more?"

He was quiet for some time, taking breaths until he got the nausea under control. "The long and short of it, we were tortured. I got it the worst because I was the biggest man, and they thought I was the leader." He pointed at his eyebrow. "This is from a divot in the concrete courtyard outside the cells. The guards dragged me straight through it with my hands tied behind my back. I'd be thinking, 'Here it comes, here it comes,' and boom, my eyebrow slammed into it, then they'd hold my legs up to scrape it on the other side." He said. "I can't go on." His head in his hands, he wept, shoulders shaking.

She touched his shoulder. "I'm sorry, I feel for you."

Turmoil. His guts churned as he wiped his nose. "This doesn't make sense. I served on a spy ship. It was boring. I had volunteered to be a frogman, but they assigned me to this dull duty monitoring electronic transmissions." His forehead broke into a heavy sweat. "It's not logical. Maybe I heard this story somewhere and made it up as my own."

She pointed. "You didn't make up this bullet."

His tears were also real. "I don't want to remember." He clutched his stomach. "I'm going to puke."

The doctor grabbed a wastebasket.

He threw up.

It was decayed material, undigested.

Book IV
An Unexpected Reunion

Chapter 28
The Chronic Mental Health Clinic

Summer 1982

Dr. Rameriz was greeted by the smell of coffee and unwashed clothing when he walked into the Boulder mental health office. The noon therapy group members dwandled about while others shuffled down the ramp outside. The wood floors were scuffed and sloppily mopped. It was his first job after finishing a doctorate in psychology at C.U Boulder. Didn't pay well, but after two years of supervision, he could be licensed as a clinical psychologist and open a practice. Had to start somewhere – the chronically mentally ill treatment program was the bottom.

The reception desk was empty so he sat his briefcase beside a stained fabric chair in the waiting room. He didn't lean back or it might soil his white shirt. He watched people with mental illnesses shuffle out, some with dull, drugged expressions. A few looked happy, too happy. He straightened his tie, then stood to open a window. Needed some fresh air in here. He inhaled the scent of blooming lilacs.

"Are you Dr. Alan Ramirez?"

He turned around. "Yes."

"Hi, I'm Shonna, the office manager." 60-ish, oversized colorful dress, gray-black curly hair, and big warm brown eyes. "I'll get you set up in your office, but Mr. Conrad wants to see you first. He's waiting."

Curt Conrad, the director, had hired him over the phone. Alan thought, *Guess I'm not the only desperate person working in this old, probably haunted, house.* He followed Shonna's chunky form down the hall. A flutter of nerves in his stomach said this meeting might be the first and last. Maybe the director changed his mind, and he could get out of this smelly place. It had a faint hint of alcohol puke. He knew it wouldn't happen, they were desperate for psychologists, especially those with testing skills. He needed the job.

The meeting with the director turned out to be the start of something he could never have imagined.

157

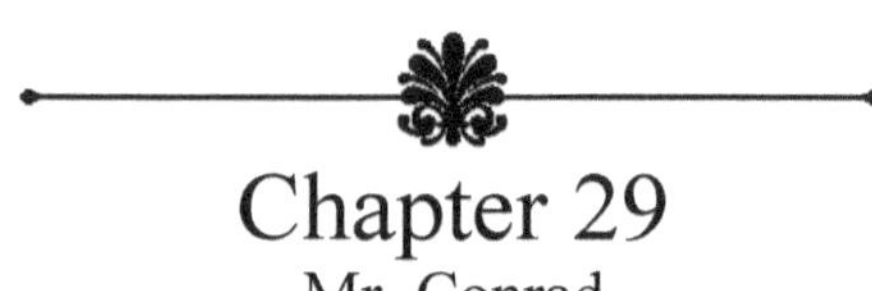

Chapter 29
Mr. Conrad

Mr. Conrad stood from behind the battered and scarred pine desk and extended his right hand, a warm smile on his face. "Nice to meet you, Dr. Ramirez. Welcome aboard."

They shook. His missing three fingers felt creepy. "Call me Alan. Nice to meet you, sir."

"Please have a seat." He pointed at a shabby chair.

Alan noticed he had black curly hair like his own. He was six feet tall, but Mr. Conrad was much bigger, over 6'4", and had the build of a pro football player. Didn't fit here. He should be the CEO of a major corporation but was the director of this poorly funded program for the chronically mentally ill. Conrad wore a 1920s working man's cap and heavy black-framed glasses, making it hard to see his eyes through the window's reflection.

"I like your beard." Alan smiled. "Wish I could grow one like yours."

"Are you partially Asian or Native American?"

"Yes." He grinned.

Mr. Conrad looked confused.

"My mother is Korean." He rubbed his bare face. "I can't grow a beard or even a mustache. I'm jealous."

They chatted for an hour, Mr. Conrad asking about his education, where he was from, his family, and all that. "I grew up in Cortez. My mom still lives there. We were poor, and I went to college on scholarships, equal opportunity grants, and loans. I owe the bank a fortune. My adoptive dad died when I was twelve. He rolled a Caterpillar off into a canyon."

He had never met his real father. "She got pregnant by some American guy, and he abandoned her, then she met my ass-hole adoptive father." He shouldn't have mentioned that, it made his emotional integration and skills as a therapist suspect.

It piqued the director's interest. He wanted to know more. "Was your adoptive father abusive?"

"By his standards no. I've been through psychotherapy, group therapy, Gestalt therapy, and hypnotherapy. I think I've worked through it." He shrugged. "He wasn't mean to Mother, he worshipped the ground she walked on, she's beautiful and probably about your age."

Conrad's face brightened momentarily, then he looked ill. He stared at Alan a moment and then glanced at a trash can.

Alan leaned back. That was strange.

His face red, Mr. Conrad apologized. "I'm sorry. Certain memories make me nauseous. I wasn't expecting that."

He wanted to demonstrate his therapy skills. "Hum, would you like to talk about it?"

Conrad shook his head. "No."

That was it. End of discussion.

Dr. Ramiz settled in and took over intakes and assessments. Fascinating subjects. One man came in with long golden necklaces and several crosses around his neck, claiming he was sent by God to convert the masses. "Doc, you gotta help me. I know I have bipolar disorder and when I'm up, you can't believe what I get done. I can preach and teach and convert people like no one else, but the downs, the downs get to me. I'm up for three or four days like a ball of fire doing the Lord's work, then it hits me and I can't get out of bed. Please doc, I need help."

Alan explained that the best treatment was medication along with cognitive therapy where the person learned to talk to themselves logically and realistically.

Mr. Evangelical said, "I'll do anything, but you have to assure me that the medication won't take away my highs. Man, I feel wonderful, and I get so much done for the Lord. You wouldn't believe it. But the downs are awful. I want something that just gets rid of them."

Dr. Ramirez explained that the medication would level out his moods, and he would be more stable, but it would likely also reduce the days of high energy.

He stood. "Thanks for your help. I'm gonna pass." He walked out.

Shaken, he talked to Mr. Conrad about the prospective patient.

He said, "It's not against the law to have a mental illness. As long as he doesn't hurt anyone or himself, he can cycle up and down all he wants." He patted him on the back. "Dr. Ramirez, I can tell you are a compassionate man. I'm happy you came to work here."

The Director was nice but generally alone in his office. Every morning, Alan stopped in to have a cup of coffee and chat. Occasionally, they went to lunch together. The other six staff members, all females, except for the therapist who served the county jail, were intimidated by the director.

The psychiatric nurse said, "He's very private and his face often has a scowl as if he's angry."

Alan said, "Cindy, I think he has a lot of body pain. He said he was in a bad car accident when he was younger and from the looks of him, he probably played college football."

One morning, he asked Mr. Conrad, "So how did you lose your fingers?"

He looked down at them with sadness. "It was a farm accident." He didn't go into detail.

Alan said, "I grew up stacking hay. I was always scared of the bailers." They had growing up on a farm in common and sometimes talked about farm animals and crops. Alan told about the time he and a buddy jumped on the backs of steers and he got bucked off into a plow. Couldn't walk to the house. "My adoptive dad said I didn't have a lick of common sense."

Little by little, he got to know Mr. Conrad, but it was one-sided. He told him about his nasty divorce battle and his struggles with dating. He decided it wasn't worth it to try to find a woman. Conrad was a good listener and a politician when it came to answering personal questions, evading them with ease.

"Were you ever married? Do you have kids?"

Mr. Conrad shook his head. A soft sadness in his eyes. "No, it never worked out." End of conversation.

Fridays after work, Mr. Conrad was more energized than usual and strode out to his new black and gold Corvette. Alan jogged to keep up. "You seem excited, where are you going?"

He stopped and looked at Alan. "My Krav Maga club. It's how I deal with stress." A quizzical look. "Want to come? You can ride with me."

He'd been wanting to ride in the new Corvette since he took the job. "Sure." He hopped into the passenger side. "What is Krav Maga?"

A slight smile. "It's the world's toughest martial art. Hope you like it. I'll tell the guys to go easy on you."

"I ran track in high school. Won the low hurdles at State my senior year, but I didn't do contact sports."

A slight smile came on Conrad's face as the engine roared to life.

The other club members were kind to him. He wasn't too bruised at the end of the session, but Conrad and the others were. He was a triple black belt master and could hand it out as well as take it.

Alan said, "I need a drink, my whole body hurts."

"I don't drink alcohol, but we can stop somewhere if you want."

"It's okay. I'll go home and take a hot bath."

When he dropped him back at the mental health center, he said, "Thanks, Curt. I'd like to join your club if it's possible."

"You're welcome, Alan. Let's plan on next Friday."

Chapter 30
Korean Book Study

Alan didn't particularly enjoy working with the chronically mentally ill. His internship was with children and families, and he felt underqualified for this role.

Curt constantly praised him along with other staff. "You're making slow progress, even though it may not feel like it. We haven't had a patient need hospitalization in three months."

The staff psychiatrist was an admitted bipolar but brilliant. He loved working with the chronics because he could constantly tweak their medications. "This should help with the dry mouth and your shuffling gate," he told a patient. "Don't drink or you'll wind up at the State Hospital again." He winked and smiled when the patient slowly nodded.

The psychiatric nurse was equally into it. Cindy enjoyed making the patients eat a cracker after popping their medication into their mouths. "Good for you, now don't tongue it. I'm going to watch until you've chewed the whole cracker." Some of the patients still managed to. They'd sell the pill on the street to buy alcohol or street drugs. She often stopped into Dr. Ramirez's office to talk. "Seems like you and Mr. Conrad are becoming friends."

Cindy's chest wobbled up and down when she walked. She needed a bra, and he wondered what it would be like to fondle them, then mentally slapped his face. "Why do you say that?"

"I see you leaving with him on Fridays." She caught his eyes. "The rest of us are a bit jealous."

"It's nothing. He invited me to join his martial arts club. We don't talk about anything personal, but he seems like a nice guy."

"Does he date?" She was interested.

"I don't think so. Says he never married. He seems gun-shy around females."

"So are you."

"Huh. Yeah, I went through a bad divorce. I'll never do that again."

He gave a slight laugh. "The main cause of divorce is marriage."

A subtle leer rode her face. "Do you have a lover?"

It surprised him. She was cute with short blonde hair and blue eyes, but he hadn't thought about taking her out since she had ten years on him. Plus, it would be too complicated to be on the staff together if it didn't work. "Nope, and I don't want one." He was learning from Curt. Keep it brief and impersonal.

She left with a disappointed look.

He told Curt about it the next morning.

"Smart move. It would cause problems. She's been divorced twice and is man-hungry." He explained that when staff got physically or romantically involved, it could cause jealousy, rumors, and so on. It would be particularly difficult if one party didn't want to continue. "Alan, I can tell you are maturing." He thought for a moment. "I go to a Korean Book study every couple of weeks. There are some cute women your age. You're welcome to go with me if you want."

"You know Korean?"

"Yes, I served on a spy ship during the Korean War, monitoring the communist radio traffic, so I understand and read it. I'm not fluent, but I get by."

"I didn't know you were in the Navy."

He looked out the window. "It's in the past."

Alan understood Korean because his mother used it with him, but he had refused to speak it. He was the only part Asian in the Cortez schools and was brutally teased as a half-breed. He hated that part of himself. He finally made a friend when a black student enrolled in ninth grade. They became best buddies. Darnel was a stud athlete and stuck up for him when others teased and harassed him. He was killed in Vietnam. Alan hadn't had a close friend since. He wanted to be friends with Curt, and the Korean book study would give them another thing in common.

They started going to the book study, riding in with the rumbling, tight-cornering Corvette. The young ladies often came out to admire it. He took them one by one for a ride but wasn't interested. "They're too young for me. Most are your age."

"How old are you, anyway?"

"I'm forty-nine. How old are you?"

"Thirty and already divorced." He was embarrassed and couldn't bring himself to ask any of the cute Korean women out, although his mother would have been ecstatic. One evening, the youngest member boldly looked into his face. "I love the green and gold specks in your brown eyes. You're handsome."

His face felt hot as hell. "Thank you."

She glanced at Curt. "You two have the same eyes, are you related?"

Curt laughed.

Alan grinned as he glanced at Curt. "Maybe we're brothers from different mothers." He tried to inspect his brown eyes to see if he had green and gold specks. Hard to tell with the glasses.

Curt had taken a stunt driving course and could drive like a highly trained State Trooper. Scared the piss out of Alan a couple of times when he suddenly did a U-turn and sailed back past a following dark sedan. Alan begged him to show him how.

"I'll let you drive it some time and if you're competent, maybe I'll start training you. It's an art."

He often probed when Alan struggled with a patient, saying, "There's something inside you that is inhibiting you. Talk to me." It was almost like he was the psychologist.

Alan told him everything about himself, but Curt revealed little. Made him curious. The man was a mystery.

For fun, they often spoke Korean in the office, making other staff members look at them with questions in their eyes. Curt laughed and told them what they said. They were becoming friends.

Alan started riding his bike to work to save gas. Curt came out one hot afternoon and admired his Schwinn road bike. His Peloton wasn't new, but it was fast. They started going out for twenty-mile rides on Sunday afternoons when the weather was nice, and they'd come back sweating and laughing. They high-fived when they beat their previous time.

Alan told Curt that he played guitar and sang. "I thought about going to this open mic at a bar, but I'm too shy. I get nervous and either forget the cords or lyrics and make a fool of myself."

"I've been playing the guitar since I was twelve. I write songs and sing. Maybe we could get together."

Alan's heart opened like a sunflower. "That's exactly what I've been meditating to have happen, someone to play and sing with. When can we get together?"

A few weeks later, he took his guitar over to Curt's house. "You're my first guest. I never have anyone over."

They liked the blues, country, and ballads. Curt played a couple of his own songs, and Alan wanted to learn them.

When playing music, Curt was more open and relaxed. He mentioned personal things, his deceased mother, father, and grandfather, and the dogs he had raised. He talked about the orchards and growing up in Cedaredge. One night he told about his first girlfriend, Darlene.

"One weekend, I was back in Cedaredge and my mom asked me to pick up bread and milk at the store. I saw my old high school enemy, Bud Hamilton's, 1950 Ford pickup parked at the Cedaredge Merc. It was dented and the front bumper was missing as if he crashed into something. I almost didn't go in. I told my dog, 'Screw it, I'll just ignore the butthead when he calls me Cunt-rad. Someday, he'll push me too hard, and I'll clock him.'

I picked up the milk and started up the bread aisle. Their backs to me, Darlene and Bud were arguing about bread. They were using the baby carriage as a food cart. Darlene held a loaf in her hands, and Bud grabbed it. "That's too expensive, put it back!"

"No! You always want the cheapest brand. I'm not putting it back."

They struggled over the loaf, smashing it.

Bud slapped her cheek. It wasn't a tap.

Darlene stumbled back and shrieked.

That did it. Nothing like a damsel in distress to get my blood up. Three quick strides and I stepped between them. "Well, look at the big man, hitting a woman."

Bud looked up, his breath wreaking of whiskey. 'So Cunt-rad's back in town. Heard you got kicked outta the Navy for being a retard.'

He shoved me, and I stumbled backward into Darlene who bumped the baby carriage, nearly tipping it over.

Bud growled, 'Stay outta my business.'

I held the milk bottle by the neck. I meant to just tap his forehead, but Bud lunged to tackle me in the same instant. With a loud crack, the bottle shattered on top of Bud's head, splattering milk and glass everywhere. Bud dropped to the floor, out cold.

Darlene exclaimed, 'Good. I'm glad you finally came to get me. Let's go.'

I started walking backward. 'No Darlene, I didn't come to get you.' I put my palms up between us. 'I heard you fighting, and stepped in when he slapped you, that's all.'

She had an enormous smile as she pushed the baby carriage down the aisle at me. It was loaded with cans, milk, and meat. The baby squalled loudly. She said, 'God, how I've dreamed of this day.'

I got to the end of the aisle. 'No Darlene, I'm starting college. I can't afford a wife.' I cut left and trotted up the next row.

The manager headed down the bread aisle. 'What happened? Why is milk all over the place? Who broke this bottle?'

Darlene laughed. 'Well, Bud is drunk again, and he smacked himself in the head with the milk bottle. Serves him right.'

I waved at the cashier as I went by.

She asked, 'Couldn't find what you were looking for?'

I laughed. 'No, I got what I've wanted for a long time.'"

Alan laughed and laughed. They were becoming friends. Someday, he'd ask why he left the Navy instead of retiring with twenty years. It would wait.

Chapter 31
Near Wreck

The time passed quickly. Alan had another year to meet the supervision requirements to sit for the State and National Psychologist Boards. He started thinking maybe he'd stay on with the mental health center after the hours were documented just to see Curt every day. He asked if he could work part-time and start working with children and families privately.

Curt said, "Pal, do what is best for you. I'd be happiest if you stay full-time, but I'd love to have you for even a few hours a week if you decide to open a practice next year. You are an intuitive therapist and an incredible diagnostician."

They had a routine of doing things together: Krav Maga on Fridays then on Saturdays, Curt took him for a spin in the Corvette and taught him stunt driving. Afterward, they played guitars, and on Sundays, went for a bike ride, weather permitting. It was probably a boundary violation on both of their parts but, heck, they were lonely and had no other friends. Who would complain? Every couple of weeks, they read a Korean story and enjoyed the cute women flirting with them, but neither invited a girl to dinner or a movie.

"Hey, Pal, why don't you take one of these sweet women out?" Curt asked. "The one named Ara has her eyes on you."

"Why don't you? I'm still coming off a rotten divorce. What's your excuse?"

He became quiet and strummed his guitar. "Listen to this chord pattern, think of words and feelings it reminds you of." He began playing a sweet melody and humming along.

Alan cocked his ear, listening intently. "It's a Korean love song. I can almost see a young couple together with yearning in their eyes." His mother had sung it to him since he was a baby.

Curt smiled and began singing in Korean, "Arirang, Arirang, Arariyo, you must pass over Arirang Hill. My love please hang in there and be well."

Alan harmonized.

When he finished, there was moisture in his eyes.

"That was beautiful. Where did you learn it?"

"I'm not sure." He looked away. A tear ran down his face and he wiped it with the back of his hand. "I woke up in the middle of the night, hearing a young girl singing."

Alan stood. "I think you need a hug."

Curt stood and reluctantly accepted it. "Okay, thanks, I'm good." He waved him away.

The rest of the evening, they played blues songs, some of them sad, others angry. Something was opening inside the man.

The next day, there was a skiff of snow so Curt suggested they take the Corvette for a spin on the Peak to Peak Highway instead of riding bikes. "I'll take it easy because of the snow." The engine roared to life and Curt burned rubber out of the parking lot. He grinned. "I'm a teenager when I get into this car."

Alan slapped the dash. "Me too." He drummed his hands on his knees to the music on the stereo.

A pickup pulled out in front of them at 9th Street. It was heavily loaded with gravel, and the driver drove slowly. Curt tried to pass when it was clear, and it sped up until the next curve and yellow lines, then slowed way down again.

At the next opportunity to pass, the driver again sped up when Curt punched it. The pickup swung into the other lane, blocking them. Curt nearly tried the right side but the guard rail and Boulder Creek made the attempt dangerous.

Alan yelled, "Don't wreck!"

Suddenly, the tailgate fell open and gravel, screws, and nails tumbled out, slamming the front of the Corvette like hailstones. They heard pings on the front and gravel hitting the undercarriage. A rocks cracked the windshield.

Curt honked furiously as he braked.

Alan stuck his hand out the window and flipped the driver off. "What the fuck is wrong with you!"

Curt stopped when he had the chance. Breathing hard, he said, "That was intentional. Look at him, he's still going. Wait, he stopped. What the fuck?" Curt wanted to see who it was, chew him out, and tell him he was losing stuff, creating a hazard for other drivers.

He drove to the truck cautiously, and the driver took off, dropping crap in front of them. More gravel, loaded with nails and screws shook out. Curt did everything possible to dodge them as he hit the brakes. Rocks zinged into his paint job and windshield, even bouncing off the side windows. Suddenly, Curt had trouble controlling the car and they nearly hit the guard rail. "I have a flat front tire." There was nowhere to pull over. They had to keep going. The pickup crawled along. The driver looked back with an evil grin.

Finally, there was a small pull off and Curt was able to get over. Two flats, one in front, one in back. The tires were ruined. They'd have to hitch a ride back to Boulder.

Alan exploded, hurling curse words.

Curt was cool and calm, although his face was white. "I've been harassed before." He told of the time his brake line was cut, and he crashed his old Lincoln convertible. "I sure loved that car."

"Man, you need to level with me. What the hell is going on? Why would anyone do something like that to you?"

"No, it could endanger your life."

Chapter 32
Cool

The Corvette wasn't in the parking lot. Alan figured it was in the body shop. When he brought morning coffee, Curt's head was on the desk as if exhausted. He raised and without looking at Alan, messed with his new Apple IIe computer, mumbling to himself. He said, "Thanks."

Alan sat a few minutes, shrugged, and went to his office.

Curt hardly spoke, not even to Shonna.

She came into his office. "Dr. Ramirez, what is wrong with Mr. Conrad? He won't look at me or anyone else. Usually, I can make him laugh." She fluffed her multicolored robe out as if she were an African queen and sat down in the chair fronting his desk.

"We drove up the Boulder Canyon yesterday and got stuck behind this pickup with a load of gravel. The tailgate fell and his car was hit by the rocks and there were a lot of nails and screws mixed in it. The paint was chipped and his windshield was broken. We ended up with flat tires and had to hitchhike back." He shrugged. "I guess that's it."

She shook her big head and rolled her eyes. "Well, thank you for telling me. He won't say anything. It's like he's all curled up inside himself. At least now, I can tell the staff something."

Friday evening, he drove to Krav Maga, and Curt didn't look at him. They didn't play guitars, ride bikes, or go for a spin. Alan stared out his apartment window. The shadows were long in the yard. It was turning autumn and the monarch butterflies were passing through as they did every year on their way from Canada to Mexico. One paused to rest on the window sill. Its wings opened in a leisurely way, then closed again. Moisture rose in his eyes.

It went on. The next week, Curt didn't go to the Korean book study, and the women asked where he was. "I don't know. His Corvette suffered some damage, and I'm not sure how he's getting to work."

"Why doesn't he ride with you?" Ara asked.

He figured to burn the bridge with her before she crossed it. His tone was gruff. "I offered. You'd have to ask him."

She looked hurt. Ara glanced sadly over her shoulder as she walked away.

Alan felt bad. She was a lovely woman. He needed to be nicer.

Another week went by and Alan couldn't stand it. He parked in front of his desk the next morning. "Curt, I know you're upset about the damage to your car, but don't take it out on me or the staff."

He looks uncomfortable. "I'm not. I'm keeping you safe."

Alan took a deep breath. "Safe from what? You said someone once cut your brake lines and cars have harassed you when you're driving. What gives? Man, I care about you. You're my only friend, my buddy."

Curt sighed. "Maybe someday I'll tell you, but I'm not ready." He gave a slight shrug. "My car's supposed to be fixed tomorrow. Want a ride to the Krav Maga?"

"Of course."

He acted like nothing happened. They started playing guitars and biking once more. Curt tried to get him to talk to Ara and made him stand close by while he joked with her, asking questions about her life and her dreams. She kept trying to catch Alan's eyes.

He was terrified. She was smart and lovely. She made him want to hold and kiss her. He tried not to think about her. It didn't work. His mind was nearly consumed with her, with Ara.

A couple of weeks went by and on Sunday, they took a bike run up to Lyons on the back roads. Curt kept looking back as if expecting something. On the way back to Boulder, a gray jeep peeled out from a gravel side road and barreled down on them.

They split. Curt went left and Alan rode right into the bar ditch, ending up tangled in a barbed wire fence. Curt stood on the pedals, pumping with all his might. The jeep hit his back wheel. It flipped him, and he flew clear over the fence.

Alan was too shaken up to get the license plate. He ran to his buddy. "Are you okay?"

His cheek and left arm bled. "I'm alive if that's what you mean."

"Jesus, that driver tried to kill you. If you hadn't dove over the fence, he would have run you over." He looked around. "It's a good thing these are thick cedar posts. If they were steel T bars, he might have rolled through them."

"Yeah, and then he would have come back and run over you."

Alan ripped off his T-shirt and tore strips to stop Curt's bleeding arm. It was deep. "You need stitches. Think you can ride your bike?" He looked down. His pant leg bled. He pulled it up. Barbed wire had punctured the skin. It wasn't bad.

"Yeah, I've been hurt worse." Curt was curiously calm. He stood and checked his bike. The rear wheel was slightly bent. He braced it and with tremendous strength, straightened the wheel with his bare hands.

"Geez, you're stronger than hell."

Curt got on his bike. "You should start lifting weights with me. I lift three or four times a week." He started peddling. "Let's get on the main road. If that jeep comes back, we'll get his plates."

After urgent care stitched his arm, and they were back at his house, Alan said, "Okay buddy, it's time you level with me. What the hell are you involved with where someone is trying to kill you?"

A slight shrug. "Listen, I'm exhausted physically and emotionally. Give me some time and I'll tell you." He stopped and looked into his eyes. "I'm sorry for getting you involved. That's why I've been a loner for so many years."

"What is the why?"

"Listen, if some agent ever tries to interview you, don't tell him anything. If they think you know what I know, you'll have a target on your back as big as mine." He looked the floor. "I'm very sorry for getting close to you."

"Hell, man. You can't let some idiots keep you from having a life. I'm committed to being your friend. I love you, man, you're like the father I never had. Don't friggin' cut me off again."

He clenched his jaws. "Okay. I won't." He turned and went inside.

# Chapter 33
San Diego Hospital

Curt found a rear window unlocked. Quietly, he pushed it up and crawled into an office at the naval hospital in San Diego. His records at the VA showed only that he was a seaman third class, that he had washed overboard and presumed lost at sea, and was also a former POW with a brain injury. When he tried to get his medical records this morning, the staff said they didn't have records going back that far. "They're microfiched." The young lady offered to order them.

"Please, I'd appreciate a copy." He took a two-week vacation and left Dr. Ramirez in charge of the mental health center.

There wouldn't be anything new in them, but he thought maybe, just maybe, his complete medical records were hidden in the building. Wandering through the darkened halls, he dodged security. It was thrilling, unlike his home life. If caught, he'd say he was a former patient and didn't know how he got there. They'd just kick him out. In the basement, he saw a door marked 'Medical Records' and jimmied it open. A vast room, it was the size of the University of Colorado's library. He used his flashlight to alphabetically search files.

There were rows of file cabinets in the basement of the naval hospital. He couldn't find any of the other four men's records on the mission with him. He flipped through the Cs, looking for his name. He found it! Curtis A. Conrad. Nervously, he scanned it, only to realize it was some other navy man's file who served in Vietnam. His records, like his buddy, Carl's, were not there.

Disappointed, he retreated the way he came and slipped out the rear window. A security guard's flashlight beam lit up his face. "Halt, what are you doing out here?"

"Just wandering around. I was treated in this building for my injuries."

"Are you Navy?"

"I was."

"Why are you here?"

"Don't know. It's like I just came too."

"Have you been drinking?"

"I don't drink."

The guard smelled his breath. "You haven't been drinking and you don't smell like marijuana. Come with me. Did you drive here or take a bus?"

"I parked out front."

The guard escorted him to the rental car. "You should come back in the morning and ask to see a psychologist."

"Sure. That's who I was looking for."

Curt slid behind the wheel laughing. *At least I had some fun.* But he was frustrated. What happened to the other men on the mission? If only he could remember their names besides Carl's maybe he could locate one and learn how they ended up as prisoners. He meditated on the men he served with. There was a guy named Taylor, but he couldn't remember his last name. A name popped up. Adam Amspoker. We called him Spooker. Wonder where he is?

At the motel, Curt scanned the San Diego phone book and found several Amspokers. *I'll call in the morning.* He did a hundred pushups, practiced air Krav Maga, and then took a hot shower.

Visiting the naval hospital brought up memories of the troopship and being treated here. He remembered the hours and hours of interrogations, and how Naval intelligence alleged he was brainwashed to believe he was on a secret mission to defuse a nuclear bomb. "Hells bells, I never had a brain injury, and I wasn't brain-washed. I'm as sane as the next guy."

After the clinic doctor removed the bullet from his shoulder, he had gone through physical therapy for a frozen pelvic floor with minor improvement. Later, a surgeon performed hip surgery for an impingement syndrome. It helped with his hip pain and stiffness so now, he walked without a limp.

After breakfast and coffee in the morning, he called every Amspoker in the phone book. Finally, an older-sounding woman said Adam moved to Portland, Oregon, and gave him a phone number. "Would you mind calling to let him know I'm on the way?"

On the trip up I-5, Curt remembered getting injections of a hallucinogen. Weird shit, his brain had whirled with crazy images, then more shock treatments and the counter-conditioning with Antabuse and drinking while he told the story of his POW experience. They were determined to make him forget the top-secret mission, and it had worked. Until now.

He realized a dark blue sedan followed his rental car. *I'll shake him in the next town off the freeway.* He turned off at Willows. It wasn't easy because he wasn't in his Corvette. It took over an hour to finally ditch the tail, so he spent a night in Redding instead of driving the full sixteen hours to Portland.

It was irritating in the morning when he saw another plain sedan behind him on I-5. "I've got to use cash from now on. They're treating me like a criminal. Why aren't they spending resources on real crooks, or tracking down Vietnam War deserters?"

Two men tailed him in the plain gray sedan. Then the first agents rejoined, staying behind the first tail. It took nearly three hours to ditch them. He managed it simply by luck. In a Medford, Oregon subdivision, a garage door was open and he drove in. Screeching to a halt, he hopped out and hit the door closer. He watched from the window as both tails drove by.

A lady came into the garage, yelling, "What are you doing in here?"

"Sorry, Ma'am. My house looks just like yours. Could you please hit the opener?"

Adam agreed to meet him for coffee in Portland but he was nervous. "They're always watching me, probably you too."

"Yep, I had different ones following me most of the way here." They stared at each other, cautiously, calculating, worrying. Curt asked, "Besides Carl, do you know what happened to the other two men on our team?"

"Yeah, Taylor committed suicide and Jack was killed in a suspicious car accident. I quit the VA because they were using ECT and drugs, hoping I'd commit suicide."

"Someone tried to take me out in a car wreck, but I'm not sure who. I've got huge memory gaps. I still don't remember the briefing and how we got captured by the North Koreans. Do you?"

Spooker's eyes closed, and his face paled. "It was shortly after Truman recalled MacArthur. There were six of us in the aircraft carrier briefing room. You were an extra in case someone dropped out. They said it might be a suicide mission and we may be captured and tortured."

"Go on please."

"We had five men on our team. You were added when a guy learned his wife was pregnant so he didn't want to go. Two were to stand guard once we located the bomb, two to dig it up, and a weaponeer to remove the nuclear trigger." He cleared his throat. "We parachuted in near a southern tributary of the Taedong River which flows North through Pyongyang." His eyes looked foggy. "You got tangled in a tree and hung upside down all night until we found you. Taylor had disappeared and when we found him, he had broken his ankle so you and Carl packed him."

Curt couldn't speak. He realized his dad was right. They were sent in to save the U.S. from international condemnation. It was like a spring suddenly decompressed in his head. He jumped up and paced the coffee shop, talking to himself, *It all makes sense now. Jesus, it all makes sense—why they tried to destroy my memory, why they watch me. We were sent to defuse a nuclear bomb MacArthur ordered dropped on North Korea! If the world knew, the U.S. would be condemned and North Korea could be justified in demanding reparations.* He realized people stared at him as he paced.

Pulling himself together, he went to the table and sat down. He looked into Adam's eyes. "So that's why the Navy deprogrammed me and kept me on drugs."

Adam nodded. "Or murdered us in an 'accident.' MacArthur had nuclear authority for only two weeks before Truman recalled him. The bomb was supposed to explode on impact and pollute the entire riparian system. It would have killed millions of people." He cleared his throat. "I'm thinking it was a dud. That, or they dropped one without the nuclear trigger."

"Geez, if they didn't install the trigger, our mission was a total waste."

"I've been trying to learn the truth. It's very hard because the nuclear arsenal is shrouded in secrecy. I've been to Japan twice and South Korea once. I understand they don't install the trigger until just before the bomber leaves."

Curt took a deep breath. "So they want to keep the world from knowing the U.S. attempted to use nukes against civilians during the Korean War." He waited a moment, then asked, "How did we get captured?"

"You don't remember?"

"No."

"Man, they must have fried your brain with the ECT. You packed our detector because you're so big." He gave a weak grin. "Now metal detectors are small and light, but back in the '50s they were heavy as hell." He went on, "Eventually, you pinged a large metal object on a sand spit, and we dug until we got the nose exposed and tipped it over. Taylor just got the outer plate off to begin defusing the bomb when we heard a North Korean patrol coming through the woods. We got it covered up and spent the night hiding in the brush. In the morning they surrounded us."

"We didn't shoot? There wasn't a firefight?"

"Nope, they got the drop on us. Jack was on watch and they caught him flatfooted. I woke up to a gun pointed at my head."

Curt stared at the ceiling. "I don't think any nuclear bombs have gone off. At least nothing has been reported." He closed his eyes, slowly shaking his head. "So, potentially, a live nuclear bomb is rusting somewhere on a sand spit in North Korea that could blow at any time unless the North Koreans found it and have reverse-engineered it. Either way, it's bad news." His hands shook as he sipped coffee. "Without any of us as witnesses, the government can deny it." He swallowed the rest of the coffee. "I only remember bits and pieces."

"They tortured you the worst. I remember you being marched around outside the cells with a finger stuck up your nose." He held up his right hand, showing his missing little finger. Me and Carl too."

A look of sympathy, his eyes were moist. "You were the man. They kicked the hell out of your nuts until you passed out. They'd throw you back into your cell and you'd lay curled up and moaning for hours." Adam looked into his eyes. "Every one of us, including the Australians and Brits, thought you were the bravest, most courageous man in the camp."

With sudden pain in his groin, Curt fought tears. "I had forgotten about that." Dropping his head to hide tears, he stood. "Want some more coffee?"

"Sure."

Curt had himself under control when he returned with steaming cups. "Do you remember being rescued?"

"Oh shit, even with the ECT and LSD, they couldn't wash that out of my head. I came back to run beside you, trying to get you to drop

Carl from your back, but hell if you would. You kept saying, 'We promised we'd haul each other out.' The North Koreans were on our asses, firing machine guns. No idea how we didn't get killed. Those South Korean marines were fearless! I know they lost men rescuing us.

After we got to the truck, the South Koreans took us to different homes to recuperate. Guess their hospitals were destroyed by the communists. I was with a family for a month or more until I gained some weight. The woman was incredibly nice. She made delicious soup."

He went on. "After I recovered, a jeep showed up and took me to a troopship. At first, they thought I was some kook or a deserter because they had no records of us. No one admitted knowledge of our secret mission." He coughed. "The worst part was they interrogated me all the way back to the States and claimed the North Korean's had brain- washed me."

Curt nodded. "I'm remembering now. It was horrible. They treated me like a collaborator." He shook his head slowly.

"When you didn't turn up in San Diego, I figured you died because you collapsed when we got to the truck. Your ass was bleeding badly." He sipped coffee, then cleared his throat. "Where did you end up?"

"I think in a South Korean woman's home. I didn't remember anything about it until a doctor pulled a bullet from my shoulder and I started getting flashes of things that happened." Curt clenched his jaws. He tried drinking coffee but couldn't because his hands shook.

Adam broke the tension. "At the naval hospital in San Diego, after they injected me with LSD and subjected me to a session of ECT, I knew I had to escape. or I'd lose my mind. They wanted to make us into vegetables."

"God, no wonder my memory is like a shredded book." He caught Adam's eyes again. "What do you remember about the deprogramming at the naval hospital like the loud music, and the confusing questions they asked?"

Adam shuddered. "I don't want to talk about it. The CIA and naval intelligence interrogated us. Nothing physical but the mental torture was worse than the POW camp. They claimed I was brainwashed by the North Koreans to believe the story about defusing a nuclear bomb. I received one shock treatment and escaped the first chance." He abruptly stood. "I just saw an intelligence agent drive by. They use subcontractors these days. You have to watch carefully because they dress down and try to fit in. I'm going out the back." He paused at the door. "Don't look me up or contact me again. They'll figure we're putting two and two together, then make it look like an accident."

"Son of a bitch," Curt mumbled. He waited long enough for Adam to get away from the area before he walked to the rented car. A dark blue sedan with an agent was parked down the block. The other sedan with two men sat across the street. They were Asians.

Totally confusing and strange.

Chapter 34
The Agent

The same night as the Korean book study, soon after Alan got home, there was a loud knock on his apartment door. A man dressed in a dark suit and tie stood outside.

"What can I do for you?"

He pulled out a badge. "I'm with Naval Intelligence. We have information you've become good friends with Curt Conrad."

"Yes, so what?"

"May I come in?"

"No."

"So you're going to be uncooperative, are you?" He frowned. He had an earbud and someone was giving him instructions. Looking at Alan with piercing grey eyes, he said, "We don't know what you are talking about those nights in his house, but I'm to warn you that if he reveals any top-secret information to you, both of you might be targeted."

Alan let out a slight laugh. "What the fuck? Targeted by who? Naval Intelligence?"

"You better be very careful. The North Koreans would love to get confirmation. They might try to kidnap both of you."

His mouth fell open. "You are kidding me. I'm a nobody. I don't know anything the communists might be interested in."

He pointed his index finger at his chest as if it were a gun. "Keep it that way." He turned and walked to a dark blue sedan where another man waited.

He started looking over his shoulder like Curt, especially when they went somewhere in his gold and black Corvette or out riding bikes. Alan was afraid to tell him of the encounter when he got back from his vacation. He knew Curt would shut up, and might even fire him, hoping to keep him safe.

Chapter 35
Something I Went Through

One Saturday night they sat playing blues and heart-ache love ballads in his living room. Curt's eyes were dark and sunken into his brow. He looked burdened.

"What's going on?" Alan asked, "Everything we're playing is sad. You can tell me."

He didn't want to talk about it.

"Come on, you know my deepest struggles. We're best friends. Trust me."

He focused on Alan's eyes. "I guess it's only fair you know." He gathered eyes into his deep brown ones. "You have to agree not to tell anyone else or write and publish it as long as I'm alive. Not your mother, or if you ever marry again, your wife."

He promised.

Curt stood and set a kettle of water on the stove. "We should have some tea. He took his time preparing it. He brought out a homemade apricot pie and cut slices, heated it, and put ice cream on it while Alan strummed his guitar and sang softly. Curt had taught him Arirang, and he sang it.

"Pal, please don't play that song. It makes me want to cry."

"I know, it makes my mother cry too."

"She does?"

"Yeah, she said it is the most popular folk song in Korea. The first time you played it for me, I immediately recognized it. She hums or sings it often. Makes me miss her."

"Someday, I'd like to meet her."

"She would like you." Alan grinned. "She likes anyone who treats me well, and I've had trouble making friends my whole live since I'm half Asian."

Curt served the pie and ice cream. He took a deep breath. "Remember you've promised to never publish this or tell anyone until after I'm long gone."

Alan stuck his hand out. "It is my solemn promise."

They shook.

He inhaled and exhaled, then said, "There is something I went through during the Korean War that I've never told anyone and since you're involved now, I'm going to tell you everything I've remembered." He explained there was no way to independently verify the truth of his experience since the Navy appeared to have destroyed all evidence of the top-secret mission, including sanitizing his medical records.

"Please tell me. So far it's been a one-way street with you probing my life. I'd like to know what you went through."

Curt began – hesitating and speaking slowly. When he described the cruel commander sawing his little finger off, he sobbed. His shoulders shook. His face was reddish purple. Tears ran down his cheeks.

Alan didn't know what to do. He put his arm around him and they sat together on the couch.

He caught his breath. "I can't go on. I'll tell you the rest some other time."

Alan was shocked at the implications. If true, it explained the real reason why Truman recalled MacArthur. It had international implications even today.

He tried to get him to write and publish his story, and offered to ghostwrite it, changing all names.

He refused, "They'll come after us. We could be killed like two of the other guys who survived the mission." His expression was deadly serious.

Alan shrugged. "It would be hearsay and wouldn't stand up in court."

"You think the communists would care about that? They probably want someone to confirm that MacArthur dropped a nuclear bomb in North Korea so they can blast the news around the world."

Alan shuddered.

He patted his shoulder, "Sorry brother. Better get used to the idea." He cleared his throat. "Now you know why I didn't want to tell you."

Curt made more tea.

They sat quietly for a while.

Alan wasn't sure what would help and started strumming his guitar. He didn't mean to play it, but Arirang was in his head. He heard Curt singing along. In his mind, he heard his mother's voice and imagined how beautiful it would be if they sang together.

Tears were in both men's eyes when they said goodbye for the night.

Chapter 36
The Horrifying Story

Something in his face changed, Curt was calmer and grimaced less.

Alan understood. It was the release, the catharsis of holding something so dreadful a secret for many years. He had seen it in children when he did play and art therapy with them. One child went from nonverbal to speaking whole sentences, and his coloring changed from scribbles to well-formed, recognizable figures.

Each time Curt shared more, Alan shook with anger at the evil North Korean Commander or was sick to his stomach from watching his buddy's pale face covered with tears. It was extremely difficult to listen to and challenging to write. After each session, he wrote copious notes, then tucked them into a safe deposit box for prosperity. He had nightmares and awakened fatigued in the morning.

Cindy dropped by with her braless magnificents bouncing. "You're good for Mr. Conrad. He seems more relaxed, having you as a friend."

"Yeah, he's a good guy."

"Think he'd be interested in taking me out?"

"I doubt it."

"You don't have to be so blunt." She huffed out, swinging firm boobs with hard nipples. They were nice.

He thought of Ara. She was gentle and very intelligent. Why was he so afraid of her? Oh yeah. Divorce. He shuddered. Never again.

Alan vowed to listen and be the best friend a man could have.

Their relationship metamorphosed as if they were a close uncle and nephew. Once a week when they met to play guitars, Curt told him a little more. They had to take breaks.

Curt said he could publish the story after he was gone. But he worried that both of them might be kidnapped by the North Koreans and spirited back to be used as propaganda. That's why Naval Intelligence kept an eye on him. That's why the government might off him or pressure him to commit suicide.

Alan constantly watched for anyone who might be surveilling or following. They were in this together.

In some ways, the deprogramming was even more horrific than the torture. Alan couldn't believe the way he was treated, as if this brave man, his best friend, had betrayed his country. It pissed him off. He wanted to publish the story so the citizens would know how poorly Korean War POWs were treated.

Curt shook his head adamantly, "Alan, don't even think about it." Fear in his eyes. "I'm still being followed and Naval Intelligence doubtlessly knows we've become good friends." He looked him in the eye. "Have you been contacted?"

Alan thought about lying since it would freak him out. He might stop hanging around with him just to keep him safe. He inhaled and exhaled. "Yeah, a month ago, a man knocked on my door and showed me his badge, saying he's with Naval Intelligence. I wouldn't let him in my apartment. He warned that I might be targeted by the North Koreans." He held Curt's eyes. "I told him I didn't know anything the communists might be interested in. He said to keep it that way."

Fear flashed in his face. "Alan, I'm sorry. It happens to all my friends. That's why I have none." He looked down. "Listen, we should stop hanging out. I've learned to get along without friends."

Alan grabbed his big paw with the missing fingers. "Fuck them, Curt. You've become my best friend. Hell, it's hard to make real friends. I have lots of acquaintances, but no one like you that I can share my innermost thoughts and feelings with. Geez, man. Don't cut me off."

Curt noticeably cooled. It took several weeks of Alan gently joking each morning over coffee that he relaxed again. Alan talked him into coming over to play guitars. After a few songs, he confronted him. "Listen, you have taught me to be emotionally honest. I'm hurt because you've been avoiding me. I know it's because that intelligence agent knocked on my door, but …."

Curt looked guilty.

"Come on, be my buddy again. I think of you like you're my older brother."

He sighed. "I've been thinking about it. I'm just afraid the intelligence agents are correct – you might become a North Korean target like me." He shuddered. "You don't know the anxiety and fear of looking over your shoulder all the time."

"Hell, I already do. I've seen plain sedans following me. The other night, I was sure they were Asians."

"Shit!" He shook his head. "I was afraid of that."

Alan offered his hand. "Listen, I'm not going to let some communists screw up the best friendship I've ever had. If for some reason, they make a move on one of us, we'll kick ass on them. You got me into Krav Maga for a reason didn't you?"

He nodded with a wry smile. "It was unconscious at the time, but yes, I want you to have the skills to defend yourself."

Chapter 37
Attacked

The next weekend, Alan headed to Curt's house with his guitar. They planned to play at an open mic and wanted to rehearse one more time before getting on stage that evening. He was surprised to see Curt's garage door open. He parked near the curb and when he stepped out, heard yells and thumps. It sounded like a meeting of the Krav Maga club. "What the heck?" He approached cautiously.

Curt did a flip, catching a man in the chin with his heel as he rolled over the roof of his car. Black masked men were quickly after him, smashing at his arms and face with kicks, fists, and nunchucks.

Alan didn't hesitate and joined the melee, kicking a nun chuck man in the back, preventing him from bashing his buddy's head with the sticks. It was two against four.

Curt ducked, rolled, and grabbed a short shovel, slashing at the attackers: the crack of bones rang out.

Another pulled a knife but Alan kicked it from his hand, screaming, "Get the fuck out of here."

It went on, bruising kicks and slugs, and blood flew. Alan took a fierce kick in the face and blacked out.

Shots rang out and the masked men looked up. This new guy in a ski mask joined the battle, shooting a semi-auto at the ceiling. In the fracas, Curt got him by the arm, twisted, and broke it. Curt jerked away his firearm, and holding him by the neck, yelled, "I'll kill him!" He quickly fired two shots in the direction of the other agents.

Suddenly, they were gone.

Curt jerked the man around, kneed him in the nuts, and chopped the back of his neck. He dropped.

Hitting the door closer, he tied the agent's hands behind his back, wrapped electrical cords around his legs, and then dragged him to the kitchen door steps.

He checked Alan and patted his cheeks. "You alright?"

"Barely." He scanned the garage as he wiped blood from his nose. "What the fuck was that?"

"I think they were North Koreans trying to kidnap me. Thanks for coming in." Curt looked at the masked man on the steps. He moved slightly. "We better check him, find out who he is."

He helped Alan stand, and they loamed over the agent. Curt leaned down and pulled off his ski mask.

"What the fuck?" Alan nearly yelled. The guy was an American with a military haircut.

Curt bled from multiple wounds, cuts, and welts. "Watch him, I need to wash up." He touched Alan's shoulder. "You okay?"

He felt his nose and said with a stuffy, nasal voice, "I think it's broken, but the bleeding has stopped." He motioned to the door. "I'll stand guard. Go get cleaned up."

Curt looked better when he returned, but he was angry and scared. The man became conscious. Military haircut, black suit, and tie. Curt shook him and yelled, "What the fuck were your men trying to do to me?"

The man stared with a surly expression.

He searched his pockets for an I.D. "How do you drive without a license?" He checked for a dog tag and found nothing. The gun was a 9mm Glock, a special agent weapon. The Corvette had bad dents on the roof, doors, and hood from bodies slamming into it. Curt was pissed about his car, and held the agent's neck with his left hand. "What's your mission? Tell me, or I'll break your nose."

"Go ahead. It won't do you any good. I'll never talk."

"It's your face." Curt popped him, and his nose cracked off to the side. "You can be brave, or you can be smart and save yourself a lot of pain. I'm not calling the police. I'd rather torture it out of you."

"Fuck you!" His nose gushed blood.

Curt untied the electrical cords from the agent's legs and once freed, spread them. "Alan, hold his legs."

The man kicked at him, and Alan busted his nuts. As the man squirmed in agony, Curt unbuckled the man's belt and pulled off his pants and underwear.

"You'll get to experience what I did in the POW camp if you don't talk." He cut the end of an electrical cord, peeled the wires back, and wrapped the bare ends around the man's scrotum, then used the guy's belt to lash his legs back together. "You have one chance to tell me what your mission is and who sent you before I plug it in."

The agent's eyes went wide. "No, please."

"Then talk. I learned a lot about torture in North Korea." He held the plug near an outlet.

"We were told to rough you up and scare you so you won't talk."

"Talk about what?"

"I have no idea."

Curt briefly inserted the plug. 110V was a helluva lot stronger than the 12 volts the North Korean commander subjected him to.

The agent fought crying out.

"What are they afraid I'd talk about?"

"I don't know, some mission you were on during the Korean War. They don't tell us much."

"What agency are you working for? The CIA, FBI, Navy Intelligence, who?"

He didn't speak.

"Your sex life is in my hands." He narrowed the gap to the outlet. Brave sucker, this one. Curt plugged it in and let the man whimper a half minute before pulling it out. "Tell me what agency put you on this task. Who are you working for?" He grabbed a hunting knife from his workbench and cut off the man's suit jacket and shirt, ripping it into shreds. He had an anchor tattooed on his chest with U.S. Navy under it.

Tears ran down the agent's face.

"You've got high pain tolerance. Bet you went through lots of tests and training to get on this special team, huh?"

No response.

"I asked you a question."

"Fuck you." His face twisted with anguish.

"Guess you enjoy pain." He picked him up by his broken arm.

He moaned.

Curt wrenched it.

The agent caught his breath after a moment. "Does the agency matter? It's the message. They want you to keep your mouth shut."

"About what?"

"Hell if I know. Something to do with the Korean War."

"What else did they tell you?"

"To make sure you understood that if you ever told anyone what you did in North Korea, you'd pay the price." He glanced at Alan.

"They think you've been telling him."

Alan kept quiet.

"I've already paid the price." He showed his missing fingers.

He stood the agent up and pressed an elbow into his throat. "I'm going to let you go. When your bosses interrogate you, say you met one angry man who doesn't know what the hell happened in Korea. I have no memory of anything other than monitoring radio transmissions on the spy ship. The Navy deprogrammed me. They used LSD and ECT and erased all my records. It's only because agents keep tracking me and doing shit like this that I know it has international significance. If the dumbasses were smart, they'd leave me alone. They're the ones forcing me to try to remember. You ought to tell them that."

The agent tried to shake his head. His voice was choked and strained, "Fucking government." His eyes held tears.

Curt let off some pressure.

"Man, take some pity on a fellow serviceman, my arm is broken, and it hurts like hell, and my nuts are on fire. You won, okay? You and your buddy kicked ass on four of the toughest North Korean agents along with me."

Curt blinked. He glanced at Alan.

"It makes sense," Alan spoke quickly. "The government wants to intimidate you and keep you scared."

He let off the pressure on the man's throat but grabbed the broken arm. "What do you know about the North Koreans?"

"Ouch, shit." He caught his breath. "Known operatives are working in the country. We've been told to make sure they don't kidnap you, or…. His eyes shifted back and forth between Alan and Curt.

"Or what? You'll kill me in an accident?"

"I'm sorry man. That's the way it works."

Alan said, "Curt, the government wants you to die in an accident or commit suicide."

Curt shook his head. He turned to the agent. "What are you going to tell your agency when they find you?"

"You don't remember jack shit, and they're wasting their time, just like the North Koreans."

Chapter 38
The Caring Home

They were too shaken to play guitars. Alan had just purchased a large bottle of red wine and went to his pickup for it.

Curt's legs and hands trembled so badly, that he gulped a glass down. He shook his head. "Now you know why I've been afraid to be your friend. This is the third incident. They're ramping up the pressure." His neck and face turned red from drinking the wine.

"I'm in this with you to the end." Although the attack scared him, Alan was excited. "This is giving me a real purpose, a reason to be alive. I've wondered why the hell I ended up working with the chronics. I think it's fate."

"Fate my ass. You make your own choices." He sipped a second glass. "Interesting, this merlot doesn't make my throat tighten." He smiled thoughtfully. "Maybe I can have a glass now and then."

They talked for hours, trying to come up with a plan, and gradually relaxed. Alan said, "Well, my friend, you might as well tell me everything now. I'm wearing a target on my back just like you. I'm sure that agent will inform his superiors that I came in and helped kick ass tonight."

"I'm thinking that." He shook his head. He told him about going out to San Diego and then looking up Spooker in Portland.

"Have you remembered anything else? Like about the South Korean home where they nursed you back to health?"

It may have been the wine or the bonding that happens from the heat of a battle, a battle they won. Curt said, "Yes, I dream of the girl that took care of me, I can't remember her name, but she was sixteen, and I was eighteen. Her mother and grandparents encouraged us to fall in love and…" His voice faded.

Alan poured them more wine and found some cheese and crackers in the kitchen. "Cheers. Here's to remembering, even if it's painful."

He told Alan about the tiny home with three sleeping pads, and the old Korean doctor treating him. The girl nursed him back to health.

They taught each other their languages, played games with her and her grandfather, and she made clothes for him. He laughed as he told about the outhouse incident. "We used to sing Korean folk songs together."

Curt went to the kitchen. "I have a roast in the crockpot. Are you hungry?"

They ate. The red wine smoothed everything.

"I thought you were allergic to alcohol."

"This merlot doesn't seem to affect me like others. My face is hot, but I feel fine. Actually, I feel good, considering we just fought off five men." He looked at Alan. "You're my pal, my best friend."

Alan said, "The girl sounds lovely. Very sweet and kind." He rubbed his bare chin. "So did you...?"

Curt sighed and took a deep breath. "Yes, we were both virgins. It was incredibly sweet and loving. I'll never experience that again." Tears ran down his cheeks. "God, I loved her, and I still do. If there was any way in the world, I'd go to Korea and try to find her."

"Oh, man, I feel sorry for you. So you've been in love with her all these years." Alan took a breath. "That's why you've never married."

Shaking his head sadly, he nodded.

"You might be able to go to South Korea and find her."

He had a faraway look. "That would be a challenge. She's probably married by now."

Alan patted his shoulder. "Don't give up hope."

"How about you? You seem to be terrified of getting involved with another woman after that ugly divorce you suffered through."

"I am."

"What about Ara in the Korean book study, the girl that loves your eyes?" He smiled. "Ara is intelligent. She makes insightful comments, and it's obvious she's attracted to you. She has a masters in international relations and would probably be a good wife. You should ask her out."

Alan shuddered. "I don't even want to think about it."

Chapter 39
Cheap Black Suits

Misun Ramirez unlocked and opened her apartment door to see two Asian men in black suits. She backed away, but one grabbed her wrist and dragged her inside as the other slammed the door shut with her keys hanging in the knob.

They led her to the couch. One sat at her side while the other jammed a chair into her knees. He sat facing her, his legs pressed hard against the outside of hers. Leering into her face, he spoke Korean, "You nursed an American seaman back to health during the war. What did he tell you his mission was?"

"I don't know what you're talking about."

The man squeezed above her knee, his fingers gripping like a vise. "You and your mother helped Seaman Curt Conrad recuperate. He went by Phil Brown when you first met him. He told you plenty. What do you know?"

Misun steeled herself. "I was sixteen when South Korean marines brought him to our house. He was virtually unconscious much of the time because the doctor had him on morphine."

He slapped her. "You want to keep that pretty complexion? Talk!"

"Ow! Who are you? Are you North Koreans?" Blood ran from her nose.

He backhanded her, knocking her down to the couch. "I'll ask the questions. Now talk!"

The other agent sat her up, holding her shoulders tightly.

Although both nostrils bled, she smelled garlic-pepper kimchi on their breaths. A favorite in North Korea.

The agent slapped her again. "Open up you Americanized whore!"

He grabbed her left hand and squeezed her fingers. They cracked against her wedding ring as the other agent held his hand over her mouth to muffle her screams. The stale smell of cigarettes, garlic, peppers, kimchi.

"You make any noise and I'll slash your cheeks." He held a knife.

She tried to grab her bleeding nose. It felt broken. The other agent held her arms pinned to her sides. Through sobs, she said, "I'd tell you if I knew. I haven't seen him since he left in an Army jeep. It's been years, I hardly remember him."

"Yeah right." He snarled. "You loved him and wanted to go with him to America. Yet you don't remember what he told you? Aren't you the tough Korean bitch? We can take your old mother in and after we torture her. She'll tell us everything about him. You better think about whether you want to protect Curt Conrad or your momma." He slammed his heel into the top of her foot.

Feeling the bones crack, Misun fought a scream. Tears ran down her cheeks. When she finally caught her breath, she said, "If I knew what he did, I'd tell you. I hardly remember his face."

"Seaman Conrad dropped out of the American VA services and is the director of a mental health center in Boulder. We know American agents tail him. We think he knows something very, very important. Tell us what he told you!" He stomped her other arch.

Gritting her teeth, Misun told herself that if Curt could endure torture, so could she. But she couldn't stop the tears from tumbling down her cheeks. Closing her eyes, she fought through the pain. The man crushed her hand again. "Owh! Please stop."

"Talk!"

"I don't know anything about his history or his mission other than he was an American seaman we took care of. You'll be arrested for assault and battery for this."

"Ha, the local cops won't touch us. They think we're CIA." He pulled out a real-looking ID. "Do you take us for fools? Your son has befriended him. We're sure he's told you all about him."

The other agent said, "We know you haven't dated since your husband died in the construction accident because you fell in love with seaman Conrad when he recuperated in your momma's home. We think you're still in love with him." A twisted smile. "Do you deny that?"

"I haven't seen him and my son has only told me that he has a job at a mental health center." She thought, *I wonder if it really is my Curt Allen Conrad?*

"Yeah right." His tone became pleasant. "So simply tell us what you know about Conrad. What was his mission? What has he told your son?"

Both feet had broken arches. She sat with eyes closed, frightened and enraged at these nasty Korean men whose breaths reminded her of the men back home. She was sure they were from North Korea: it was more than their cruel attitudes, it was their poor teeth, the smell of regional pepper-garlic kimchi, and the outdated cut of their unkempt suits. "You could have asked nicely without hurting me."

"We are asking nicely. Please go on."

"Can I have a tissue?" Blood from her nose was ruining her white blouse.

The nicer agent got toilet paper and gave it to her.

Once she had the bleeding under control, Misun said, "My son said he went to CU Boulder. He practices Krav Maga and lifts weights. They long-distance bike ride." She looked at the agent playing the good guy. "He's sick and tired of intelligence agents following him."

The mean agent squeezed her fractured fingers.

"Ouch!"

The nicer one said, "Go on."

Catching her breath, she said, "All I know is someone is trying to kill him and my son. My son doesn't know why. He said Curt is very private and says little about his private life."

The cruel agent released her fingers. "What has he remembered about his mission? He parachuted into North Korea with four other men." He took his heel off of her left foot.

"That is all I know. I haven't told my son that I may know his boss if he's the same man." She sat still, anticipating another painful ordeal.

The nicer agent got her a glass of water.

"Kamsahamnida," she took a drink.

"Chonmahnehyo. What else?"

"My son said his parents and grandfather are deceased. He doesn't have any close friends."

"He took a trip to the Pacific coast recently. Why?"

"I don't know. My son hasn't mentioned it."

"Curt met a man he was in the Navy with." He looked at her, asking pleasantly, "You know nothing about a mission in North Korea?"

"No. We had trouble communicating since I didn't understand English."

The mean one squeezed and twisted her wrist very hard. "You're either playing games or so gullible you don't realize Conrad lied about his activities. Stupid Korean whore. He visited the Naval Hospital in

San Diego and didn't go near a beach, then he met a man in Portland, Oregon before flying back. You shouldn't trust these American warmongers. Capitalist pigs lie, they cheat and steal, especially from us." He twisted her wrist.

It felt like he dislocated it. She suppressed a scream, but gasped. "You're hurting me."

He twisted it again. "So you're one of those Yankee-loving twats looking for a green card. You married the second American you met. Is that what you're trying to tell us?" He twisted her wrist again. "How'd you like to be able to keep working at Walmart?"

"Ow! I didn't love my husband. He was the only choice I had at the time." She took a breath. "I'm telling the truth."

The agent playing the good guy checked his partner. "I don't think we're going to learn anything more. Let's get going before they show up."

The cruel agent pointed at her feet. "If you value your health and your son's, you better not say a word to anyone, and if you see Conrad, plan on another session. The next time we'll break your legs and arms." He stomped out the door.

The other agent apologized, "Sorry, Agent Park has a lot of anger. He was tortured by the Americans." He pointed at his head making a circle with one finger. "I tried to get him to simply interview you without any of this." He pointed at her fingers and feet. "I hope we have no reason to return." He quickly strode out.

Misun collapsed back on the couch, her mind swirling with a thousand questions. She woke an hour later. Her feet throbbed and she limped to the restroom, ran a hot tub of water, and dumped in Epsom salts.

"Oh, ah!" She worked the shoes off her swollen feet. She might need to have them and her wrist X-rayed. Her fingers felt fractured and she had trouble doing anything with her left hand. She soaked in the hot water until it cooled, ran more hot water, then eventually crawled out. In the bathroom mirror, the handprints on her face were dark. She'd have to report to her job at Walmart looking like a Japanese Geisha and she'd be hobbling like an old arthritic woman. Her left hand and wrist was so swollen, she couldn't get the wedding ring off.

Limping around her apartment as she dried off, Misun saw the agents had gone through everything: drawers and cabinets were open, and stuff was scattered on the floor. What were they looking for? Getting frozen peas for her hand and feet, she struggled to the bedroom. The dresser was stripped of contents, and her clothes from the closet on the floor. *My journal, my log of the time with Curt at Mommas!* She had it in her purse. She meant to share it with her son when he came to visit next weekend. Could they know about this? Villagers may have seen her writing in it. Communist sympathizers may have pressured different old folks to tell what they knew about Curt and her. She took two pain pills, then poured herself a glass of merlot.

Reading through it carefully, she saw notations about Curt's mission. 'We didn't get the nuke. Radiation in the rivers. Could kill millions. MacArthur. We failed to remove the trigger.' The North Koreans wanted Curt for a specific reason.

She wondered if the nuclear bomb dropped by MacArthur had leaked or blown up and the secretive government was determined to have corroborative witnesses before announcing The United States had used nuclear weapons, and their citizens were dying of radioactive poisoning as a result. She wondered what the agents meant by, 'Let's get out of here before they show up.' Who was 'They?' Was it a reference to the FBI, CIA, or the local police?

She didn't answer the phone when it rang over and over. She knew it was her son. She didn't dare tell him what happened. He might do something to get himself killed. He was somewhat of a coward until he met Curt. Now he talked about Krav Maga and sounded fearless.

In the morning, Misun couldn't handle going to work. Her arches hurt, and she couldn't hold anything in her left hand. She called Alan and told him what happened.

"You need to call 911." He'd leave immediately. It was a seven-hour drive.

Her feet were so badly swollen she couldn't walk. She needed medical treatment. In desperation, she called 911.

The paramedics immediately assumed a man beat her. They called the police.

Misun was afraid to say what happened. "I fell down the stairs last night. It was several flights." The female officer wanted to know who she was seeing. Misun said, "My husband is deceased. I'm not seeing anyone."

The officer wasn't convinced. "It looks like you were slapped around." She pointed at Misun's cheek. "This looks like a handprint."

Misun denied it, yet the policewoman referred her to a domestic violence center, recommending she stay there for safety. "You're going to need physical help. The paramedics say you may have broken arches. Do you have any friends who can help you?"

"Yes, my son is coming."

After her feet, hands, wrist, and nose were X-rayed, the doctor said Misun had several fractures, and treatment meant staying off her feet, ice rotating with heat, and pain medicine. He wrapped both feet tightly, bandaged her fingers together, and splinted her nose and left wrist. "If your feet don't heal, we may have to put them in casts and you'd need a wheelchair. At any rate, you will need a walker or crutches to get around. Do you have anyone to help you?"

Taking an Uber home, she talked the driver into helping her up the stairs and into her apartment. The man kept shaking his head. "Whoever did this to you should be in prison."

Alan was shocked to see her face. "Who beat you up?" He had dark bags under his eyes.

"I'm sure they were North Koreans."

Alan insisted she come to Boulder so he could watch her.

"What about my job?"

"You can transfer to Walmart in Lafayette."

"How about the apartment and my car?"

"We'll notify the management you're moving, and I'll take your car to a dealership for consignment. It's simple."

That night, she dreamed of making love with Curt and woke up shaking with fear, worrying North Korean agents kidnapped him.

Chapter 40
Arirang Hill

At their morning coffee, Alan told Curt what happened to his mother.

"So she's living with you here in Boulder?"

"Yes, she was injured badly and is terrified."

His face twisted with concern. "Is she okay, will she heal?"

"Her nose, both arches, and left hand were broken. Her left wrist was also dislocated. She's barely able to get around."

"Oh my god, that's horrible."

"She's tough. She's lived alone since her husband died and will heal."

He was quiet, then asked, tentatively, "Think I could meet her?"

"She would like that. She never talked about you when I was growing up, but on the way over because those nasty North Koreans beat her, you're all she talked about." Alan smiled. "She still loves you."

Curt's face lit up so brightly, the whole office seemed struck with sunshine.

Misun insisted that before meeting Curt, she could walk normally and her bruised face was healed.

Weeks passed. Curt kept asking, "Is your mother doing better?" He shaved his beard to look younger and stopped wearing the stupid heavy store glasses. Still liked the 1920s working man's hat. It was a habit.

At the Korean book study, Ara grabbed Alan's arm as he started to leave. "Will you walk me to my Four-Runner?"

Curt grinned and nodded to Alan.

Reluctantly, Alan extended the crook of his arm.

She took it.

Curt leaned patiently against the Corvette while they talked. He saw Alan smiling as he spoke with the girl. When he got into the car, he asked, "So? You ask her out?"

"She's too young." His face flushed. "She is so smart and so lovely." He shook his head sadly.

"She's twenty-five and has a master's degree. Listen, you fought off some of the most highly skilled martial artists in the world, and it's time you found your courage around women." He grinned and gave him a piece of paper. "Here's her phone number. If you don't call her, I'll bring her over some evening when we're playing guitars. She plays the flute and would like to join us."

"Think I'll wait for that to happen."

"Bring your mother."

A month rolled by before the evening came. Ara bounced in happily, pulled out her flute, and tuned it. "This is so exciting. I've been wanting someone to play with."

Curt said, "Alan is bringing his mother. He said she has a lovely voice. Do you know Arirang?"

"Yes, that's one of my favorites."

Alan knocked and then walked in, trailing his mother.

Misun shyly came in behind her son and stayed behind him. Curt stepped to one side, and she moved to the other. He stepped to the other and she shied away. He gave Alan a look as he held up his palms.

"Mom, come on. I know you will remember each other."

Eyes downcast, she stepped from behind her son. She looked at Curt's huge shoes and scanned up. She had forgotten how tall he was. When her eyes met his, she nearly cried and opened her arms, "Oh, it is you!"

They embraced and stared into one another's eyes for long moments, then tenderly kissed.

Ara started crying. "Oh, I want to be in love like that." She looked at Alan. Their eyes tangoed. He opened his arms, and they embraced as they watched the couple.

The emotions in the room swelled as if love roasted on a fire and it warmed, growing hotter by the second. At last, Curt stepped back from Misun. He dropped to his knees. "I meant to return." He took her hand. "They took everything away from me at the Naval hospital, and I couldn't write. I've dreamed of you for years." His mouth was open with awe, his lips were wet, and his brown eyes longed.

She knelt and looked into his eyes. "I waited as long as possible. But I was pregnant with your child. Corporal Ramirez begged me to marry him and I had no other option."

Alan's mouth fell open at the same time as Curt's. They gawked at each other.

Curt and Misun stood. He stared at the young man.

Alan said, "Dad?"

"Son?"

Misun pointed back and forth at the men. "Look at you, you have the same black curly hair and gold and green flecks in your eyes. You are father and son."

Ara blurted, "I thought so! You're both so handsome, I just knew you were related."

Misun took the men's hands. "Come, let's go look in a mirror together." She led them to a large hall mirror. "See, it's obvious."

Ara and Misun stood behind the men, watching their faces.

The men smiled at each other in the mirror with the same expression. They laughed and caught each other's eyes, seeing the gold and green sparkles. The scales fell from their eyes.

Alan clapped his arms around him. "You *are* my dad!"

Curt hugged him so tightly that his feet rose off the floor. "And you're *my* son." They stared into one another's eyes, then kissed each other's cheeks.

"Wow!" Ara exclaimed. "I sure didn't expect this. I feel very honored, very privileged."

She and Misun hugged.

Misun whispered, "I hope my son falls in love with you. Sing Arirang with him. It's our favorite song."

A twinkle sprang into her eyes. "Curt and I were planning on it." She picked up her flute and played the melody.

That got the men's attention. Curt and Alan grabbed their guitars, and the family sang together, harmonizing.

Arirang, Arirang, Arariyo, you must pass over Arirang Hill

My love please hang in there and be well.

Wondrous time, happy time, let us delay,

Till night is over, do not go away.

Just as there are many stars in the clear sky,

Our hearts share dreams do not deny.

When you leave through the pass,

please take me and go

Let us hold hands so together we know.

Arirang, Arirang, Arariyo

Our hearts will be one as we grow.

Chapter 41
The Cup of Peace

Curt and Alan waited in the falling snow outside of The Cup of Peace in Boulder as the women arrived in Ara's SUV. They took their jackets and led them to a secluded corner. Candles, soft Korean music with a woman and man singing in harmony, "Arirang, arirang, arariyo, you are going over Arirang hill…"

The family spoke Korean among themselves.

A waiter arrived with a white towel over his arm, serving water from a pitcher with beads on its chilled sides, speaking Korean. "Would you like to see the wine list?"

Curt said, "I don't drink."

Misun shook her head, "Neither do I."

"Oh, come on," Alan urged, "Just a glass, I love merlot. It's a nice dry wine. Have one glass with us, and I'll buy. Merlot doesn't make you choke up. This is a special occasion."

Curt didn't know what to order. The waiter suggested a bottle of fine New Zealand merlot. "It should be perfect for you."

Curt looked at Alan, and he nodded.

The conversation was stiff and stilted. Alan kept coming up with topics to talk about. "Have you seen *The Return of the Jedi*?"

Neither had.

Ara snuggled under his arm. "I'd like to see it with you."

He kissed the top of her head, then asked his parents, "So talk about what you like to do."

Curt said, "I work out at the gym."

Misun gave a quick nod. "Yoga is all I do outside of my home." She shrugged. "Well, sometimes I go to movies with a friend."

A Korean waitress appeared with the wine. She offered the first glass to Curt. He had no idea what to do.

Alan demonstrated. "You're supposed to swirl, sniff it, and then take a sip. If you like it, tell the waitress it's fine, and she'll leave the bottle. If you don't, she will bring something else." He smiled at Ara.

"Do you enjoy wine?"

"Yes, sure."

"You are lovely and smart," Misun said. "I'd love to have you as my daughter."

She blushed.

Alan's face went red. "Mom!"

"You two look good together."

"So do you."

Everyone smiled.

Curt followed the wine ritual, and the waitress sat the bottle wrapped in a white towel on the table. He said, "Kamsahamnida." Thank you.

The waitress smiled, "Cheonman-eyo." You're welcome, asking, "Do you speak Korean?"

He nodded at Misun. "I learned in Korea.

"We were so young." Misun caught his eyes. "Why didn't you return for me?"

Curt sat quietly, then said, "They deprogrammed us when we were repatriated. I didn't remember anything for many years." He caught her eyes. "But I dreamed of you."

Misun fought back tears. "I tried to wait for you, but I was pregnant with Alan."

"I'm so sorry. I forgot nearly everything for many years." He took her hand. "I owe you my life."

They toasted each other, then animated, everyone talked in Korean.

Misun said, "Your accent and grammar are perfect. I'm sure I didn't teach you."

"I took Korean in college, and if I go out to eat, I choose Korean restaurants to keep it up. I'm also in a Korean book study." He glanced at Ara. "That's where we met Alan's future wife."

"Dad! Stop it, we're just getting to know each other."

His tone was gruff, "Get off it, Alan. You've known each other for more than a year. The two of you are the most talkative at the book study. You constantly looked at each other and smiled. You were too afraid to ask her out."

"I didn't want to go through another divorce."

Ara gazed into his eyes. "You won't."

Alan nearly crumbled. "Ara, I think I'm in love with you." His lower lip trembled.

She kissed his lips. "I love you too."

Misun never drank, and her face flushed. She told Curt what he looked like when the South Korean soldiers first brought him to the house. "You were in horrible condition. We thought you would die. A Korean doctor took off your big toe because it was crushed and hanging by the skin. He also dug a bullet from deep in your bum. He shot you up with morphine and antibiotics, and warned us to not get close since you were on the edge of forever."

Curt shook his head. "I have no memory of it, but please tell me."

She described caring for him, cleaning his wounds, and helping him to the toilet bucket. "You had cuts, punctures, and burns all over your body—all were infected. The doctor rigged an IV for morphine and antibiotics. He kept missing your vein and there was blood all over." Her face blanched. "I remember when he cut off your toe. You hardly flinched."

"Huh." He held up his right hand. "I'm sure it didn't hurt like when the communists sawed off these one at a time."

Ara gasped and pushed closer to Alan.

Misun held his stubs. "They were horribly infected when the soldiers brought you to our home. I rubbed herbs on them four or five times a day. They had puss pockets under the ragged skin. We were afraid you'd lose your hand."

"Kamsahamnida." He sat quietly listening as she told of his slow, painful recovery, until he asked, "How's your family?"

"They are well but getting old. My grandmother died of cancer. Grandfather's hearing is going, and Mother has arthritis in her back from working at the fish market." A slight grin. "It took three of us to get you onto the bucket."

His face went red. "You hand-washed me? You wiped my butt?"

A soft giggle. "I learned to detach. You were smelly."

"I wonder if I'd remember more if you took me back to your home? I'd love to thank your mother and grandparents."

She caught her breath. "They would enjoy that. Unfortunately, my uncle is gone. You may not remember him but you were kindred spirits. You and Kim Chin-mae liked each other. You talked about battle strategy and eventually, he was promoted as the head of President Park's bodyguard." Her face went sad. "He was killed during an assassination attempt."

"Go on, Mom, tell us more." Alan's face was animated.

"Grandpa loved playing flower cards with you. You were our greatest success because you were in the worst condition, and you were so gracious and thankful for even the smallest things. You even tried to help me cook and clean. I couldn't believe it because Korean men think housework is beneath them."

She took a breath. "I try to go home once a year and send some of my pay." She held his eyes. "They even have a bamboo floor and a bathroom. Korea is now a modern country thanks to the United States. And we're free, unlike the North."

They finished the bottle, talking and talking in Korean. Alan ordered another.

Misun pulled the gold chain from her neck and handed it to Curt.

His eyes went wide. They teared. "Wow, I can't believe it. My class ring."

"I've worn it since you gave it to me. I went to town and traded a sack of flour to an old woman for the chain."

He pointed at the bullet. "What's this? It looks like an AK 47."

"The old Korean doctor pulled it from your buttocks. I talked a man into drilling a hole into it so I could hang it with your ring."

Curt's face wrinkled as he fought tears. They hugged each other and again looked into one another's eyes with a sense of awe.

Alan put his palm out. "Can I see it? Mom never let me touch it."

Curt handed it to him. He and Ara read, "Cedaredge High School, 1950." He smiled as he gave it back. "This is a treasure."

Misun put the chain back around her neck and patted her chest. "This is where it belongs. I feel naked without it." She mentioned she kept a log of the time he was there. "I made friends with a boy named Bitgaram who was conscripted by the North Koreans as a guard at your POW camp. He was rescued at the same time as you. He told me everything he witnessed. He said you were incredibly brave, and the commander tortured you the worst. It's in my journal."

"Think I could read it?"

"It's your story."

"I'd like to read it too," Alan said.

Ara touched his forearm. "Can we read it together?"

Curt smiled. "All of us can read it as a family." Then his face changed. "You better give it to me for safe-keeping. I have a wall safe."

Chapter 42
Sensual Hot Springs

Cindy plopped down in the chair in front of his desk, her pert breasts jiggling. "You and your father are so easy to read. Both of you are in love. I'm jealous."

Dr. Ramirez didn't know what to say. "You need to find a new husband."

"I've tried. Do you know any single men my age?"

He leaned back. "You know, there are a couple of guys in the Krav Maga club you might like."

Shonna popped in, her big brown eyes as wide as her toothy smile. "You and your father's faces are shining like a full moon. I'm so proud of my boys." She laughed. "I'm gonna give both of you away at your wedding."

Dr. Ramirez laughed. "It will be a pleasure."

Curt wanted to take everyone to the Ouray hot springs. Alan drove Ara's Four-Runner so they could ride together.

He didn't speed. "The State Patrol has an office in Montrose and they frequently cruise this section." Montrose was a larger version of Delta with more economic activity. They had a Russel Stover candy factory and a Kmart.

Elk grazed in the meadows outside of Colona. As they entered Ouray, Misun pointed out the public hot pool. "I thought that was where we're going."

Curt said, "I think you'll like another place. The natives called it the Spirit Cave, a space to cleanse your soul."

The Wiesbaden Hot Springs Lodge's delicate feminine bedrooms were decorated in the late 1800s Victorian style. Curt suggested they sit in the spirit cave. The mineral spring was very hot, and Misun slowly sat down in steaming water up to her hips. A slight smell of sulfur rose in the mist.

Ara said, "This is probably good for healing infections."

"You're right," Misun said, "I wish we had something like this when we were nursing our soldiers."

The only sound was the occasional drip of condensation from the flat stones above their heads. It was shadowy with only a dim light, dark and romantic. She kissed Curt as sweat dripped, and ran from their foreheads and cheeks.

Ara followed suit with Alan.

"We should go to our rooms," Misun suggested.

They wrapped towels around their bodies, and as they stepped into the sunlight, it hit them like a baseball bat, blinding them. They laughed, guiding partners to the rooms.

The morning woke them with the percussive sound of blackbird wings as if a change was coming. He pushed between her legs again and she said, "Curt, I'm sore, aren't you?"

"Yes, I'm sore, but I've dreamed you back into my life and now you're here." He probed so gently that she surrendered, wanting to possess and be possessed by him, lying back to enjoy every slow stroke that built in her body with a pulsing vibration like a coming earthquake. Suddenly, she trembled with an explosion that rippled up and down her body, rattling her spine. He filled her beyond the brim and her cervix lapped up his sperm. When she came to, his juices dripped from her, leaving wet spots across the white sheets.

He said, "It felt like something magical happened."

Misun looked into his loving eyes. "Yes, I believe I may be pregnant."

They drove up the highway to Grand Mesa. Curt stopped at an overlook above Cedaredge to point out the mountain peaks. They got out to look.

"That snow-capped point to the far south is The Lone Cone outside of Durango. To the east near Paonia, the range is called the West Elks, and to the west is the Uncompahgre Plateau." He turned and held her close, saying, "Misun, I love you and I want to live with you. I want to have another child with you and grow old with you." He dropped to one knee, holding her hands gently. Reaching into his pocket, he pulled out a box to reveal a large, perfect, oval diamond that sparkled in the sun. "Will you please marry me?"

A spoonbill lifted in the wind into clear skies.

Moisture filled her eyes as she bowed with her hands steepled. "Oh yes, Curt, I give my heart and my life to you."

It was too sweet, too romantic and Ara began weeping softly.

Alan took her hand as he knelt. "Although we haven't dated for long, I'm taking my parents' advice." He pulled out a ring identical to the one his father gave to his mother. "Ara Ling, you are my path across forever. I will always be loyal, and I will always love you." He took a breath as he looked into her eyes. "Will you please marry me?"

She glanced at his parents. They nodded with wide smiles. "Yes, oh yes, Alan. When I first saw you walk into the Korean book study, my heart jumped into my throat. You are the only man I would ever marry."

Misun exhaled. "We should have a double wedding in Golden, Colorado, symbolizing fifty years of love."

Curt said, "It's already been thirty-one years for us. Let's go for seventy."

Chapter 43
The Frightening Drive Home

Alan drove home with Ara tucked in close. He felt like the adult because his parents smooched in the rear seat. It was weird. He turned up the stereo so he couldn't hear their kisses. Glancing in the rearview mirror, he saw a dark sedan behind with two men in the front seat. He didn't mention it.

After he gassed up in Avon and pulled back onto I-70, the blue sedan crept up again. There was another one, a gray car with two figures pulled along beside him. They were Asian. He said, "Dad, I think we're in trouble. Look to the left and in back of us."

Curt sprang to life. "Alan, we have both the North Koreans and Naval Intelligence on us. Pull over and let me take the wheel."

"I can handle this." He punched it.

The Asians dropped back behind the blue sedan.

Curt directed, "We need to get off the freeway at the first chance. It's easier to lose them on a four-wheel drive forest road."

The dark sedan rear-ended them, trying to run them off the road and cause a wreck. The Asians hit the rear side of the dark sedan and sent them into a spin.

Alan jerked the wheel. "This is crazy, they're trying to protect us."

"They want us alive." Misun's hands shook.

Near Dillion, Alan whipped the Four-Runner onto an off-ramp. He led the two cars around the town and up alleys, following Curt's directions. He headed back to the freeway and when both cars were in close pursuit, did a sudden, police-style U-turn and sailed back past them, going the wrong way. Cars swerved and honked.

He spun onto an off ramp and only slowed when they hit the town.

"Wow!" Ara exclaimed, "You're a great driver."

"Dad taught me." He felt oddly calm.

They headed for the mountains. The noon sun bathed the forest ahead in sunlight, creating a green glow. Risking dead ends, he took progressively narrower and rougher roads. "Is this full-time four-wheel drive or do I need to get out to lock the wheels?"

Ara said, "It's full-time." She pointed, "Use this button to shift into low." She was cool and calm, impressing the others.

The road grew rugged with tire-piercing boulders, and eventually, the two sedans gave up. Curt said, "I wonder if they'll have a shootout. This is wild, having both sides after us."

"I thought our government was supposed to protect us, not try to kill us." Ara shook her head. "The North Koreans may have saved our lives."

Afraid to return the way they came, Alan kept driving. No one was familiar with the area. They got lost in the many forest service and old mining roads. "We might have to spend the night up here, and it's going to be cold." He stopped at an overlook.

They stood outside, shivering in the chilly wind.

Curt carefully examined the terrain. "Over there," he pointed. "I'd guess that ravine might have a road. If we're lucky we'll see someone else out four wheeling and get directions."

It took an hour to find the passage into the ravine. By the time they were back in Dillion, they were hungry, and it was dark. They decided to return to Boulder through Breckenridge and Fairplay, fearful that somewhere along the freeway, their enemies waited. They stayed at Curt's house, one always alert and on watch.

Chapter 44
Harassment

Shonna gushed when she learned both men were engaged. "Please invite me to the wedding. I want to give you away."

Curt laughed, "Mothers don't give their sons away."

Her big brown eyes opened wide. "This one does."

After work, Curt walked straight up to the dark sedan sitting a block away, jerked the driver's door open, and punched the man's face. Dragging the agent out, he splattered on the pavement like a bag of vegetable stew, tearing the shoulder and knees of his suit. Curt took a Krav Maga stance. "If you follow Misun or my son, if you harass them in any way, I'll kill you."

The agent sat up and wiped blood from his lips. "You're an idiot. You could kill me and there'd be a hundred right behind me. You can never hide, and you better not tell your fiancé anything about the mission."

"What mission?"

"You know what I'm talking about."

"The navy deprogrammed me. There is nothing in my Navy records about a mission, and I don't remember a thing about my service in Korea."

"You better hope." He stood. "We're watching you, your son, and Misun Kim. We know she nursed you back to health."

Standing, he said, "If it was me and I cared about the woman, I'd never see her again." He wiped his face, slid into the car, started it, and without another glance, drove away.

Two weeks later, agents pounded on Ara's apartment door. She checked through the peephole and didn't open it. She shoved a heavy chair against it and called Alan.

"I'm on the way." By the time he arrived, the agents were gone, but everyone was upset. "You need to move in with me." He saw her frightened eyes. "Have you told your parents about any of this?"

"No, they would freak out and come get me. They'd try to hide me away and forbid me from marrying you."

"What do you want?"

"I want to move in with you, and I want you to take me to and from work from now on."

Curt insisted everyone move in with him. "I have two spare bedrooms, and it will be safer."

The men installed motion lights and alarms. Everyone was on edge. They took turns standing watch at night.

There were no direct incidents for the next weeks, although they periodically spotted someone following them.

Misun discovered she was pregnant. "I'm too old. I'm 47, our baby could have Down's Syndrome. Either I have an abortion, or we get married right away."

Curt was ecstatic. "We'll get married."

A few days later, Ara announced, "I'm also pregnant."

The family conferred. It was too dangerous to raise children where both the North Koreans and Naval Intelligence could attack them. They'd head for Canada.

They applied for South Korean Visas, and Curt listed his house. They sold the cars, then donated all but essentials to the Humane Society in Boulder.

Momma was overjoyed that Misun was coming home with Seaman Curt Conrad and her grandson.

The wedding at the Golden Chapel was a simple affair since they had little time to plan it. Along with Ara's family, the guests included the mental health staff, the Korean book club, and the Krav Maga club.

Shonna proudly escorted Curt and Alan down the church aisle dressed in a black and gold robe like an African queen. Krav Maga club members in fighting uniforms lined the center aisle as Misun and Ara walked forward. A silver-haired woman performed the ceremony.

The family harmonized for the audience, "Arirang, arirang, arariyo, we are going over Arirang hill."

Sealing their marriage with a kiss, Curt said, "I remember clearly now, and I remember everything you've told me except when I was knocked out on morphine."

She squeezed his hand. "We'll sing Korean lullabies to our twins."

"Twins?"

Misun nodded. Curt laughed happily. "We'll give them oranges and chocolate when they do something good."

Cindy kissed each man too long and too hard. She smiled at Alan. "Thanks for introducing me to Ramon. He's a stud." Her big boobs bounced.

Ara and Misun looked happy for her.

Ramon saluted Curt. "Thank you for being our trainer."

They roared away in Ara's Four-Runner. Curt wanted to ensure that neither American intelligence nor the North Koreans could tail them. Taking side roads across the Colorado Rockies through snow and blizzards with chains on the tires, they wound through Utah, and across the mountains of Montana.

Curt mentioned, "I'd like to talk to Adam Spooker one more time. He said he was trying to find out more about the nuclear bomb that was dropped."

They met at Multnomah Falls on the Columbia River and went for a walk. Misun and Ara asked Adam to take a family photo with her camera.

Curt asked, "Adam, have you found out anything more about the nuclear bomb that was dropped on North Korea we were sent to defuse."

Adam had a sick look on his face as he shook his head. "I'm nearly certain they didn't insert the nuclear trigger. Otherwise, according to everything I have learned, it should have exploded when it was dropped."

"You mean our mission was unnecessary?"

"Maybe." He shrugged. "There's a small chance a nuclear bomb is deteriorating in that river basin feeding to P'yŏngyang. Who knows if it might still release radiation and kill millions?"

"Or the North Koreans removed the trigger and reverse-engineered it so they can produce nuclear bombs." He took a breath and exhaled. "They have one now." Curt held up his hand with the missing fingers. "So, it's possible everything we went through was a stupid mistake, a military communication error."

Adam took a deep breath. "Hate to say it, but it wouldn't be the first time."

Chapter 45
South Korea

In Vancouver, BC, they sold the SUV to an excited small dealer of 4x4s. "These Four-Runners sell for a premium here. I can get those rear dents popped out with no problem."

Misun couldn't contain her excitement. She was returning home with Curt, the man she had loved since she was sixteen. And she carried his twins.

Momma met them at the airport. Misun was dumbfounded because she walked past her. "Seaman Curt Conrad!" She kissed his cheeks, saying in Korean, "I knew you would come back and marry my daughter. You promised." She saw Alan. "And you must be my grandson. They hugged.

"And who are you?"

"I'm Ara, Alan's wife." A sweet smile.

"Welcome to the family."

She turned to Misun and gently patted her growing tummy. "My child and grandchildren are home. I knew someday you would bring him back from over Arirang Hill."

President Park had promised Misun after her uncle was killed during an assassination attempt, that he would do everything he could to help her relocate to South Korea if she wanted. He kept his word and had his office create new identities for everyone. Curt's Korean first name was Kwan, meaning powerful and strong. He and Alan took the last name, Kim. Alan became Gi, meaning brave.

Citizenship papers were issued along with South Korean passports. Soon, they were married in traditional Korean style. Misun's grandfather hobbled up to hand her a golden hairpiece. "Chin-mae wanted me to give this to you when you married."

She felt like the real Korean Princess Pyeonggang, and Curt was her Ondal, a hero who saved his country. She sensed her grandmother's ghost at the wedding, smiling and saying, "I told you he was waiting for you to bring him back to life." She was no longer a gwisin, a ghost trapped on earth. Her life was complete.

She made Curt a new calligraphy:

$$고생 끝에 낙이 온다$$

Curt read aloud, "At the end of hardship comes happiness."

When the twins and Ara's child were old enough, they read from Uncle Kim Chin-mae's old gold-trimmed leather-bound book of Korean folk tales. *The Weeping Princess* was their favorite.

They loved taking the children to the overlook near the village spirit pole to watch the spoonbills taking off to explore their world.

Epilogue

It was Christmas Eve, 2020, and, despite warnings from the Centers for Disease Control to avoid gatherings due to COVID, the whole family assembled at the Kim's home in Westminster, Colorado. Curt, now eighty-seven, lay dying of cancer. He was propped in a hospital bed placed in the living room with the Christmas tree, a morphine IV in his arm, watching the grandchildren open their presents.

"Let me see it, Ji-a, bring it to me." She was six, from their daughter, Eun.

Ji-a handed *The Invasion of the Cow Snatchers* game to Curt and he chuckled as he figured it out. Ji-a sat on the side of his bed, explaining how to fly your UFO over to snap up a cow.

Misun asked their second son, Tae, now thirty-seven, to help her to Curt's bed. She had developed multiple sclerosis after they bought the home just east of Rocky Flats in Westminster. After their diagnosis, Alan learned about the potential source of Misun's MS and Curt's cancer. The real estate agent had not informed them about the radioactivity from the near Chernobyl-like meltdown of plutonium at the Rocky Flats plant. It was too late: they were already sick and couldn't afford another home since housing prices had skyrocketed. Misun had problems swallowing, speech difficulties, and painful muscle spasms that inhibited her movements. She needed help to get to Curt's side.

Although he was sixty-eight, Alan said, "I've got her. She's tiny." He easily lifted Mom onto the bed so Misun could lay beside him to watch Curt play the six-year-old's game.

Ara leaned against his side and whispered, "This is so hard."

Misun looked up into Curt's face, catching his eyes.

He winked. "This is kind of fun." He handed the game to her and flicked his chin at Ji-a. "Show Grandma."

As the child skipped around the end of the bed, he lay back, closed his eyes, and clenched his jaws with pain. It was end-stage bone cancer originating in the prostate that metastasized before the VA doctors caught it. The children were still angry he kept going to the VA because he fought every inch to get them to run tests. Had he seen someone at Samaritan Hospital, he might still be kicking butt at Krav Maga.

Misun rubbed his chest, feeling his scars. "Curt, this is so hard to see you suffer." His big arm, now flabby and weak, came around her shoulders. It reminded her of when he was on morphine at Momma's house seventy years ago.

They lived in South Korea for twelve peaceful years until Misun's mother passed away. Seoul exploded into a busy, hectic city of ten million. By 1995 the North Koreans and the United States seemed to forget them since the nuclear bomb had not gone off, and they returned to Colorado. Tae was a physics scientist at CU Boulder, married, and had two children. His twin Eu, was a financial analyst for JP Morgan. She and her husband also had two children.

Alan and Ara had one boy named Hye. He was divorced and only in the last two years had developed a relationship with his son, Curtis, who was now fourteen. They were proud of all of the kids and grandchildren.

It was noisy since the grandchildren played loudly and the adults talked over them, yet Curt dozed from the morphine. Misun knew it wouldn't be long. Hospice wanted to move him to the hospital this week but agreed he could stay home through the holidays because he protested, "I don't want to die in a hospital. I want to die at home with Misun in my arms."

She hoped he would make it to his birthday on New Year's. He would be eighty-eight, an auspicious number: yin and yang, the double hee, eternity. She had a feeling they would go together.

Misun wanted it quiet so Curt could rest. Struggling for breath, she sat up, her hand folded over the stubs of Curt's missing fingers.

"Can everyone please go downstairs? There's plenty of room for you to talk, and the kids can play. Your father needs a nap before lunch."

Alan was the peacemaker. He stood. "Let's get everyone down to the family room since the kids are done opening presents. Ara made sweet red bean pancakes, and we can toast soju."

They herded the children downstairs, but Hye's teenage son, Curtis, hung back. He walked quietly to the old people lying on the hospital bed and handed Misun an orange. "I don't know either of you well, but I've heard stories about your courage."

Misun coughed. Her neck was hot, and her throat felt funny. She looked up at the handsome boy with dark curly hair. He was as tall as Curt before cancer curled his spine.

"Grandpa Alan told me how you nursed him back to health, then how you finally found him." Moisture in his eyes. "You fought the North Koreans and the U.S. intelligence to be together." His fingers touched Curt's leg. "I just hope I have the courage and the strength to find a love like you."

Misun offered her hand and Curtis took it by the tips, kissing the back of her hand. "I wish I could know you better." He turned and fled downstairs.

Everyone was surprised Grandpa Conrad made it through Christmas, but they were concerned because Misun was becoming sicker and sicker. She had lost her sense of smell and taste. The three children stopped by on New Year's Eve to wish Grandpa a happy birthday. They brought kimchi and sweet red bean pancakes. The grandchildren stood quietly as if understanding.

Fearful Curt would die, Misun hadn't left home since before Christmas. Besides, she had the flu or something, and it made it hard to breathe, especially with the MS. She lay next to Curt whose face was pastel gray, his breathing shallow.

The hospice nurse said softly, "It won't be long."

Ara and Alan held his hands.

The Christmas tree stood with multicolored lights and ornaments they collected from all over the world on their travels: A small camel from Egypt, a bear from Russia, a lama from Peru, and many others from all around the world.

Misun coughed. She had a fever and was short of breath as if her lungs filled with fluid.

Alan said, "We should take her to the hospital."

The hospice nurse spoke, "I've tried. She won't leave his side."

"She may have Covid. One of us may have been asymptomatic at Christmas. Everyone should have worn masks."

They had guilty expressions.

Misun raised her feverish head as she gasped for air. "I'm so happy you're here – Daddy and I are going home together at midnight." Her silver river of hair sparkled in the Christmas tree lights. She asked for a chocolate and an orange.

Alan located a Hersey's kiss and peeled an orange, giving it to her.

Misun unwrapped and held the chocolate just under her husband's nose. "Want a kiss?"

A tiny upturn of his lips. She held it in her teeth and then to his mouth.

As the silver ball came down in Times Square, a rasping gurgle, a slight shiver, and Curt was gone.

Misun lay her head on his chest and closed her eyes. Dreaming of the night they walked together overlooking the wharf above their tiny fishing village, she followed him over Arirang Hill.

Alan pulled the calligraphy from the wall.

고생 끝에 낙이 온다
"At the end of hardship comes happiness."

The End

Afterword
History

etween 1910 and 1945, Korea was occupied and exploited by the Japanese, and by the end of World War II, it was one of the poorest countries in the world. Korea was divided at the 38th parallel with the U.S.S.R. taking control of the north while the U.S. controlled the south. In 1950, Soviet-equipped North Korean troops massed north of the 38th parallel, and on Sunday, June 25, North Korean ground and air forces poured into South Korea. By the end of the summer, the Republic of Korea and U.N. troops had retreated to a toehold around Pusan, in the southeastern corner of the peninsula.

The United States strongly considered using nuclear weapons to turn the tide. In July of 1950, President Harry S. Truman authorized the Strategic Air Command to send 10 atomic-capable B-29s carrying assembled bombs without their plutonium cores, to Guam. They were soon augmented by 10 more bombers. At the time, the Soviet Union had five atomic bombs while the U.S. had 299, however, there was a realistic fear the Soviets would quickly retaliate if the United States used nuclear weapons and the consequences to civilians would be devastating.

On September 15, 1950, U.N. forces made an amphibious landing at Inchon, 20 miles west of Seoul. They retook the capital and severed the North Korean supply lines. By October, the U.N. troops had pushed across the 38th parallel and taken Pyongyang, the capital of North Korea, and advanced to the Yalu River.

On November 25, 1950, nearly 300,000 Chinese soldiers invaded across the Yalu River forcing U.N. troops into retreat. MacArthur immediately demanded authority to bomb Chinese bases north of the Yalu. He also asked for discretion to use atomic weapons in Korea and submitted a list of targets for which he wanted 26 atomic bombs and another eight to drop on invasion forces and enemy airpower. In an interview published in 1964, by Bob Considine in the book,

General MacArthur, MacArthur said: "I would have dropped between 30 to 50 tactical atomic bombs on his air (the enemy's) bases and other depots strung across the neck of Manchuria from just across the Yalu at Antung (northwest tip of Korea) to the neighborhood of Hunchun (northeast tip of Korea near the border of the USSR)." The goal was to prevent a land invasion of North Korea for at least 60 years.

Initially, a city of one and a half million, Seoul changed hands four times before the lines stabilized north of the 38th parallel, across the Han River. By the spring of 1951, only two hundred thousand people lived in the city.

In March 1951, U.S. intelligence intercepted clandestine conversations from General MacArthur to the Tokyo embassies of Spain and Portugal he planned to expand the Korean War into a full-scale conflict with the Chinese Communists. When the Chinese again massed new forces near the Korean border and after the Russians put 200 bombers into airbases in Manchuria, MacArthur requested a "D-Day atomic capability" to retain air superiority in the Korean theatre. Later, on March 24, MacArthur publically taunted the Chinese for failing to conquer South Korea and threatened to attack mainland China unless they gave up.

Given the dire military situation, on April 1st, Truman authorized nine nuclear bombs with fissile cores (nuclear bomb triggers) to be transferred into Air Force custody and transported to Okinawa. On April 5th, the Joint Chiefs of Staff gave orders for immediate atomic retaliation authorizing MacArthur to use nuclear bombs if the Chinese launched airstrikes originating from their bases. The same day, the chairman of the Atomic Energy Commission, Gordon Dean, transferred nine Mark IV nuclear capsules to the Air Force's 9th Bomb Group, the designated carrier for atomic weapons.

What happened between April 5th and 11th is the subject of hot debate among historians. There is no official record the U.S. used nuclear weapons in any conflict after World War Two, however, it is clear MacArthur wanted to. He pledged to end the Korean War quickly and end the possibility that any communist nation would ever threaten America again. Although it cannot be verified, the author believes it was during these two weeks, that the man who gave this account parachuted into North Korea to defuse the nuclear bomb ordered dropped by MacArthur.

On April 11th, President Harry S. Truman relieved General Douglas

MacArthur of his command. It remains the most controversial public confrontation between civilian and military authority in United States history.

There is no external evidence that a nuclear bomb dropped in the 1950's exploded. However, on October 14, 2006, it was announced U.S. intelligence detected radioactive debris above North Korea. At the time, The White House said it had no confirmation the North Koreans conducted a nuclear test. One wonders if the bomb that Curt Conrad's team was sent to defuse finally rusted out.

The End

About the Author

Danyl A. Doyle is a former resident of New Zealand, now living in the Colorado Rocky Mountains. He is an "over-educated farm boy" of mixed race. Despite learning disabilities and mild autism, he became an English teacher, a Ph.D. psychologist, and a businessman. He enjoys traveling as a professional speaker. His stories and poems have been published in The Winged Penny, The Southern Quill, The Milkbarn, and The Wilderness House Literary Review.

Please, out of the kindness of your heart, leave an honest book review. I would genuinely appreciate it.
   Feel free to email me with any comments or questions at dandoylechannel@gmail.com

Danyl A. Doyle